# 2020

## A Dystopian Thriller

R.D. Power

*Dedicated to:*

*My son, Kevin*

# PROLOGUE

After a long winter in Rapid City, SD, spring had arrived on April 27, 2020 with a flourish. The long lost sun had burst to life, melting away the last snow; a warm zephyr blew away the dank air; flowers sprang forth from the earth and returned the color to the world. What a perfect day to be alive! Oh, and Dr. Timothy Sharp, though not diabetic, received a generous dose of insulin, went into a coma, and died, and Elaine Wood and her eight-year-old son, Matt, were killed in a car crash after their brake line was cut.

# CHAPTER 1

A monstrous bang put a sudden end to Tessa Sharp's nap and presaged a premature termination to Delta Flight 3166. She stared wide-eyed at a spear of some sort that had pierced the thin skin of the airplane. Buzzers blared, people screamed, and the steward went tumbling down the aisle as the plane nosedived.

Tessa closed her eyes and opened them again, trying to force herself to awake from this nightmare, but it was all too real. Too petrified to scream, she glanced around the cabin and saw panic and disbelief on the faces of her fellow passengers on the small Dash 8. *This can't be happening!* she told herself.

She felt a tear run down her cheek. How depressing to make it only to age twenty-five, never having been in love—at least not since eighth grade, and that didn't really count— never having had a child, never having accomplished anything really. Hadn't even made a ripple. "Please, God, help us," she whispered. Her heart hammered so fiercely, she could feel each beat through her ears.

After what seemed like an eternity in the dive with Tessa expecting everything to end all the while, the plane finally leveled out. It shuddered and bounced around, but at least it seemed under a semblance of control.

"Assume ... sh ...tion!" shouted the steward from the front of the cabin as he scrambled to a seat and put on his seat belt.

Tessa asked, "What did he say?"

"He said, 'Assume the crash position,' as if that'll do us any good," answered a man three rows back across the aisle. He'd been drinking heavily before all this and seemed more irritated than perturbed at this point. "That'll just mean my head'll end up in the ass of this sissy baby in front of me."

Said sissy was Mort Wood, who was traveling with Tessa to Syracuse. "Why me? Why me?" he moaned between sobs.

The aggravated man continued, "You know, when American Airlines went bust last month and left me with a worthless ticket, I was rather peeved, but what're you going to do? Delta had lots of seats. So what if I had to pay again? That's life nowadays. But I draw the damn line at exploding engines."

Tessa leaned forward and looked out the window. Her jaw dropped when she saw black smoke streaking out from a shattered engine. The propeller was gone, except for the part that had penetrated the cabin.

The man went on, "I'll bet they haven't had this piece of shit in for maintenance since the 1990s."

"Oh, shut up!" said a weeping woman from back in the plane somewhere.

"Compared to seven years ago, there are only one-third the number of flights, but three times the number of crashes.

That's a nine times greater chance of doing what we're just about to do. Did you know that, lady?"

"For God's sake, have some consideration. You're scaring everyone," said the lady.

"Me? I would've thought the prospect of hurtling into the earth at three hundred miles per hour would overshadow anything I might say."

"Shut the hell up!" said the weeping woman's husband.

Tessa looked out the window; the ground was close now, but she could see no evidence they were over a runway. As her panicked reason began to consider how much this might hurt, the plane touched down—actually, smashed down—onto the runway.

"Woo!" the irritated man screamed. "We made it! I can't fucking believe it. What do you say, hero?" he said, tapping Mort on the shoulder. "You can stop crying now. I thought pieces of the tire on the landing gear were going to shoot right up my ass." He turned to the manifestly gay steward, who was walking down to aisle to check on the passengers, and said, "What's that feel like getting rubber up your ass?"

"Shut up, asshole!" said half the plane.

The plane rolled to a stop. Tessa was so relieved, she belatedly started weeping. She was dressed warmly in her dark blue sweats, but found herself shivering.

The steward opened the door and let down the stairs. Mort beat the women to the exit. "Be careful; watch your step," the steward said.

"If I was careful I'd have never taken this G D airline," the irritated man said. He shook the hand of the pilot and said, "This an everyday occurrence for you?"

Descending the stairs, Tessa looked at what had been the engine. It continued to smoke; most of the housing was gone. The wing was scorched underneath. She shook her head and quavered. Finding the pilot, she hugged him and thanked him.

The twelve passengers and three crew grabbed their luggage from the cargo hold and walked a safe distance from the plane. They waited and waited, but no emergency crew showed up. Just as they decided to walk, a police car came. The officer told them they had to hike the half mile to the terminal and drove away.

"Welcome to Syrafuckingcuse," said the irritated man amidst the grumbling of other passengers.

As they slogged into the terminal, some passengers were met by crying relatives, but Tessa had no one; no one anywhere after her father's murder four days prior, save a great-aunt in Ontario. She felt so forlorn at that moment, tears streamed down her face.

A man in a shabby suit waylaid her, presented his card, and said, "Seymour Abramsky, attorney at law. I understand you were just in a crash. It's extremely upsetting, I know. You should strongly consider suing the airline for emotional distress or whiplash. I heard the landing was really rough; if you're lucky, you'll get whiplash."

"Go away," she said, but Mort took his card.

"Don't take anything from them, not even free tickets," advised Seymour. Mort nodded as he gave the man his information. Turning back to Tessa, Seymour said, "Lady, you should reconsider. This could mean big bucks."

"For who?" she said as she walked toward the exit to search for a cab. Mort followed.

Tessa noticed a lot of people crying in the terminal, most of them airline or airport employees. Others were angry, mostly passengers judging from the suitcases they were carrying. "What the hell do we do now?" yelled one livid man.

"Hell if I know," said another man. He was looking forlornly at the screens showing arrivals and departures. All now said "Cancelled."

A fight broke out across the concourse. A security guard ambled past her, away from the tussle. Tessa asked, "What's going on?"

"They just announced the airport defaulted on its loans; it's bankrupt. No more flights in or out. Everyone's laid off. I'll be damned if I try to stop a fight. Not my problem anymore."

She shook her head and hastened to the exit. On the way, a woman accosted them, holding out her card, informing them of her legal expertise and asking if they were on the Delta flight from Detroit. Before Mort could answer, Tessa said, "No." The lady withdrew her card and went to another person.

Exiting the terminal, they were set upon by several desperate taxi drivers, but Tessa flung them an angry peremptory wave and got into the nearest one, Mort following. Tessa gave the driver the address, and he pulled out.

The cabby thanked her for choosing his cab and went on to tell her he'd been a bank manager before the depression, and his wife had been a city planner. They'd been run out of Utica when his bank went bankrupt and many depositors lost their savings. "It wasn't my fault," he claimed—so said every banker. "The FDIC ran out of money and the federal government refused to step in because it had no money either, so customers lined up to get their cash. It was just like 'It's a Wonderful

Fucking Life'—pardon my language, but I'm still bitter about it—except no goddamn angel saved me." She tuned him out; she had her own problems. She was still trembling from the crash landing.

The two got to their destination, collected their bags, and stood in front of a house, a depressing house. Leaned against the house on either side of an ugly green metal door that clashed with the yellow paint peeling off the house were drab grey cast iron slabs decorated with graffiti. The front windows were boarded up with plywood, also embellished by vandals. The yard was bursting with overgrown weeds, the only sign of life about the place, unless one counted a yellowing mugo pine to one side of the door and an all but departed shrub of some sort to the other. A splintered board here and there suggested the remains of an ancient fence. There was a mound of dirt that looked newly dug just to the left of a crumbling cement walk to the front door; if it'd been big enough to hold a body, she would have left right then.

Nervous, Tessa walked to the door and knocked. She put on her fetching smile, smoothed her auburn hair—which looked rich brown in dim light but had a lovely red hue in bright light—and tried to make her breathtaking aquamarine eyes sparkle. The door opened and out jutted a handsome, dark-haired head, which eyed Tessa, said, "Fuck off, Red Bush," and slammed the door.

"That didn't go as well as I'd hoped," noted Tessa. She knocked once more.

"Red Bush?" said Mort.

"Never mind." The face appeared again and Tessa said, "Come on, Kevin. Let us in. We're in big trouble."

Kevin Idle, looking beat in faded tan jeans, a ratty burgundy shirt, battered sneakers, and a three-day-old beard, said, "I have an acute case of apathy, plus I'm not in the market for more trouble, thanks. Got plenty already. Try next door."

"We just traveled all the way from South Dakota to get your help," she said in a pleading tone. "Our plane almost crashed."

"That's a sad story. Boring, too. Get lost."

Suddenly a van screeched to a halt in front of the house. Kevin reached out, grabbed Tessa's arm, and yanked her inside. As four armed men bolted out of the van, Kevin yelled to Mort, who was standing in shock looking at the assaulters, "You have one second before I shut you out."

Mort's considerable talent at fleeing overcame his considerable skill at cowering and he trundled inside, as the men started shooting. One bullet clipped Mort's right shoulder as Kevin closed the bullet-proof door. He fell to the floor screaming and whining.

Kevin took a garage door opener off a hook on the wall and pushed the button. An explosion outside prompted Tessa and Mort to shriek, but once they stopped, there was only silence, apart from Mort's whining. Kevin went to the door, opened it a crack, and grimaced.

"What happened?" asked Tessa, trembling.

"This," said Kevin as he pulled the door wide open. Through the smoke, the three made out bloody pieces of flesh strewn everywhere, including one revolting mess slowly oozing down the door. "I think I got them."

The van had been blown halfway across the street. A small crater had taken the place of the mini grave.

"Oh, Jesus!" exclaimed Mort, retching.

Tessa shut her eyes in terror. Kevin said, "Told you I got trouble. They were from a Mexican gang that I'm currently at loggerheads with."

Tessa opened her eyes, trying once more to wake herself from her continuing nightmare. Still trembling, she stood speechless, not even blinking.

Kevin went on, "You look impressed, Sharp. I guess the place just needed a splash of color." He looked outside again and said to Mort, "You left your suitcase out there, tubby. Not much left of it. I think I see a pair of your skivvies covering a Volkswagen across the street." He looked back at Mort and said, "You puked all over my carpet, douchebag." He checked Mort's wound, noted it was little more than a scratch and added, "I'd pick you up and toss you out, but I seem to be fresh out of forklifts, so pick yourself up and bleed somewhere else. It should be safe to leave now."

Tessa, at last able to speak again, asked, "How did you make that explosion?"

Kevin answered, "Want the recipe? Dig hole, add a soupcon of C-4, insert detonator, replace dirt, pat down, add four Mexicans, explode, let cool, spread Mexibits evenly over lawn."

He walked out to the front yard, saying, "You two, out of my house and out of my life," but before they could react, a beat-up pickup pulled up in front of his house. Two armed men jumped out pointing guns at Kevin. Falling to his knees, he cried, "Please don't shoot, oh, please don't shoot!" Tessa stepped behind the door and looked out the crack.

"I guess someone beat us here," said one of the men as he surveyed the carnage. "What caused this?"

"A b-bomb," answered Kevin in a panicky voice.

"What a fucking mess," he said to his companion. Turning to Kevin, he said, "The skinny bitch and fat bastard dead?"

"Yeah, pieces of them," he said, pointing a shaky finger here and there. "Some, some guy blew them up right on my, my front lawn," said Kevin in a more panicky voice.

But just then Mort burped and vomited. The men looked in the house and saw him.

"That must be the fucker there," the hit man said, as Mort belatedly stepped out of sight.

Whimpering, Kevin said, "Go in and get them, but please don't hurt me. Plea-he-he-he-hese!"

"Oh, Jesus, he's giving us up," said Mort to Tessa. "Your big, brave bodyguard, who we traveled across the country to hire, is actually crying. We're dead; oh, Jesus, we're dead!"

Tessa looked on in shock. She told herself, *What was I thinking? I know how useless he's always been. Now I see he's a coward, too. That rumor about him being a Navy Seal was a sad joke that's going to end up killing me.*

The man said to his colleague, "Shoot this pathetic wimp and I'll go in and finish them off."

"No!" exclaimed Kevin. "I'm just a carpenter. I knew the girl in high school, and I hate her guts, and I never met the fat one. Kill them; I don't care. But you don't need to kill me. Oh, God, I don't want to die!"

The men laughed at the weeping man, and one walked up to Kevin and pointed his pistol at his head. Tessa was getting set to run out the back, but Kevin suddenly grabbed the gun, blew a hole through the hit man's forehead, turned the gun on the other one, and did the same. It took about a second.

He stomped back into his house. Glowering at Tessa, he said, "Who the hell were those guys?"

"That's why we're here. We have killers after us," said Tessa.

"I gathered. Why? … Wait! I don't care. Both of you, get the hell out!"

"We'll pay you ten grand," said Tessa.

That got his attention. So did movement outside. A teenager ran to the pickup, which was running, got in and drove it away. "Hey, I was about to steal that!" Kevin yelled.

Just then, a black SUV screamed to a halt in front of his house. He rushed to the open door to shut it. Good thing, for two men burst out with submachine guns. Kevin managed to close the door just as the shooting began. In a fed up tone, he said, "I see you still have your well-honed talent for pissing off men," as he went to his closet and took out a handgun with a suppressor. "These two look like pros. Go out the back and keep going. Don't come back."

"Are you crazy? They'd kill us before we left the yard," said Tessa.

"I got a posse after me already. One's enough."

A window broke upstairs, followed immediately by a thump. "What was that?" asked Tessa.

Kevin looked to the sky; he hated stupid questions, she recalled, and always gave a saucy reply to them. "Unless I miss my guess, that was the sound of a herd of turtles stampeding on my roof." He gave Tessa the pistol he'd taken from the hit man and said, "One's upstairs dealing with a little surprise I set up, but you can bet the other one will try to get in down here, or they wouldn't have made noise upstairs. The doors are bullet-proof and the windows are boarded up, except for mom's bedroom window—she insisted on being able to see outside—but a grenade will open anything. Be ready and shoot whoever comes in."

"I've never used a gun. Why don't you shoot them?"

"I deplore violence," he said. "If you want, I'll stay here and you sneak up on the guy upstairs and take him out."

Kevin ran off toward the staircase with Tessa pleading, "No, Kevin, I can't, I can't! Come back!" He disappeared up the stairs.

A loud blast from the back of the house elicited screams from Tessa and Mort. Mort ran for the closet. Tessa thought that was a good idea and followed, but Mort shut the door and held it shut. "Open up!" she shouted.

"Drop the gun," said a cold voice from behind.

She followed the command and turned to face the hit man. He raised his gun, but was distracted when a man came tumbling down the stairs, ending up in a lifeless heap at the bottom.

"Shit," said the hit man as he crept toward the staircase, trying to see upstairs while keeping an eye on Tessa. Apparently deciding to earn his money and get out quickly, he turned back and pointed the gun at Tessa's head. She only had time to gasp before she heard a pop and the hit man fell dead. She looked to her left and saw Kevin holding a smoking gun.

"Christ almighty, I should get a kickback from the undertakers," said Kevin.

"No! No! This *has* to be a nightmare," she said.

"Well, wake the fuck up before I die," suggested Kevin.

All this was too much for Tessa, who collapsed to her knees, then to the floor and blacked out.

She opened her eyes, she knew not how much later, to see Kevin stepping over her, carrying three cases of canned food. He headed into the garage. Sitting up, she noticed Mort sitting on a chair, fidgeting. Kevin returned, stepped over her legs, and headed downstairs.

Tessa got to her feet and walked to the top of the basement stairs. Kevin came up with more food. "Help out, Red Bush," he said as he brushed by her.

She walked down the stairs and looked around for more food to carry up, but saw none. There was a hole in the concrete floor, but it was empty.

Kevin called down, "Bring up the frigging crap dap. We need to get the hell out of here."

She saw a four-roll package of toilet paper. She grabbed it and walked up the stairs. "I couldn't see any more food," she said.

"What little I had hidden away is already in the truck. I told the chubby chap to help me, but he won't budge from the damn chair. Throw that into the truck and get those boxes of ammunition in there," he said, gesticulating toward the hall closet. He was carrying the handgun, a grungy rifle with a silencer, and the machine guns to the garage.

In the garage was an ancient Dodge Ram whose main feature was rust. She tossed the toilet paper into the bed of the truck, put her suitcase and pocketbook in the back seat, and went to get the ammunition. Passing Kevin in the front hall, she said, "I was worried for a minute that you were going to let us die. You're a great actor. Were you even scared?"

"Let's just say it's fortunate I'm wearing brown pants."

"Thank you, Kev. We'd be dead now if not for you."

"Fine. Now I'll take you somewhere, then drive as far away from you as I can." He picked up a large desert camouflage backpack, which was already packed, and brought it to the truck with Tessa following.

"You can't leave us."

"Can; must; will." He turned to tell Mort something, but paused to look at him quaking and breathing fast. "I've never seen him look like that," he observed to Tessa.

"You've never seen him before."

"That must be why."

"He's the nervous type to begin with. Seeing a bunch of men blown to pieces probably didn't sit well with him. Didn't do me much good either."

"Tough," he sympathized. Turning to Mort, he said, "Haul yourself up and get into the back seat of my truck. Move it or I leave you behind."

Huffing and puffing, Mort got up and walked to the truck. Tessa got into the front passenger seat. Kevin peeked through small, shattered windows in the garage door. He opened the door, hurried to the truck, got in, and drove out.

# CHAPTER 2

"Why not steal that one?" asked Tessa, gesturing to the SUV still parked out front as they drove past it.

"Don't care for the color," he said in his sarcastic tone. "It's too new; almost certainly has all that anti-theft and satellite tracking stuff in it, and I don't have time to disable it. Some enterprising punk will have it before dark."

Looking at the horrific scene they were leaving, Tessa said, "You'd think someone would call the cops."

"Someone probably did; they'll be along any day now."

"You were living with your mother, right? Where is she?"

"Fuckers killed her three weeks back."

"Oh, Kevin, I'm sorry. My father was murdered four days ago."

"Shit. Sorry, Tess. Same guys after you?"

"Probably. Did the police catch your mother's murderer?"

He chuckled bitterly and said, "They showed up two days later and asked me where I was, who could verify it, how much money I got in the will, life insurance, and on and on. I was informed that the number three class of murders nowadays is

15

parricide; people killing their elderly parents to get their money and belongings. I told them I was almost sure I know who did it. They jotted the information down, but as far as I know I'm still suspect number one. I'm not worried, though; with the backlog of murders, I'll die of old age before they ever investigate."

"So, you took matters into your own hands."

"You're damn right I did. I should've been here protecting her, but we needed to eat, so I was at my job protecting the rich SOBs from the riotous rabble. The gangs found out she had food, more than likely because she was so big-hearted, she couldn't say no to all the starving children who came to her door looking for food—the parents always send their kids to do the begging. So a gang attacked the house when I was at work. They got in, killed her, and took all our food, except for the stuff I had hidden in the basement floor. They also stole everything else worth anything, including our prehistoric computer, TV, dishes, towels, knickknacks, even our toilet paper—I got more yesterday. All they left was the big furniture that would've been too much trouble to take.

"I confirmed what gang it was—the Mexican mob—and I've been killing them since. Those four made thirteen. And last week, I killed two Asian pricks who tried to kidnap a girl in the neighborhood I was hired to protect, so I'm probably on their hit list, too. Beat that."

"Okay," said Tessa. "Mort—oh, maniac killer Kevin, this is fat fuck Mort—Mort built a super battery that will be worth a lot of money. He was working in my father's lab and built the prototype according to my father's design—the idiot doesn't recall what the particular formulation was at the moment.

Word got around and someone showed up to steal the prototype and stop the technology."

"Someone?"

"God knows who. Could've been sent by Exxon or Eveready or General Electric or Con Edison or the Arabs or the solar industry—"

"How do you know they want to stop the technology if they stole the prototype? Maybe they just want it for themselves."

"Because they killed my father and tried to kill Mort, the only two people who can reproduce it."

"The only two people who can contest their ownership of the patent. Presumably they can reverse-engineer it."

"Whatever. We're running for our lives either way."

"These guys can't be too professional if they missed Mort. He looks hard to miss."

Tessa explained, "They tampered with the brakes on his car, which ended up killing his wife and son—but don't feel bad since Mort is happy about it."

"Elaine was the she-devil," said Mort. "I was her punching bag. She was a psychopath. I'm not just saying that; she was diagnosed by two psychiatrists. And her kid was just as bad. I could see early signs that she had passed her defective genes on to him. Little things: he'd torture the frogs he caught; he'd go crazy with anger over something meaningless. And big things, too: he was incapable of showing any real affection for me or Elaine. He's better off dead than going through life as a psychopath. They—"

Impatient with Mort's rambling, Kevin cut in, "So, the killer or killers tried to make it look like an accident with Mort. How did they kill your father?"

"I don't know. The police said he just died in his sleep."

"How do you know he was murdered?"

"Because they stole the prototype and targeted Mort. Way too much coincidence. And they stole everything else having to do with the battery from the lab and from my father's apartment. Nothing suspicious there, eh?"

"What did the police say?"

"A drunk dying in his sleep? Nothing too unusual about that. They couldn't possibly devote the manpower to something like that. Or maybe he killed himself; his employer's going out of business and alcohol's a depressant. If they investigated suicides they'd have no time for anything else; there's a rash of them these days. As for the robberies, there's an epidemic of them, too, and they don't have the manpower to investigate. And Mort's brakes? Their car was twenty-one years old; the brake line just wore out. They probably didn't even look for evidence of tampering. Maybe if we actually had the blueprint ..." Here she glowered at Mort.

Kevin said, "Par for the course with the cops. Either they don't have the manpower to investigate, or they were paid off by the murderers. Either way, you lose. I think we can treat today's fireworks as evidence someone means you harm. You said your plane almost crashed?" She nodded.

"What happened?"

"The engine blew up," said Mort.

"They probably did that, too," said Kevin.

"I hadn't thought of that," said Tessa. She considered for a moment and continued, "But I don't see how; we weren't even scheduled to be on that plane. It was a last minute change."

"Oh. Maybe a missile? No, probably just shitty maintenance because there was no one at the Syracuse airport to kill you in case the plane made it there. You got there before they figured." He turned right. "I wonder how they tracked you two to my house?" Tessa and Mort shrugged. "They came in shooting. No more trying to cover up murder. When you ran, you forced their hand. They're panicking."

"So you'll help us?"

"With what I'm dealing with already, I wouldn't, except for the ten grand you promised. New dollars, not the old shit, right?"

"Uh, yes, presuming we can figure out the formulation."

"That's quite a goddamn proviso, Red Bush, since hefty bag doesn't know what he did. I think I'll cut my losses. I have my hands full, and I can't deal with your shit, too."

"But he can probably figure it out if we can keep him alive and get him to a lab."

"Just how much is this battery worth, anyway?"

"Tens of billions," said Mort.

Tessa winced. She didn't quite trust Kevin, and now his price for helping would go way up.

"Billions?" said Kevin as he rocketed his outraged eyes to Tessa. "You offer me ten thousand bucks when your payoff is tens of *billions*?"

"Potentially. Chances are it will come to nothing."

"Didn't you tell me not five seconds ago he can probably figure it out? Which is it, Red Bush?"

"Stop calling me that, pothead. Now that I see how dangerous it is, I'll be happy to offer more."

"Now that you see how dangerous … Listen to yourself! You offered me that money *after* two guys tried to kill me. You knew damn well how dangerous it was, but you thought nothing about putting my life on the line."

"That's not true; I don't want to see you hurt."

"Yeah, I know; you'll just close your eyes when I get shot."

"I came to you out of desperation. I know how much you hate me, but you're the only one I can think of who can help me."

"Stop the flattery. I'm blushing." He pulled the truck to the curb and stopped. "Out of here."

"Please, Kevin, don't leave us like this, or we're dead. We'll give you a hundred thousand."

"Out!"

"How can you say no to a hundred thousand bucks? Got people lined up to give you jobs? You're so desperate, you're dragging around food and toilet paper. How can you possibly justify saying no?"

"If I felt I had to justify myself to you, I'd repeat that I already have two gangs after me, so you're not safe with me anyway, and chances are the battery will come to nothing, and I hate your guts, but since I don't have to justify myself to you, I'll just tell you to piss off."

"Please, Kev. I might be killed!"

"Just leave Fat Fuck to fend for himself."

"No!" screeched Mort. "Don't leave me alone."

"That battery is my father's invention. I'm not leaving it to Mort."

"Get out of my truck."

She gave him a pleading look, but he returned a cold stare. Resigned to his rejection, she said, "At least tell me where I can go to get help."

"I know this guy who might do it for a price."

"If you ignore my incredible debt, I have eight newbucks."

"Tell him your story, but don't let on Mort doesn't know what he did. Tell him he already has the battery, and you'll pay him a hundred thousand new dollars to protect him until you can sell the thing."

"He probably won't believe me."

"Probably not. But since you're pretty, he might take sex as a goodwill gesture."

Tessa leered at Kevin. "Who is he, your ex-cellmate?"

"Funny. He's an ex-Green Beret who I've heard is the best bodyguard in town. Name is Jonny DiLoreto. I don't know if he's as good as everyone says, or if everyone thinks he's so good because he's always bragging, but he gets away with charging a hundred newbucks an hour for his services."

Kevin drove on. They approached a park overgrown with weeds, overflowing with litter and overrun with rats, and he pulled into a parking space. Tessa saw men and women with grey skin, missing teeth and vacant eyes, coughing, drooling, and spitting. Seeing her gawking, Kevin said, "Junkies so desperate for a fix they'll overcome their normal stupor and crawl across a field of broken glass to jump the next person they see to get money, a watch, a ring, a necklace—anything to help them score their next fix. Stay here; they'd happily twist your head off to get what they crave. Lock the door."

21

"Where are you going?" asked Tessa. He leaned over, opened the glove box, and took out two cans of Heinz beans. "I thought you said the junkies are dangerous."

"Stay here."

He crossed the field walking toward a grove of pines. Sure enough, three junkies followed him. He stopped and pointed his gun at them. They walked away.

Curious, Tessa followed, staying close enough to get his protection if needed, but far enough to escape his attention.

He changed direction upon spotting a young woman with short blonde hair. She was cute; Tessa guessed her age at maybe seventeen. Tessa hid behind a tree.

The woman knelt before him and said, "What do I get today?"

"HB."

"I'd prefer DMBS."

"Sorry, all gone. HB or nothing."

She shrugged, unzipped his pants, and reached in to pull it out. Tessa looked on, mouth hanging open in shock.

An effeminate man, attired shabbily, walked by saying, "Try the wild side for once, Idle."

Kevin returned, "Can't get past the turn of a man's ankle. Or his bag. Hey, did you hear Kentucky's banned homosexuality? You no longer exist in Kentucky, Stevie."

"Troglodytes," said Steve as he continued on his way.

As the girl earned her beans, Kevin yelled to Tessa, "Get lost, Red Bush. Give us some privacy."

She stepped out and said, "In the middle of the day at a public park? You're disgusting, not to mention desperate."

A huge black man came up to her and said, "Looking for work, babe? You could earn a lot."

"Fuck off," she said, which she learned was unadvisable after he put his large hand around her neck and squeezed.

"On your knees, bitch. I'll train you good."

"Oh, for fuck sake!" said Kevin as he pulled away from the girl. "Here you go, Crystal," he said as he handed her the can and zipped up. He jogged over to the man and said, "Stay cool, George. She's with me." He handed George the other can of beans.

"Fuck off, Idle. I can make a bundle off her." He pulled out a needle.

"No!" screamed Tessa.

"It'll make you feel real good, bitch. Then you can make me feel real good."

Kevin pulled out his gun. "I'm through asking. Now I'm telling. Drop the needle." George let it fall. "Now, let her go."

George threw the can at Kevin and pulled Tessa in front of him. The can hit Kevin in the chest. He yelped. George went for his gun, but Kevin shot him in the left leg. He went down, dragging Tessa with him. Kevin came up to George and pointed the gun at his head. "Let go now!"

George submitted. Kevin picked up George's gun, which had fallen to the ground, and tossed it out of George's reach.

"Come on," he said as he took Tessa's hand and pulled her up.

Tessa held onto Kevin for a moment out of anxiety. Then she let him go out of revulsion.

"Next time I see you, I'll kill you," screamed George.

"Yeah, get in line," said Kevin as he took back his beans and rubbed his sore chest. Heading back to the truck, he said to Tessa, "You just had to stick your nose in. Christ, you're nothing but trouble."

"What is she, maybe seventeen?"

"Birth certificate not required."

"I can't believe I'm associating with you."

"I do it as a public service; I'm helping to keep pretty young things alive by giving them a simple means of earning some food."

"That monster probably did to her what he tried to do to me. Get her hooked on heroin and keep her in thrall. It takes perverts like you to keep him in business."

"Yes, Sister Tessa."

Tessa saw the girl cowering behind a tree and called to her. "Come with us. We'll get you away from him."

"Jesus, Sharp, what are we going to do with—"

"Shut up, perv. What's your name?"

"Crystal."

"Come with us."

The girl walked with them. "You want me to finish, Kev?" asked Crystal.

"No!" answered Tessa. "You don't need to do that anymore."

"Who the hell is she?" asked Crystal.

"No one," said Kevin.

"Well, No One," said Crystal, "if I don't do this, I die, unless you got a bunch of money to give me." Tessa looked down. "Just what I thought. Typical rich bitch; full of advice, but unwilling to really help. I'll have you know, Ms. Holier

24

Than Thou, his cock saved my life more than once; I'd have died of starvation without it."

"Yup, I'm a bonerfide hero," bragged Kevin.

Tessa pulled out two dollar coins and handed them to Crystal. She took them without a thank you, saying, "I better get back and help George, or he'll be real mad at me."

"I just winged him; he'll be fine. Here's his HB."

"It would help me deal with him if you give me a few DMBS," said Crystal.

"I have none."

"Any CBR?"

"I'm low on food, Crystal. Good luck."

She turned and ran back to George.

"That two bucks will help with her next score," said Kevin.

"Who says she'll use it for drugs?"

"What do you figure she's going to do with it? Start a college fund?"

"Maybe buy a DMBS. I figured out HB is Heinz Beans. What about the other letters?" asked Tessa.

"Dinty Moore Beef Stew, Chef Boyardee Ravioli. Street currency. Speaking of food, I just realized you left that pig alone with our food supply! Let's run."

They got to the truck, where two junkies were helping themselves to the toilet paper. Kevin fired into the air, and they walked off with two rolls of toilet paper each. Mort was cringing in the back seat. Looking inside, Kevin saw five empty cans of beans and two of chicken noodle soup on the seat. His hand was in another can of beans.

"You son of a bitch!" Kevin barked. He opened the back door and pointed his gun at Mort, who screamed.

"Kevin, don't!" pleaded Tessa.

"The fucker finished off six HBs and two CCNs." She put her hand on his hand and pushed it down. Kevin holstered his gun and yelled, "You fat, greedy pig. That stash is the last of my food. You ate three days' worth in ten minutes. Get out. I'm going to show you what your intestines look like." He reached in to pull Mort out, but Mort was pretty much immovable when he wanted to be.

"Kevin, stop this," urged Tessa.

"If you even look at any more of my food, you die. Understood?"

A terrified Mort nodded as he swallowed the last of the beans.

"Why the hell did you leave him with the food? That's like leaving, uh …"

"You in charge of a whorehouse?"

"Perfect. I'd be most attentive to quality control."

"Yes, I just saw your definition of quality: a teenage junkie in the park. Losing your food is your fault for getting your jollies with a child prostitute. How can you live with yourself?"

He pretended to cry and said, "I'm just a shit stain on the underpants of life." She lifted her eyes. He went on, "You're supposed to be a genius, but isn't it incredibly stupid to be constantly insulting the person who represents your only current chance of staying alive, a person who already hates you and wouldn't lose a wink of sleep if the hit men succeed in their mission?"

"Get over yourself, will you? That you're still pissed I dumped you eleven years after the fact shows how petty you are. I've never regretted my decision. You were a complete loser back then; you couldn't go a day without grass or hash or booze or cigarettes or sluts. Some things never change."

"So how have things worked out for you, Sharp? No rings, I see. Mr. Right not cooperating?"

"I'm in no hurry. I don't even need to ask about your love life; I've just seen it."

"I could have a woman like that." He snapped his fingers.

"As long as you pay. No woman with any class would be interested."

"Like you, you mean? If I wanted to meet a woman like you, I'd go trolling downtown with a can of pea soup."

"If I wanted to meet a guy like you, I'd just shoot myself up with heroin and hang out at parks."

"I hope the hell Jonny is there. I can't wait to get rid of … Oh, shit."

"What?" She saw him looking at a dangerous-looking man crossing the street toward two young teenage girls.

"That crazy bugger is back on the streets," Kevin said as he started toward the man. Tessa followed. "He tried to kill one of the girls here last Tuesday; he was choking her to death until I smashed him in the face. As far as I can tell, he thinks God has chosen him to cleanse the world of prostitutes, and he thinks any young woman is a prostitute. Should be in a mental hospital, but they're all closed."

The man beset the girls, hollering, "The sexually immoral shall be in the lake that burns with fire and sulfur."

The girls screeched and tried to run, but he grabbed both and hurled them down to the ground.

"None of the daughters of Israel shall be a prostitute!" the insane man shouted as he fell on them and put an arm around the throat of each and squeezed.

Kevin dashed to him and, in a scary voice, bellowed, "I am the god of hell-fire, and you're pissing me off!" He kicked the man in the face. The girls scrambled to their feet and ran away crying. Kevin took out his handgun.

"Kevin?" said Tessa. "This would be murder."

"How many women will this lunatic kill?"

"It's not your right. He's sick."

"Tell that to the parents of the next teenager he comes across. They've found the bodies of three young women who'd been strangled in the last few weeks. This is the most likely culprit."

"Call the police."

"I called them last time, yet here he is."

She could voice no further objection.

Kevin shot the man in both knees. The man screamed out in pain. "That ought to slow him down," said Kevin. The man continued to squeal, so Kevin kicked him in the head once more, saying, "Shut the hell up." That knocked him out.

As they headed back to his pickup, Tessa said, "He might die there."

"Good."

She couldn't disagree. "You saved their lives, Kev. One minute you're this disgusting pervert, the next this dashing hero. I can't make you out at all."

A small man walked by in the park. Kevin reached into the truck, got a can of HB, and jogged over to the man. Seeing Kevin fast approaching, the man pulled a revolver. Kevin put up his hands, then showed him the HB. He exchanged the can for something that Tessa couldn't see.

Back in the pickup, Kevin pushed in the cigarette lighter. She saw he was holding a cigarette. "I don't believe it," she said. "You traded, like, one-thirtieth of our food supply for one cigarette?"

"No, I traded one-thirtieth of *my* food supply for one cigarette. I'm a Kool man; they don't come cheap."

"You're a fool, man … Don't smoke that thing in here."

Kevin lit up.

"You're back to disgusting." She opened her window. He closed it and pushed the power window lock. "Idle! You're such a child."

He chortled, blew smoke on her, pulled out of the parking spot, and drove downtown. She opened the door a crack to get rid of the smoke. He unlocked the windows.

"Shit, I need gas," Kevin said as he came up to a Texaco station. "Jesus, I hate lining up for frigging gas, then paying six-ninety-nine a gallon."

"That makes you different from everyone else," Tessa replied sarcastically.

They had sat in line for twenty-seven minutes, and Kevin was next in line when the man at the pump started hollering and cursing.

"They're out of regular," Tessa said as a security guard came to calm the man down under the threat of a whack with his night stick.

The man pulled off to the side to line up to pay. There were so many stolen credit and debit cards circulating that paying at the pump had been suspended years earlier at most gas stations.

The lineups were even worse at stations that still permitted paying at the pump.

The security guard yelled to the people lined up for regular, "If you want regular, you have to line up at those pumps."

That induced a group groan and not a few choice vulgar words from the drivers on the south side of the station. Kevin pulled up to the high octane pump. He cursed again at the eight-ninety-nine per gallon price. At that price, he told Tessa, he could only afford five gallons; he had forty-seven newbucks in his pocket and no more available credit. He got to three-point-seven gallons when the pump ran dry. A stream of curses greeted that event, and the security guard returned. Kevin gave every indication he was going to grab the club the man was flourishing, but Tessa said, "Kevin!"

The drivers behind him began bellowing and swearing and beeping their horns in protest. All three security guards rushed over to get them to leave. Kevin let more execrations flow as he pulled ahead and parked to join the next line up.

Worried about what an obviously impatient Kevin might do in the queue to pay, Tessa accompanied him. She counted six people in front of them. Not too bad; or it shouldn't have been. The only man the multi-billion-dollar Texaco Inc could presumably afford to pay was slow and belligerent. One woman pulled out a wad of old dollar bills, which were used as pennies since the new coin dollars were issued at a rate of one per hundred old dollars. This, too, caused cursing and another waving club. The man at the till insisted on recounting every one of the four hundred-plus bills.

It took sixteen minutes to get to the second spot in line. The line behind them now extended out of the store. The woman in front of him made the mistake of complaining about the lines, so she was shunted to the back of the line by the security guard at the insistence of the clerk.

"Kevin, watch what you say," Tessa warned as they stepped to the counter. He'd been so frustrated by all the goings on that he'd neglected to dig the money out of his pockets.

The clerk exercised his authority once more by saying, "Next!" and taking the next person's credit card.

That did it.

"I'm next, asshole!" screamed Kevin.

The security guard came to the rescue once more, threatening Kevin with the truncheon.

"Back of the line!" said the clerk.

In the blink of an eye Kevin snatched the club, smashed the guard over the head. As the guard fell unconscious to the floor, Kevin grabbed the clerk by the lapels, dragged him over the counter, and administered one, two, three, four, five, six, seven punches to the face in quick succession before letting him go to collapse onto the guard. The crowd behind burst into spontaneous applause.

Kevin smiled as Tessa took his hand and pulled him out to the car for the getaway before the other security guards found out what happened. They drove off with Tessa chastising Kevin for risking their lives. "If the police arrest you, where does that leave me?" she said.

"Away from me. I can live with that," he responded.

On the way to DiLoreto's, Tessa looked to her right and said, "Oh, look, it's a mother and two little children. Husband probably left her high and dry." A small boy dressed in rags held up a sign that said, *We're starving. Please help us!* The mother was holding a baby girl in her arms.

Kevin drove by, saying, "That's the first baby I've seen in months. I thought they stopped making them."

"Stop!" she insisted. "We have to help them."

"No, we don't."

"Stop, you heartless bastard." She pulled the wheel to the right. He put on the brakes, but not in time to avoid jumping the curb.

"What now?" asked Kevin.

"We give them some food."

"I have maybe half a week's worth of food as it is after pus pocket back there ate my other half-week's worth in ten seconds flat. And what about the family around the next bend? Give them some, too? There's no shortage of people who'll gladly take our food and leave us to starve."

"Is this what we've come to in this country?"

"We've come to this: if we help people who can't do anything for us in return, we join them begging in the streets. There's still welfare for the desperately poor and food kitchens for the starving."

She turned, got to her knees, and leaned over the front seat to get three cans of CCN.

"No!" said Mort. "We'll starve!"

Ignoring him, Tessa stepped out of the truck, walked to the mother, and gave her the soup. The woman thanked her profusely. Tessa returned to the truck feeling good about herself, and Kevin drove on. When they came up to the next starving family, Kevin sped up. Tessa shook her head. Kevin was right, she realized, and that was depressing enough to start her tears.

# CHAPTER 3

Kevin pulled to a stop across the street from a dive called DiLoreto's Place. All three exited the truck and entered the establishment.

Kevin told Tessa, "You'll like his looks. Who was that actor you used to adore who played Kirk in *Star Trek*?"

"Chris Pine."

"Well, this guy looks exactly like Chris Pine will after a lawnmower runs over his face and he's been dead for a week. That's him working on a bottle of gin."

Tessa looked at him. Even without the tracks of old stitches that embroidered his face, he was repulsive, but he was big and fearsome, which was what she needed.

"Frankenstein-looking motherfucker, eh? You think I'm scary? He starts where I leave off. He carries a shrunken human head on his belt. But he's handy if you need someone to crush a man's skull. Hey, Jonny!" said Kevin.

"Fuck off, Idle."

"Nice to see you, too. I bring you some business."

"Why? Since when do you turn down business? What's the story?"

"I got survival issues to get past."

"I heard you got the spicks and chinks after you. Pretty stupid, Idle."

"Can't disagree there. This is Tessa Sharp and Mort, uh—"

"Mort Wood," said Mort.

"You got a bean on your shirt, Wood," said Jonny. "Looks like you don't often miss your mouth with food," said Jonny with a loud laugh at his jest.

Picking it off his shirt, Mort went to deposit it into his mouth, but Kevin grabbed his hand, saying, "That's my bean, you acre of shit." Mort closed his hand to keep his prize. Kevin attempted to prize it open, which he eventually did, but the bean was smeared all over Mort's hand. With Kevin glaring at him, Mort licked it off.

"I'll beat you to a pulp—"

"Kevin!" reprimanded Tessa. "It's a bean! Listen to yourself."

"Listen to myself? Are you out of your mind? I'd go nuts in no time."

She furrowed her forehead and shook her head.

Without mentioning that the prototype was stolen, Tessa and Mort described their plight. Jonny readily agreed to the hundred grand payday. A sticking point was a down payment. Jonny mentioned that Tessa just might be in possession of an acceptable down payment, "Something you sit on every day," as he put it. He didn't laugh when Tessa handed him a chair. They finally settled on a hand job, with "future considerations" once they were safe.

As Kevin was leaving, she mentioned to him that she would never forgive him for leaving her behind and for making her humiliate herself with a man who was exactly the cad that his face advertised. He informed her, "Fuck you," and he walked out.

*

As Kevin got set to drive away, he looked up to see Jonny stride out of the bar fearlessly with Tessa and Mort cowering behind him. Out of the blue, a man stepped out from the alley beside the bar, raised his gun, and shot Jonny in the back. Two nearby pedestrians fled. Tessa and Mort turned and looked at the killer with horrified faces. Kevin grimaced, thinking *that's the end of Tessa* and feeling a pang of remorse, but a brown Mercury came out of nowhere to run down the killer. Tessa and Mort ran back toward the bar as the car screeched to a halt and a man jumped out. He shot at them, but missed. Cursing, he jogged toward the bar.

"Oh, for God's sake!" cried Kevin. "Dueling assassins." He put his pickup in drive and stomped on the accelerator. He steered the Ram onto the sidewalk and rammed into the man, who was thrown dead to the pavement twenty feet away. The man in the Mercury jumped out and started firing on Kevin, who stepped on the brake, turned his truck ninety degrees, pointed his revolver, and shot the man three times through the passenger window.

Kevin got out of his truck and ran into the bar. "Tessa?" he called.

"Kevin?" she replied, sticking her head above the bar. Up came a fat head beside hers.

"Come on. Let's get out of here."

"What about the killers?"

"I lectured them, and they promised to behave themselves." She smirked. "They're dead, for Christ's sake."

"And Jonny?"

"Forever cured of his bravado. Unless you want to follow his example, follow me now. If you're not in the truck by the time I take my foot off the brake, I leave you behind." He walked out. Tessa ran and Mort lumbered after him. Kevin checked one of four bloody bodies for booty. "Check them," said Kevin.

Tessa and Mort gave disgusted looks and stayed still.

"God, you're pussies," said Kevin as he rifled the dead man's pockets. "This is your mess, and you're not getting away with leaving all the dirty work to me. We need their guns, ammunition, and anything else of value we can get off them. Tessa, check the car and that truck. Wood, check those two bodies."

Tessa and Mort reluctantly did as ordered. Between them, they collected four guns, several clips, and fifty-seven new dollars from the dead.

Kevin said, "There's obviously a price on your heads to bring all these people out gunning for you. They're even starting to bump each other off, so the price must be pretty high. The guy who shot Jonny seemed to be professional, but the two in the car were clowns. I mean, this one shot at Mort and missed. That's like jumping out of a row boat in the middle of the Atlantic and missing the water."

"Are you going to help us now, or are you going to palm us off on another loser who lasts one minute past the hand job?" asked Tessa. Kevin laughed, so she went to him and rubbed her hand on his face.

"Get that filthy thing away from me," he said. "Shit, now I smell like essence of Italian bag."

"Serves you right."

"The only other person I know who might be able to handle this is a former Delta Force dude."

"He sounds promising."

"I should mention that I heard he killed his own brother just for a case of kernel corn. The only thing worse than blowing away your brother is blowing your brother. Not sure how to find him, though."

"Never mind. I think you should help us. You owe us for almost getting us killed."

"That's you through and through, Red Bush. I've saved your life how many times today, yet I owe you? How spoiled and self-centered do you have to be to think like that?"

"Please, Kev, help us," said Tessa in great distress. "We're sitting ducks. Please don't leave us." Seeing him waver, she tried another tack to secure his help. "Our battery goes way beyond us, Kevin. Just consider what this breakthrough could mean to our country and to the world. The end of our energy dependence on fossil fuels, which means a much cleaner environment, and the end of Arab oil money that funds terrorists around the planet.

"Think of everything that's tied to the price of oil, especially the transportation of everything we buy. With this battery, we can slash the cost of *everything*. We can power

38

houses, factories, malls, you name it, for a fraction of the current cost. And it means a huge new North American industry that we *will* keep here and not ship off to China. Our battery could be just what our economy needs to get out of this never-ending depression. This could easily be the most important invention of the century. We can't let it die!"

Kevin nodded. She clutched his forearm and squeezed. He looked to see Mort chewing on a Snickers. "You get that off one of them?" He nodded. "You get anymore?" Kevin asked. Mort shook his head, but Kevin walked up to him, put his hand between Mort's fourth and fifth chins to hold him still, and checked his pockets. Pulling out two more candy bars, he said, "You're a big fat fibber," as he let go of Mort's neck and tossed another Snickers to Tessa. He kept the Milky Way for himself.

They heard a siren in the distance. "Let's get out of here," said Kevin. "Are the keys in the car?" he asked Tessa. She nodded. "Okay, you drive behind me."

"What for?"

"I want to have a mini parade," he said as his eyes went north. "Wood, get into the back of the truck and be our float ... Follow me down the street so I can siphon the gas out of it without the busybody cops detaining me for depriving these gentlemen of their lives."

*

They drove a couple of miles to an abandoned strip mall, one of dozens in the city. Kevin pulled the Ram up beside the car. He went to the back of the truck and took out a plastic hose. After removing the Mercury's gas cap, he put the hose down the pipe and sucked on the end. When the gas commenced flowing, he hurriedly put the other end into his gas tank and started spitting with an imprecation or two. "I feel like a cigarette," he said to get a reaction from Tessa. She merely smirked. He unwrapped and ate his Milky Way. "Gasoline and Milky Way go together like shit and ice cream."

With his gas tank topped up, Kevin took the tube out of the Mercury and lifted it to empty the last drops into his gas tank before rolling it up and tossing it into the bed of his pickup.

Gesturing to Tessa's purse, still on the back seat, he said, "Give me that."

Tessa asked why.

"I love the way it sets off my eyes … The bad guys keep finding you; one of you must have a bug on you. Could be in your purse."

She retrieved her pocketbook and dumped the contents onto the truck bed. He looked through it, but found nothing suspicious. Holding her smart phone, he asked, "This hasn't been on, has it?"

"No, it ran out of batteries in Rapid City." He dropped it onto the ground and stepped on it. "Hey!" said she.

"Just in case; it's useless to you anyway. Let's check your suitcase and your well fed zeppelin."

All she had in her suitcase were clothes and toiletries. He grabbed a pair of lacey, black panties and put them in his pocket. "Hey!" said she.

"Just in c—" was all he got out before she fished them out of his left pocket. "A little to the right," he said. She gave him a woman's oh-you're-such-a-pervert! look.

All Mort had that raised Kevin's eyebrows was a smart phone that was on. Mort clutched it in his hand and put his hand in his pocket. "Give me that," requested Kevin. Mort didn't comply, so Kevin put his pistol against Mort's forehead and said, "Pretty please?"

"Have you ever won an argument without putting a gun to someone's head?" asked Tessa.

"There was the time I won when I held a knife to someone's throat."

Mort handed the phone over.

"How long has this been on?" Mort looked down and shrugged. Glowering at Mort, Kevin handed the phone to Tessa, who was a wiz at anything electronic, and said, "What can you tell me?"

Tessa examined it for a minute, then held the display up to Kevin and said, "He's called this number four times in the last week."

"Who're you calling?" asked Kevin. Mort wouldn't answer. Turning back to Tessa, he asked, "Any today?"

Looking at it for another moment, she said, "Yes. Just after we landed. I saw him talking on it. He said he was calling his mother."

"What the hell is going on?" he asked Mort.

"Nothing!"

"I ought to end you right now, you bastard!" He put his revolver up to Mort's head once more and said, "You in on this somehow?"

"No!" cried Mort, trembling.

"It wouldn't make sense," said Tessa. "He's been a target, too."

"Maybe the guy who missed the Atlantic missed on purpose." Still with his gun to Mort's head, he demanded, "Explain."

"Uh … I'm not in on anything. It's just …" Mort hesitated.

"Time's running out for you," Kevin warned.

"Just after her father got to the School of Mines, a man approached me and said he was from BYD Company; it's a Chinese company that makes lithium ion car batteries."

"So he was Chinese?"

"No, he was maybe Middle Eastern."

"Go on."

"He said they were interested in our research. He told me if I gave him the heads up if we made a breakthrough, he'd give me ten thousand newbucks. I didn't see a problem with that, since we'd be looking to sell the technology anyway. So, when I made the breakthrough, I called him and told him I had a battery with energy densities more than a thousand times greater than the Li-ion type."

"That was my father's breakthrough, asshole," said Tessa.

"Did you tell him it was her father's design?" asked Kevin. Addressing Tessa, he said, "That would make him a target."

"Yes, I told the man it was Tessa's battery—I mean, Tessa's dad's battery," said Mort.

Kevin said, "Why four calls?"

"First I called to tell him I had the battery prototype. He said he wanted to see it. I said I'd need to check with Dr.

Sharp. But when he was found dead in his bed and the prototype was stolen, I had to call to tell my contact. Then when my wife and her kid were killed, I called to say I was afraid someone was trying to kill me. He told me it was just a coincidence and to stay put, and I intended to, but Tessa insisted we come to you. So I called to tell him we'd come to Syracuse."

"And then you left your phone on."

"He told me to."

"Stupidity on such a grand scale stupefies me. Christ, your astonishing idiocy even outlasted seven hit men. You still left your phone on! Tell me, where's the helmet special people like you are supposed to wear?"

Kevin looked around.

"What are you looking for?" asked Tessa.

"A jagged pipe suitable for evisceration," he answered in his snappish way. "Seeing if any more killers might be lurking."

Tessa, too, looked around with big eyes.

"We need to get out of here right away." Addressing Mort, he said, "Do exactly what I say or I swear I'll waste a bullet on your brain, assuming you have one."

"Okay! Okay! Don't shoot!"

Kevin told Tessa, "Dial that number and make it so we can all hear what the person on the other end is saying." She nodded.

Kevin took the phone back as it rang. A man answered, "Wood?"

Covering the microphone, Kevin said, "Say yes." He put the phone up to Mort's mouth.

"Yes," said Mort.

"I told you not to call me again."

Again covering the mouthpiece, Kevin said, "Tell him, people are trying to kill you."

"But people are trying to kill me," Mort said into the phone.

"I'll send help right away. We really want your battery, so we'll keep you safe, I promise. Just leave your phone on, and we'll find you."

Kevin ended the call. He looked around again to spot any trouble, but apparently saw nothing of concern. Getting into the Mercury, he told Tessa and Mort, "Get in the truck and follow me. Now!" He shot out of the parking lot. Turning left, he drove for half a mile and pulled over to the curb in front of a bar. Tessa pulled in behind him. Taking the keys, he exited the car and slid into the passenger seat of his truck. He told Tessa, "Drive up to the next street and turn left, then do a U-turn and pull up to the stop sign." She followed his directions.

"I presume you left his phone in the car?" asked Tessa. He nodded. "So we're watching to see if more hit men show up?" Another nod. "Wouldn't it be safer to just get far away from here?"

"I want to be one hundred percent sure Mort's not lying, and we need to learn whatever we can about who's after you."

At Kevin's behest, Tessa donned sunglasses and a scarf to hide her auburn locks. The hit men were looking for a redhead and a fat man, and they would be close to any upcoming action. Turning his head to Mort, Kevin said, "Get down."

"Why?"

"Just do it!" Mort ducked. "And stay down."

They sat and watched for eight minutes. Mort started snoring in the back.

A pair of white men walked out of the bar and eyed the parked car. They scanned the area, dashed to the Mercury, and got in.

"They're trying to steal the car!" observed Tessa.

"This complicates things."

The thieves got the car started and peeled out.

"Should I follow?" asked Tessa.

"I guess. The more we learn, the safer we are. Let him get a little ahead … Okay, go."

"Should you be driving?"

"I might need to shoot. He's turning. Speed up; keep him in sight."

Two minutes later, they pulled to the curb a hundred feet behind the Mercury, which was paused at a red light. The light changed, and the Mercury proceeded straight.

"Okay, let's g—Wait!" Tessa saw Kevin was looking at a black Nissan pickup truck fast approaching the intersection on the street to their left. "Let's see if he follows our stolen car."

Tessa saw a handsome black man at the wheel of the Nissan. He went through the red light and turned left behind the Mercury.

"Follow him," said Kevin.

She said, "Gladly. If he wasn't trying to kill me, I could really go for him."

She pulled out and followed. The Nissan turned right, then left, then right again and slowed to a crawl in a decrepit neighborhood. Tessa stopped about three-hundred-fifty feet in back of the Nissan. She saw the stolen car in a driveway, the two car thieves still inside. Suddenly, the Nissan accelerated and skidded to a halt in front of the house. A man popped out and riddled the car with bullets from a submachine gun. Tessa put her hand to her mouth and gasped.

"This is just the sort of thing that gives killers a bad reputation," said Kevin. "If you end up with the handsome man, don't try nagging him out of his bad habits."

"We should've just left the car behind. What good did witnessing this horror do us?"

"We confirmed Mort's story, and we learned that they shoot the minute they get near, without even confirming they got the right targets. That tells me they're nervous; they must know you have protection that could get them killed. Let's get out of here."

They drove to a commercial part of town, a long stretch of auto dealers, strip malls, fast food outlets, and gas stations. Three-quarters of the establishments were out of business. Weeds were encroaching on the parking lots, plastic signs were broken, and the buildings were in shambles. Most were gutted. Thieves had even carted away bricks, leaving little more than rubble where sturdy buildings had stood only a few years prior. It looked like a war zone. Shaking her head in dismay, she drove on.

One of the businesses still thriving was Wal-Mart. Tessa said, "Look at the lineup to get into Wal-Mart."

"Didn't they have lineups out west?"

"I didn't have to deal with them much; I don't have a car, and I got room and board."

"It's part of life here now, though it's not half as bad as a couple of years back. Once I saw a line here that wound right around the building. We better try to get some food," said Kevin. Tessa pulled into the parking lot and drove around for several minutes before beating an old lady into a parking spot. The woman cursed at her and continued her search.

A man came up to Tessa and said, "Two bucks and I make sure no one touches your truck."

"Two seconds and she'll drive over you with my truck," replied Kevin.

The man gave him the finger and looked for someone else to accost.

"Okay, Tessa, line up and bring back some food."

"Why, because the woman shops?"

"No, because the woman respects my command." She laughed. He tried, "Because the woman doesn't like the feeling of my hands constricting her throat." Knowing he would never hurt her, she narrowed her eyes and crossed her arms in defiance. So, he tried, "Because if the woman doesn't shop, she doesn't eat."

She hadn't needed convincing anyway. She'd already witnessed Kevin's behavior in line today.

Kevin said, "Take Wood."

"I'm not standing in that lineup," said Mort.

"You're the one who put the hit men on our tail and who ate half our food supply. I want you far away from me."

"Kev, as you know, we have murderers after us," said Tessa, "and they're looking for a redheaded woman together with a fat man."

"Ah, shit. Just go yourself, then."

"What should I get?"

"Fresh fruit and vegetables, or cans or bottles of fruit, vegetables, and meat. Nothing that needs refrigeration or cooking since we're on the road."

Kevin and Mort sat back and closed their eyes as Tessa got out of the truck and joined the lineup. About thirty feet ahead, a fight broke out where a man had attempted to cut in line. Security guards dragged him away screaming. People were coming out with carts overloaded with groceries, and the people in line were hurling abuse at them. Tessa asked a woman in front of her why.

The lady answered, "Half the problem is rich jerks hoarding. Get a six-week supply just in case the food stops coming. So what if there's nothing left for the next person in line?" The lady yelled at a man who was pushing one overflowing cart and pulling another, "Hey, did you get everything you needed, asshole?"

Tessa stood in line for forty-four minutes before getting into the store. The first thing she noticed was there were no carts left. The second was the lineups to check out were as bad as the lineup to get in. The third was the unimpressive selection of food and the many shoppers voicing their disapproval as wary security guards hovered close at hand.

Tessa checked out the fresh fruits and vegetables, but besides a few rotted potatoes, half-eaten apples, and crushed tomatoes, there was nothing left. Hurrying over to the food aisles, she managed to get a case of Libby's Wax Beans, a case of Bumble Bee Light Tuna, three cans of Del Monte Pear Halves, two cans of SPAM, and one dented can each of Green Giant Asparagus Spears, Hormel Chili, Del Monte Green Peas, and Dole Tropical Fruit Salad.

Piling the individual cans on top of the two cases, she carried the heavy load to the back of a long checkout line. She put her pile on the floor in front of her and shoved it forward with her foot when the line moved.

She looked to her left and her eyes widened as she stared at a TV. "Is that a movie?" she asked the woman behind her.

The woman looked and saw the torch and head from the Statue of Liberty in the midst of smoking debris. The banner under the picture said, "Breaking news: Statue of Liberty destroyed."

The woman said, "That's CNN. I think it must be real."

People up and down the lines gaped at the news. Many began to cry.

# CHAPTER 4

When Tessa got back to the truck, her shirt was ripped and her elbow was bleeding. Kevin got out of the truck and looked at what she was holding.

"A can of asparagus and a case of wax fucking beans? That's it?"

Fuming, she hollered, "First of all, there was almost nothing left in the store. Second, I had a lot more until some big asshole knocked me over and took it from me not a hundred feet away while you two shitheads slept. I had to fight him for what I have left."

"Where is the bastard?"

"He drove away."

"Jesus Christ, Tessa!"

"It's not my fault," she said, as tears of ire flooded her eyes. "He pulled a knife on me when I fought back."

"Alright, calm down." He took the food from her and put it into the truck. They got into the truck, and he backed out and pulled away. "How much money do we have left?"

"Twenty-six bucks."

"Now that we have more food, can we eat?" asked Mort.

"If I catch you eating any more of this food, you're dead, and since you ate a three-day supply, you don't get any for three days."

"Three days! I'm already starving."

"You'd make a lousy African," said Kevin, turning out onto the avenue. "People there ask, 'When's dinner, Mom?' and she says, 'Six-thirty, next Tuesday.'"

"I don't give a shit about Africans; I'm hungry."

"Wood, you've already stored up a shitload of fat against the uncertain food supply, which was forward thinking, but by the same token, you ain't getting any more food."

"If I don't get food, I don't make the battery."

"Shut up, ass," said Tessa. She turned to Kevin and told him the Statue of Liberty was destroyed. He turned on the radio, which confirmed the news. Speculation was already rampant that Muslim terrorists had blown it up.

An outraged Kevin said, "That's what we get for laying off most of our fighters. Never mind defending the free world; we can't even defend ourselves anymore."

"Were you laid off?" asked Tessa.

"Yup, along with half the rest of the Navy, half the Marines, some of the Air Force, and most of the Army."

"I read about some cutbacks to our armed forces because we were closing bases all over the world."

"Yeah, retrenching to stoke the gaping public service, health, and social security maws."

"But why would they lay off Navy Seals?" He lowered his head momentarily. "You were never a Navy Seal, were you?"

"I was a cook."

"A *cook*? I don't believe you."

"Don't care what you believe. The government put thousands and thousands of highly trained killers out of work, without the pensions they were promised, and without any help to deal with the aftermath of war on the body and psyche; and without any jobs to go to. Now they're causing trouble everywhere—big shocker—and marching on Washington."

"So you got a job protecting a rich enclave." He nodded. "A cook? Come on. Tell me the truth."

"Rich folk got to eat, too." She frowned. "After eight months of desperate searching, leeching off my mom, and finally stealing food and other things just to survive, I got hired by the Loomis Hill Neighborhood Association. They set up a gated community in 2017, I think, to protect themselves from reality. Pay was shit, but enough to feed me and mom, and anyone who came to her door for handouts."

"And Crystal."

"And Sabrina and Valentine and Danielle—"

"Stop."

"The fuckers fired me two days back."

"Why?"

"For bringing my problems to their doorstep. The Mexican mob figured out I was sniping their leaders and was apparently displeased. They knew I worked protecting Loomis Hill, so they sent two guys there after me. I killed them, but not before they injured one of the rich douchebags and ruined some property."

"Why has everyone become so malicious?"

"Good people: to survive. Bad people were malicious to begin with; the turmoil makes it much easier, that's all." She shook her head in disgust. Reverting to the employment topic, he asked, "What about you? Are you working?"

"Not yet, no."

"No jobs for engineers?"

"I'm not an engineer."

"Last I heard you were in Cornell taking engineering and working on your father's research project."

"I quit in October of my fourth year."

"Why?" he asked as he slowed for a red light, looked around, and drove through it.

"It was a terrible situation at Cornell. The university had shut down my father's battery research. I had devised a computer model that accurately predicted the energy density, performance limitations, life, and other characteristics of a battery. The model systematically tested dozens of different formulations and quickly narrowed them down to the most promising candidates. That enabled us to seriously cut testing time, so we could zero in much faster on what worked and what didn't. We were *so* close to a breakthrough. Yet, they shut us down. It disappointed me, but devastated my father."

"So, why was the program shut down?"

"Lots of programs were being shut down at the time, as the economy tanked. Suddenly, fifty thousand dollars a year for tuition was a questionable proposition—as if it shouldn't have been all along. And with free online courses from some of the best universities in the world, why pay? Students stopped applying; gifts dried up; programs had to go. We thought we were just one of the casualties. His drinking got a lot worse at that point. Partly because of that, I suppose, he got careless. Turns out he'd been cheating on mom for years with a series of coed grad students. Mom found out when he left his phone out, which he'd never done before." Tessa hesitated, and her eyes filled with tears. "When mom found out, she was so devastated that she, she killed herself."

"Jesus, Tess, I didn't know. Shit, that's awful. She was a fine lady."

"I hated him so much, I quit Cornell and left town to live with my aunt in Ontario. All this only made his drinking worse. The final straw was when he found out the university had gotten a gift of twenty-five million dollars from some Saudi prince just before we got the ax. Dad was convinced the money had a string."

"Lose the battery research," Kevin deduced.

"You got it. My father went ballistic, and they ended up firing him. His only offer was from the South Dakota School of Mines and Technology."

"Where the Saudis tracked him and kept up to speed with his research, and when he made the breakthrough—"

"Break through his skull! It's the Saudis after us!"

"Probably. Or possibly that Chinese battery company."

After considering these possibilities in silence for a few minutes, they continued their discussion.

"So, you never finished college?"

"I did. I went out to Colorado College." He laughed. "Shut up. It's a good college." He laughed again. "Shut up."

"What's your degree in?"

"Women's studies."

He laughed. She hit his chest.

"I'm sure employers lined up to lure you in," he said.

"My college shut down for good this year. Mine was the last graduating class. I couldn't believe it when I found out. Now what's my degree worth?"

"Same as before: nothing," answered Kevin. "What did you pay for this degree of yours?"

"Never mind."

"Two hundred grand?"

"Close enough. I had to do two years there to get my degree."

He laughed once more and said, "So you transferred from a great school to a nothing one and from a great discipline to a shit one all to piss off your father?" A morose nod. "At a cost of two hundred grand?" An embarrassed nod. "Which you still owe?"

"Yes, and the government was careful to make sure all college loans became payable in new dollars, even though all their bonds were payable in old dollars."

"Pretty dumb for a genius."

"It broke his heart, which was what I wanted at the time." Tears rolled down her cheeks. "Now he's gone, and all I have is a worthless degree, a pile of debt I can't possibly repay, and a guilty conscience."

"My school is closing, too," said Mort. "Last year there were more professors and administrators than students."

"Hard to believe the prestigious South Dakota School of Mines and Technology is going belly up," said Tessa.

"Jesus!" cried Kevin as he suddenly swerved into oncoming traffic. Tessa and Mort screamed, as Kevin swerved back to the right side of the road, just missing a dump truck that blared its horn.

"Why the hell did you do that?" asked Tessa.

"To practice for when I visit England … To avoid the manhole. The cover was gone; if I'd hit it, it would've ruined my suspension, and there's no replacement parts for Chryslers anymore. People have been swiping manhole covers and sewer grates for years here. Someone melts them down for the steel, I guess. A little kid died last year when he fell into the sewer, and they cause dozens of accidents a year."

They drove back downtown. "Where are we going?" asked Tessa.

"We need to get out of town, but we have almost no money and almost no food. What we do have is a few guns that we can turn into cash and food." While halted at a red light—only because a car in front of him had stopped—he looked at her, grasped a handful of her gorgeous hair and piled it onto the top of her head.

She slapped at his hand and said, "Cut it out." She shook her head to get her hair back the way she wanted it.

He asked, "You have anything skimpy in your suitcase besides black panties?"

"None of your business, creep."

"You know when your father did his sabbatical in Singapore when you were in tenth grade specifically so you could experience an Eastern culture and learn Chinese?"

"No, I forgot all about the most interesting experience of my life. And technically there is no language called Chinese; I learned Cantonese."

"Do you remember it?"

"Why?"

"Jesus Christ, just answer a question for once, will you?"

"I don't get many chances to practice it, so I've likely lost a lot of it, but I can probably understand it well enough. Why?"

\*

The armed man at the door stared at a striking redhead outfitted in tight blue jeans shorts and a halter top. Her hair was gathered on top of her head, leaving her lovely face uncovered. "I'd like to bite those succulent tits," he said out loud in Cantonese as she and her partner walked up to him outside the musty old shop. "And I could lick those legs forever." She understood and fought back an impulse to knee him in the groin. In English the man told Kevin, "I have to check you."

"I have a few special gifts for sale. They're in these bags. I also have my Colt 1911, which is not for sale."

The man took the bags and the Colt and said, "Wait here."

He came out a minute later and said, "Step inside and wait at the door until the other customers are done."

Tessa and Kevin looked on as a white man dressed in a nice suit that had seen better days stood talking to an old Chinese man. He was trying to pawn a Rolex, but wasn't happy with what the Chinese man was offering. He left without making a deal. Next, a woman with a bottle of HE Tide attempted to trade it for a case of tomato soup."

Chan said, "I don't take liquid Tide. It's always watered down."

"Never been opened. Look."

The man checked the bottle and said, "Four CTS."

"Eight."

"Five. Take it or leave it."

They made the trade. "What's in there?" asked the lady.

"Used cooking oil."

"People buy that?"

"Sure. Good biofuel. Who's next?"

After the woman left, the burly guard locked the door and frisked Kevin. He turned to frisk Tessa, but she said, "Don't even think about it." She turned slowly as he studied her fine form; there wasn't room to hide a toothpick in her outfit. He nodded to her, muttering in Cantonese, "I could ram that sweet ass all day."

She bit her tongue. Kevin stepped up to Chan and said, "In plastic bag number one I have three guns: two Berettas and an FNH. What'll you give me for them?"

"You know I don't trade in guns."

"Yes, I do. And what can't I have for the guns you can't take?"

"You can't have a case of CCS and a case of Maling Peas—"

"Shove the Chinese shit right back up your ass."

"Got lots of Maling, but not much else."

Kevin looked at the small pile of canned food and said, "I'll take the CCS and that case of DCC."

"Done," said Chan.

"Really? Fuck, I must've settled too soon."

"Too bad. Hand the guns over." They made the trade. "What about the Colt?" The gun lay on the counter between the two men; it had been unloaded.

"Not for sale, but I have two Uzi submachine guns." He opened the bag and showed Chan the merchandise.

Chan glanced at his bodyguard and said in Cantonese, "Get ready." Addressing Kevin, Chan said, "Hundred newbucks. Take it or leave it."

"Leave it. Two hundred."

Tessa said, "Kev, I'm bored."

"Shut up, bitch. I'm doing business here," Kevin replied.

"But it's hot in here," she said in a whiny voice as she turned away from the men, took a clip out of her hair and bent over slowly to let it fall. She stood upright, turned, and shook her head to clear the hair from her face, bouncing her bosom in a most enticing way. All three men studied that maneuver. She sidled up to Kevin and said, "Let's go, baby."

"I said shut up."

"Don't be mad, Kevy." She kissed him.

"Take your pretty little ass out of here while the men do business." He slapped her rear. She yelped, gave him the briefest, *I'll get you for that* look, and wiggled to the front door.

Chan told his bodyguard in Cantonese, "Don't let her leave."

The guard seized her, twisting her around and holding her across her breasts while squeezing her rear against his crotch. She screeched and stamped on his foot. He let go and took out his gun. She ran to Kevin's side.

Kevin said, "I'm disappointed in you, Chan. I was hoping we could do business. You've been living here for over thirty years and you're a Triad son of a bitch?"

"Not much choice anymore. You were dead as soon as you stopped the kidnapping and killed the boss's son. And you wasted your life because it's going down again this afternoon anyway. The little girl will bring in top dollar." He turned to his guard and said, "Shoot them."

Tessa exclaimed, "He said, 'Shoot them!'"

The man pointed his gun at Kevin, just as Kevin fired the Smith & Wesson Compact J-Frame revolver Tessa had smuggled in and handed to Kevin. Down he went, shot in the heart. Kevin turned the revolver on Chan.

"Wait! We can work this out," said a now panicky Chan.

"Combination."

"That's Triad property in there."

"Combination!"

"Left twenty-seven, right three, left thirty-nine."

Tessa went to the safe and tried it; it worked.

"Made a payment this morning, so there's not much in there. You're dead anyway."

"So are you," he said as a bullet stopped Chan's heart.

"What we got?" asked Kevin.

"Uh, he wasn't lying. Three hundred twenty newbucks, some papers, and these two boxes."

"Take the cash and those boxes. They're C-4 kits that Chan assembled. Could come in handy. What's that other—"

"Nothing," said Tessa, closing the safe.

"It was weed and coke, wasn't it?"

"You have an incredibly serious responsibility right now; you can't pull it off wasted."

"I control it now; not the other way around. Those drugs represent an important source of money for us."

"No, Kevin, please."

"Open it!"

She reluctantly opened the safe. He took a large plastic bag of marijuana and reached in for the cocaine, but Tessa grabbed his hand and said, "Don't. It absolutely ruined my best friend as a teenager. I can't watch that happen to you again!"

Shaking his head, he left the cocaine in the safe. She kissed his cheek.

Kevin took his guns back, along with a hundred-thirty new dollars that Chan had on him, plus some rolling papers that were on the counter.

While Tessa collected the canned food, she said, "What worries me as I stand near you watching you kill people left and right, is I'm not running away screaming or going out of my mind. I don't know if I'm in shock or if it's become old hat disturbingly soon."

"Welcome to my world."

"I understand that we need money to get out of here, so we had to sell the guns. But you said you weren't sure you could trust him. So, why did you have to pawn your guns here?"

"Chan and the Mexican mob are the only choices in town for moving illegal guns. The Mexicans would shoot me on sight. I had hoped Chan wasn't linked to Triad; he'd been here for decades. Hey, I loved the way you bent over to distract them while you dug the gun out of your hair, then turned around swishing your hair and bouncing your tits while you handed me the gun. Where'd you learn that? Finishing school?"

She smiled and whacked his butt hard. "Slap my butt in public ever again and you die." He laughed.

The two looked out the front window, saw the coast was clear, and hurried to his truck where Mort, whom they had

61

locked out of the truck away from the food, stood waiting. "Oh, good, you got more food," he said.

Kevin unlocked the doors, and they put their loot in the back. He had a thought and ran back into the store. Curious, Tessa followed. "Can I give you a hand?"

"Sure. Put it right here," he said, pointing to his crotch.

She smacked him in his groin with her open hand, which made him stoop and grunt. "You literally asked for it," she said with a penitent smile.

Frowning, he picked up two cases of Maling canned food and limped out. He put them in the back seat, gave Mort the can opener, and said, "Eat. Maling only!" Mort smiled and got to work.

Kevin got into the driver's seat, but Tessa stood looking at two women swinging a bat at a dog. "Kevin, they're going to kill it." Turning to the people, she yelled, "Stop! Stop!"

"For God's sake, Tessa," said Kevin, "get in."

"Do something, Kevin."

"Looks like good eating to me."

"Oh, you're such an ass! Give me your gun. Give it to me!"

He handed her the Smith & Wesson. She jogged over to the women and had words with them. As one raised the bat to hit the dog, Tessa pointed the gun at her. The woman screamed, "We found it first," and swung the bat at the dog. It moved aside, but took the bat to its side and yelped. Tessa shot at her feet, almost dropping the weapon in the process; the kickback surprised her. The frightened dog took off. With the women hollering at her, Tessa ran after the dog and eventually caught it.

Kevin followed in the truck. She took the dog by the collar and led it to the truck. "Poor little thing looks so sick," she mentioned to Kevin.

"Don't get too attached then."

A man pulled up in a small white truck. He got out and said, "This your dog?"

"We just rescued it from people who were going to kill and eat it," boasted Tessa.

"It doesn't have a dog license," pointed out the man.

"And?" she said.

"And I'm fining you one hundred dollars for the infraction and charging another hundred for the required license."

"What?"

He started writing the ticket.

Kevin said, "Come on, buddy. She's telling the truth. Let this one go."

"Sorry, gotta write her up."

"Kevin, let's just go."

"He's got my license plate."

"You don't blink when gang members come shooting for you, but you're worried about a dog catcher?"

"Listen, Red Bush, the best way to get on the official radar is to not pay your fines. The bastards take that more seriously than murder because that's how they get enough money to pay themselves." He turned to the man and said, "Hey, what's it going to take to overlook this?"

"Are you offering me a bribe, sir?"

"Nope. Just offering you a reward for making sure the city is safe from rabid strays. A thank you for your fine work. What do you say to fifty newbucks?"

"I say no. But I might accept a reward of a hundred."

"Seventy-five."

"A hundred."

Kevin handed the man a hundred dollars while glowering at Tessa. Tessa looked down as the man went on his way.

"You're not giving any of my food to that mangy creature," said Mort from the back seat of the truck.

"None of the food is yours," said Kevin. Turning to Tessa, he said, "It ain't getting any of *my* food. So, what's your plan?"

"What about the Chinese stuff you …" she said, stopping when she noticed the dog had moseyed down the street.

Just then, a car pulled up, and a man hopped out and shot the dog. Tessa stood in shock, unable to move or scream, as the man picked up the dog and shoved it into the trunk. When he drove away, Tessa started bawling.

"It's just a dog—"

"Shut up, shut up, shut up!" she screamed.

She ran down the street in utter dismay. Kevin called after her, "Come back, Tessa, we have a kidnapping to stop," but she kept running.

\*

Two men with thick, black beards and black turbans stood in a doorway and made eyes at a lovely infidel coming their way. As Tessa walked by out of breath, one said to the other, "Dressed like a whore, so she must be a whore."

"How much, cow?" said his friend.

Already angry, Tessa became furious at this insult and marched up to the men, intending to set them straight and help them see, via her fists, that their ingrained beliefs were demeaning to women. But when she got close, they snatched her, covered her mouth, and dragged her inside the small store. One man locked the door.

"American women; so predictable, so self-righteous. You have no idea infidel whores are fair game. If you parade around showing all that skin, you are inviting us to fuck you."

"Help! Someone please help me!" she screamed. The store owner, another bearded, beturbaned man, chuckled. A woman in a burka went about her business of stocking shelves.

"No one here is going to help you, so scream all you want. It makes conquering you all the better." The man yanked down her halter-top. She screamed again and covered her breasts with her arms. Both men laughed. "You are nothing but a filthy whore, and we're going to give you what you asked for."

The other man put a long knife to her throat, saying, "Take off your clothes."

"No, please!"

"Now!" he yelled as he pushed the tip of the knife into her throat.

Shaking, she pulled off her halter-top and dropped it, unbuttoned and unzipped her shorts, and let them fall to the floor. One man grinned a toothless smile; the other licked his lips.

"Those too," he ordered, gesturing to her panties. Crying, she lowered them as the men fondled her breasts.

"What's—" one said as he noticed a red dot on his companion's forehead. Before he could finish, the companion was down on the floor, blood flowing out of the hole in his head. Then he, too, went down, with a bullet through the head.

*

Kevin shot the lock, entered the store, and seeing the store owner raise a shotgun, shot him twice in the forehead with his Colt. His wife began wailing and ran to pick up the knife that had fallen to the floor. As she charged at Kevin, she, too, plummeted to the floor with a hole in her head.

He turned to look at Tessa, whose left hand was covering her genitals and right arm covering her chest. He leered for a moment, then tossed her a blanket he'd taken from his truck. She wrapped herself in the blanket and picked up her clothes.

Tessa couldn't stop trembling.

"Come on, let's go," he said. Still focused on the dead people all around her, she absent-mindedly let her blanket fall open at the top. He gazed at her breasts and said, "Pink nipples; my favorite. How did you know?"

She blushed, closed the blanket, slapped him, and cried, "Insensitive jerk!"

Rubbing his cheek, he replied, "Strange custom you Canadians have for thanking someone who saved your life. How do I say you're welcome? A sock in the jaw?"

"I was just about to be raped and killed and you're teasing me about my nipples. And you just killed four more people. Do you take anything seriously?"

"Not much. Just another flaw that makes me well adapted for the shitty times we live in."

Overwhelmed, Tessa started sobbing. Kevin took her in his arms and, although she held on tight, her weeping escalated. "You're still human; it's not old hat," he said softly. He carried her out of the shop and brought her to his truck, where Mort was busy eating Chunky Soup. "I told you Maling only, pig!" said Kevin. "Get out of my truck."

Mort said, "I'll get out to stretch my legs as long as you give me your keys. I don't trust you not to drive away and leave me here."

Still having to deal with the weeping Tessa, he didn't want to argue then, so he put Tessa into the back seat and handed Mort the keys. "Stay near the truck," he warned. He joined Tessa in the back seat. She once again held him close.

After a few minutes, she calmed down and said, "How do you do this? I mean, you were a lot of bad things, but never a mean man. Now you're a cold-blooded killer … I'm not trying to be critical. I mean, you're absolutely amazing at … at keeping us alive. But how, Kev?"

"It started at military school. The place was horrible, but one teacher was a retired Navy man who saw something in me. Who knows what?"

"God, Kevin, you have more potential than almost anyone I've ever met. Why do you think I was so hard on you for throwing it all away?" She turned away from him and put on her sweatshirt.

"He took me out to a rifle range and said I was a natural. I was really good even on that first day. God knows how something like that can be inborn. He began grooming me for the Seals from that day on. By the time I finished high school, I had decided to try. I mean, I had no other plans. So I joined the Navy; his strong recommendation helped overcome any qualms they might have had about my previous behavior. And I managed to meet the entry requirements and make it through the awful Basic SEAL training course—I get exhausted just thinking back to it. Then, after that, two years of grueling training at swimming, navigation, demolitions, weapons, and parachuting before they deployed me."

"So you *were* a Navy Seal."

He pulled down the neck of his shirt to show her his tattoo of the Seal Team Three Insignia. "I qualified as an expert sharpshooter—the highest level. How do I do this? Incredibly intensive training and hard experience."

"But killing people?"

"I was in the mountains of Pakistan for my first live mission. The first time I shot a human being, I kept the scope focused on the body for I don't know how long. I'd hit him in the center of his chest from a kilometer away. I felt everything from horror to pride. I think horror was winning, but at that point the commander screamed at me to shoot the next target. So I did."

"Did it get easier?"

"Of course it did. We were killing al Qaeda and Taliban pricks who made it their mission in life to blow up innocent people. Everyone we took out saved dozens, maybe hundreds of lives, potentially at least. That made it possible the first time and easier every time out, until I actually began to enjoy it."

"Do you enjoy it now?"

"I do, for the same reasons. I'm killing thugs who live only to make life worse for everyone else. I never kill anyone who doesn't deserve it."

"But isn't it possible to go overboard? I mean, who are you to determine who deserves to die?"

"Usually it's pretty straightforward; it's the guy who's shooting at me or who crushed my mother's head or who's just about to rape my friend. But there are grey areas, and they always scare me. Has killing monsters made me one of them? I hope not, but I wonder sometimes."

"You're not a monster, but you're awfully callous about killing. There's nothing funny about killing a human being, but you almost always joke about it."

"A Navy psychologist told me snipers tend to develop coping mechanisms to deal with what they do for a living. Mine was making light of it—joking about it."

Tessa yawned and said, "Did she think that was okay?"

"Better than most other coping mechanisms she had come across, she said, but she warned me not to go overboard or she'd take away my rifle."

While putting on her sweatpants, she said, "I'll let you know when you're going overboard."

She trailed off with this and fell asleep.

Kevin moved up to the driver's seat, Mort got in, and they drove away for their next undertaking.

# CHAPTER 5

"We've been sitting here for almost an hour now," said Mort. Tessa, who'd been napping since they last spoke, awoke. They were parked on a side street under a shade tree in southwestern Syracuse just outside the recently-gated community of Loomis Hill, immediately west of the defunct Onondaga Community College. "We hired you to protect us, but this detour is likely to put us at greater risk. We should just leave it to the police and get out of here. This is none of our business."

"I don't trust the police," said Kevin.

"You watch too much TV," responded Mort. "Not all of them are on the take."

"No, but enough are, and we don't know which ones. If the Triad finds out that I know, they'll send a bunch of assholes gunning for me."

"All the more reason to get the hell out of here."

"Why don't we just go and get her?" asked Tessa.

"It's a gated community with armed guards who are all former military, and I'm barred from entering. I could get in, but I might get caught, which would bring the police. If I get arrested, Heather would be defenseless."

"Just tell the police!" said Mort.

"Mort, we're close to the old zoo, here, so shut up before I make you the next elephant exhibit."

"The old zoo?" said Tessa. "Is it gone?"

"Yup. Must be at least two years now, they closed it. Shipped off some animals. Slaughtered others. Gave the edible ones to soup kitchens."

"You're kidding," said Tessa.

"Nope. 'Hey buddy, pass the gnu balls.' 'Please, sir, I want some more lemur soup.' PETA was so outraged, a few of them broke in and freed some of the animals, including some meat eaters. One PETA moron got eaten by a snow leopard. 'There you go, kitty, taste freedom. No, go. Go! I'm not freedom. Ah!' I laughed for a week. They hunted the leopards down and killed them, but not before they killed two old people. Imagine a couple in their golden years, holding hands, strolling down a garden path at sunset, the man saying, 'After all these years, you're still as beautiful as ever. I love you more than ever … What the hell? Ah! Oh, God, take her, take her. She's got much more meat. Ah!'"

Tessa said, "That was a neat little zoo. Remember our families visited there the summer before eighth grade? We went off on our own, and you suggested we make our own exhibit banging in the forest, but I only let you kiss me. I can still see you telling people passing by, 'Here we have the horny teenage human exhibit with the blue-balled male pestering the cock-teasing female to practice producing the next generation.' God, you were funny that day. I envisioned bringing our ch … Uh, anyway, it's so sad it's gone … Isn't Heather at school? What if they try—"

"These parents have money. Most won't send their kids to public schools, especially with all the violence, with class sizes of sixty and up, and with the schools falling apart. She's taught, along with a few dozen others, by private tutors who are mostly laid off school and college teachers. Buggers pay them barely above minimum wage."

Tessa said, "I know we can't just let this happen, but can you really protect her without the police?" He shrugged. "Obviously they're doing this for the ransom?"

"Actually, no. They want to sell her."

"What? In China?"

"Maybe."

"But not before raping her," said Tessa with repugnance.

"Hell, no. That would cut her value by ninety percent."

Two black Geely sedans with opaque windows drove by. Kevin said, "That's them." He let them get a little ahead and pulled out to follow.

"You're going to get me killed!" said Mort. "I demand we leave Syracuse now."

"Shut up," said Tessa and Kevin in concert.

Approaching a fortified gate, the sedans came to a halt. A Chinese man lowered the window and handed an envelope to one of the guards, who proceeded to open the gate for the two cars.

"That son of a bitch!" said Kevin.

Both cars drove in, and the man closed the gate. Kevin drove up, lowered the window, and said, "Open up, Lombardi."

"You're persona non grata, Idle. Drive on out of here." Kevin got out of the pickup. Lombardi went on, "I have four words for you, Idle: back in the truck, asshole."

"I have four words for you, Lombardi: learn how to count."

"Huh? Just get out of here. I don't want trouble."

"You got trouble, Lombardi." Lombardi and his partner drew their guns. Staying calm, Kevin said, "You got a cushy job here, boys. What do you think the neighborhood association would think of you two accepting a bribe to let the Triad in?" They looked at each other uncomfortably, but held their ground. "If I drive away, I'll find high ground and uncork my Accuracy Rifle and zero on you two."

"Open up," said Lombardi.

Kevin got into his truck and drove through, showing them his middle finger. He drove fast up Howlett Hill Road and took a left turn.

"They took the next left," pointed out Tessa.

"There are probably four or five of the bastards. I can't take them all on close up. And if they see me, they'll use her as a shield."

He drove up the road, turned onto a short street that ended in a circle, and stopped. Grasping his L115A3 AWM rifle fitted with a scope, he ran through some woods, stopped between two houses, lay on his stomach, and pointed the rifle. Tessa ran up to see what he was aiming at. About two-hundred yards away, the black sedans were parked in front of an impressive house. Two men were standing near the cars. Then two men came out dragging a blonde girl. One of the men had his hand around her mouth. "You can't hit them at this distance with that old thing, can you?" she said.

"This is touching distance for a sniper, and this old thing is worth more than my house. I stole it off a dead Brit in Pakistan."

Tessa heard a pop and saw one of the men holding the girl go down. She gawped at Kevin. "Good shooting for a cook," she said.

"Quiet. Some of us got hits to do."

Another pop; then one more. Looking back to the house, she saw three of the four men sprawled on the ground. The other pulled the girl between him and Kevin and took her to the car.

"Shit!" said Kevin. He was unwilling to chance hitting the girl.

The man managed to get behind the car and shove her in; he got in and drove away.

Kevin dashed to his truck; Tessa followed and only just managed to get in before he took off, heading back toward the gate. Mort had switched to the back seat, apparently figuring it might be safer, so Tessa took the front passenger seat.

They hit eighty on a short straightaway. She closed her eyes, and Mort screamed as they sped up to the stop sign. Tessa could've sworn they were on two wheels turning the corner just in front of the Geely. The kidnapper stood on his brakes to avoid a collision, then tried to get past Kevin's truck. To head the kidnapper off, Kevin accelerated and changed lanes. "Seat belts, everyone," said Kevin as they approached the gate. The two guards who had opened the gate jumped aside.

With their truck just ahead of the Geely, Kevin warned "Hang on," and jammed on the brakes. The kidnapper braked, but hit the back of his truck, swerved, and lost control. The car flipped onto its driver side and stopped just short of the gate. With Tessa again closing her eyes and Mort still screaming, Kevin's truck hit the brick gate. The front airbags in the Ram deployed, which saved Tessa and Kevin injury. Mort was on the floor in the back. He'd been crushed into the front seat when the crash occurred. Well padded, he suffered no serious injuries, but was nevertheless moaning.

Kevin reached in front of Tessa, lifting the depleted airbag to get into the glove box. Clutching his 1911, he got out of the truck. Glancing in the Geely's windshield to size up the situation, he clambered up onto the car, hauled up the door, and pointed his gun inside. Tessa got out and ran over to the car. She saw through the windshield that the man was lying with his back to the driver door, which was against the ground. The frightened girl was on top of him, and he had her by the neck with a gun pointing at her temple. His face was bloody. Spent airbags hung all around the interior.

"I shoot her! I shoot her! Get away or she die!" Tessa heard the man say.

Then the man suddenly turned his gun toward Kevin, and she was about to scream a warning to Kevin when Kevin shot. She saw the kidnapper slumped back with blood oozing out of a hole in the side of his head.

The poor girl was screaming in a frenzy. Kevin said, "Heather, it's over. You're okay. Heather! Look at me. It's Kevin." The girl looked up. "You're safe now. Take my hand. Come on, honey. I promise I'll protect you."

She said, "Kevin?" He nodded. She reached up; he grabbed her by the upper arm and pulled her up with one arm. He let the door fall shut, turned and lowered her to the ground, and jumped down. The girl threw her arms around him, sobbing.

Even weeping, the girl was stunning, Tessa could see. With Heather still hanging onto him for dear life, he walked her back to his truck; Tessa followed. "Okay, Heather, let go now and get in. You're safe. This is Tessa; she'll help protect you."

Tessa took her hand and said, "Come on."

Heather reluctantly let go of Kevin and got into the truck with Tessa. Kevin frowned at the damage to the front of his truck. He tried pulling away the right fender, but couldn't get it off; it hung down to the ground.

The guards had abandoned their post; saving themselves from the inevitable fallout, Tessa guessed.

Kevin got in and grimaced as he turned the key. When it started, he gave a look of relief.

He backed up and turned around. The fender dragged on the ground, making an annoying scraping sound. The right-front wheel wobbled, so the truck shimmied harder as it went faster.

Shaking his head, he said, "Shit, we can't drive any distance with this."

"Can't we take the other car in front of Heather's house?"

"That would be illegal … I'm guessing they track their cars, but we may have no other choice for now."

"How come her parents didn't take extra precautions after last week?"

"Excellent question. The kidnappers did the same thing today as they did last week. I had spotted their car, which I thought looked suspicious. When they came out of the house with their captive, I shot them." He turned left. "I called her mother and kept Heather with me until the mom and her husband showed up. I told them they had to get her out of here. Obviously they didn't listen."

As they approached Heather's house, she appeared to get more and more anxious. "What's wrong?" asked Tessa. "We're taking you home."

"No!" she said. She began to cry again.

"Heather, what's the matter?" said Tessa.

"Those men ..." She was crying too hard to get the rest out.

Tessa stroked her hair. "Calm down, Heather. We'll make sure you're safe."

Heather took a deep breath and said, "He let them check me."

"Check you? How?" said Tessa.

"You know. Down here," she said, pointing between her legs.

"Who? Your father?" asked a shocked Tessa.

"Step-father," she clarified.

"He's in on it!" said Kevin.

"But why?" said Tessa.

"A beautiful blonde virgin teenager will probably go for a million newbucks in Shanghai or Dubai," said Kevin.

Tessa's jaw dropped. "He sold his own step-daughter?"

"Looks that way."

Tessa turned to Heather and said, "We won't leave you with him." Heather nodded.

Kevin pulled up to her house. The step-father emerged from the house, looked into the truck, and said, "You got her back? Thank God! But this is the second time you let this happen, Idle—"

Kevin smashed the man so hard in the face, he fell to the ground, unconscious. A few minutes later, the mother drove up, got out of her BMW, looked in horror at the carnage, and screamed to see her husband among the inert bodies on the ground.

"He's alive," said Kevin.

As Mrs. Janet Hope, who was a physician, knelt to check on him, she said, "He called to say the Chinese men kidnapped Heather. I almost died when I saw the black car on its side at the gate; I checked to see if Heather was in it, but she wasn't. They must've got away with her. Please get her back, Mr. Idle! I'll pay anything."

"Mom?" said Heather as she got out of the truck.

"Heather!"

As the emotional mother embraced her daughter, Kevin said, "Your husband arranged the whole thing."

Janet, of course, refused to believe this at first, but when Heather told her about the pelvic exam as her step-father looked on with eye teeth dripping, she fell to her knees crying. She told Kevin, "I thought after last week, we should send her to my sister in Vermont. But he said we could protect her." Looking at her husband, who was coming to, she got to her feet and kicked him in the head. Kevin laughed. She pulled out her phone.

Kevin asked her not to phone the police until they left because he'd been involved in so much mayhem recently, they were bound to hold him. He said he was pretty sure a neighbor would have phoned by now anyway and was anxious to leave.

"Won't it take them days to show up?" said Tessa to Kevin.

"No, they get a little extra from the neighborhood to see to their needs. They'll be here within a half hour."

Janet said to Kevin, "Thank you for my daughter." She shook his hand. "I have a proposition. Get her to my sister's in Montpelier, and I'll pay you a thousand new dollars."

"I'm sorry, Dr. Hope, but I now have the Chinese and the Mexicans after me; and my friends here also have killers after them. Heather wouldn't be safe with us."

"And if I try to take her and the Chinese come after her, we're absolutely helpless. I don't trust anyone else. I'll get my sister and her husband to meet you in Albany. Please, Mr. Idle." Kevin shook his head, so she sweetened the pot. "Your truck is ruined. Tell you what; take my daughter to Albany and you can have his SUV. He won't be needing it anytime soon." She opened the garage door. Sitting there was a four-year-old Toyota Highlander. Kevin agreed.

Heather went in to pack quickly while Tessa and Kevin moved their belongings to the Toyota.

Tessa wondered aloud why Janet wasn't planning to come with her daughter. Her reason was all too practical for the United States in 2020: she dared not leave a good job for fear of never finding another. Even physicians had to worry, with so many seniors having perished in the pandemic of 2017-18, with Medicare and Medicaid cut to the bone, with many patients unable to pay for their health care, and with hospitals restricting employment as a result. Her take-home pay was less than half of what it had been in 2015, what with a string of salary rollbacks and ever increasing taxes and fees.

Like most Americans, their savings had been wiped out by a brief bout of hyperinflation averaging about 60% each month—wage and price controls were imposed, which brought inflation under control but also brought about shortages of everything. She had her daughter to support and her sister's family to help, and hefty monthly payments on her house and car. To top it all off, she had recently discovered her husband had a gambling problem; she supposed he owed the Triad money, bringing about this latest calamity. Their family had been squeaking by with two incomes. Now they'd have to do with one, and she'd have to look for a way to make it all work. She simply could not leave Syracuse at present.

Kevin worried the Triad could get to the husband, even in jail. They agreed that Janet would lie to her husband and tell him Kevin was taking Heather somewhere secret, and that not even she knew where.

Janet called her sister. She was indisposed, but her brother-in-law listened to Janet's appeal and said of course Heather was welcome there. They arranged a meeting for around 7:00 PM that evening at what used to be the Best Value Inn just northwest of Albany. Dr. Hope gave Heather a thousand dollars to defray the extra expenses her sister's family would face.

Mother and daughter wept and hugged, and the four left Syracuse bound for Albany. Because the New York Thruway would've cost almost fifty newbucks to Albany, they took Route 20 east.

They made good time and found the old hotel where they were supposed to hand off Heather to her aunt and uncle. The place was a wreck. With about an hour before the meeting time, they relaxed in the parking lot with sandwiches Janet had made for them.

By 7:15 there was no sign of the aunt and uncle, so Kevin told Heather to call them. Turned out that their old car had given up at Ascutney, Vermont. Fortunately, they had friends there and were at their house. They gave Tessa directions to Mountain View Drive, about a mile off Interstate 91. Kevin furrowed his brow, but said nothing.

Heather's uncle suggested they leave the drive for the morrow, which was fine with Kevin; he had other plans for tonight.

They found a bed and breakfast establishment in Mariaville, near Schenectady. Kevin refused to consider the asking price of seventy-five newbucks per room, and was on the way out when the proprietor offered a price of one-hundred-fifty for three rooms. Tessa and Heather agreed. Kevin cursed and brought in the suitcases and his military backpack.

Heather had something important to ask Kevin, but he put her off until he accomplished his special mission for the evening.

# CHAPTER 6

At dusk, Tessa heard Kevin go out to the SUV. Curious, she followed.

He was just starting the engine. She opened the passenger door and said, "Where the hell are you going?"

"You don't want to know."

"Kevin!"

"While I'm in the neighborhood, I decided to, uh, pay my respects to the head of the Mexican mob upstate. He lives in a fancy neighborhood in Albany."

"Pay your respects with your rifle?" He nodded. "When you have us and Heather to protect? You can't."

"Can; must; will."

"Kevin, that's so irresponsible."

"With two gangs after me, I have to move out of the state, but I can't leave without making them pay for killing my mother."

"What you're planning is vigilantism; in a civilized society it's considered murder," said Tessa.

"Well, this hasn't been a civilized society for years now." She frowned at him and shook her head. He continued, "Everyone's dead in the long run; I simply help cold-blooded killers take a short-cut to the long run." Another frown greeted that remark, so he said, "Tess, I found mom bludgeoned to death on the kitchen floor." Tears flooded his eyes. "She never hurt a fly in her life; she was defenseless. But they killed her because they're fucking animals. These bastards get away with murder every day and with ruining thousands of people's lives. The police do nothing; everyone does nothing. That's why they keep doing it. Somebody has to stand up to them."

"You knock off the top dog, another takes his place."

"Yup. Maybe I get him, too."

"Then you'll never stop till they get you."

"Gotta go sometime."

"I'm coming with you."

"No—"

But she was already belted in. "You might need help to get away or something."

They drove to northeastern Albany and parked on Tower Heights outside the Osborne Pump Station. Kevin said, "A tall water tower here is the key. I scoped it out last week. It's about half a mile away from the mansion, and it's hard to climb, so they're probably not watching it closely. Plus, it'll take them a while to get here since there's no direct route except across a gravel pit, and what's the likelihood they'll try to get across that? We'll wait here till dark."

Tessa broached another subject that had been on her mind. "You should stop goggling at Heather, pervert. She's far too young for you."

"I just like looking at her adorable face. I can still see hope in her eyes; such sweet ignorance."

"Bullshit. You're just staring at her tits and ass."

"Not true; I'm also staring at her face, curves, and legs."

"That's supposed to be funny, I guess."

"What's the matter? Jealous?"

"Now that's funny," she said, laughing.

While waiting for the day's light to fade completely, Kevin turned on the radio. President Cain was in the middle of a press conference on the Statue of Liberty. Kevin immediately turned the station, saying, "Last thing I need is to listen to that fundamentalist moron."

But Tessa turned it back, saying, "Let's hear what he's going to do."

"Same thing he did when those Islamic nuts blew up our embassy in London: fuck all," said Kevin. "Nothing he can do; he laid off all our warriors."

"Shush." She turned it up.

The president was saying, "... will not stand idly by as these evildoers wreak their havoc. We will not let that happen; God will not let that happen ..."

"We and God already did!" cried Kevin.

"Quiet!"

"But we will not act in haste, strike out impetuously against our enemies. With God's help, we will assemble the evidence, identify the malefactors, and destroy them. This will take time, so we ask for your patience. But we shall prevail. The way we did against Bin Laden. With God on our side."

"See? Nothing," said Kevin. "Ever notice he says everything twice? I think his speechwriter has autism."

A *Boston Globe* reporter said, "Mr. President, two eye witnesses claimed that the torch fell onto the head, and that the debris took out the tablet and most of the left side of the structure. That might imply this wasn't a terrorist attack."

"Of course it was a terrorist attack," replied the President. "How else would the torch just fall?"

"MIT and Berkeley engineers said late last year that Lady Liberty was rotting from within."

"Absolute balderdash."

"Experts we spoke to said there was no evidence of any explosion—"

"Have any of your so-called experts been onsite to—"

"The police and National Guard won't let them near—"

"That's enough, Ms. Black," said the President. "These kind of scandalous rumors give aid and comfort to the enemy."

"Those sons of bitches!" screamed Kevin. "We did this to ourselves, and they're blaming terrorists."

"We don't know that," said Tessa. "Let's just listen." But the President would take no more questions on the Statue of Liberty.

The President was then asked about the day's riots in Washington. Feminists, gays, and lesbians were on the march, protesting against new legislation. Police and National Guard troops broke some heads, and this was causing the commander-in-chief some headaches. Responding to a reporter's question about the new prohibition against abortion, the President answered, "I asked the Lord for guidance on this emotional issue, and He assured me that we're doing right criminalizing the murder of unborn babies. I'm fully aware that those who believe that we're descended from monkeys can't understand the value we Christians place on human life, especially defenseless unborn babies, but ..."

"Oh!" said Tessa as Kevin laughed at the monkey business.

"That imbecile believes in Adam and Eve," he said.

The President's maunderings continued, "... not let them dictate their anti-Christian values to the majority. How can I possibly forgive those who do something as heinous as killing babies ..."

"What about God slaughtering all the babies of Egypt?" hollered Tessa.

"Jeez, Tessa, you looking for sense from a man who rolls around the floor speaking in tongues? Christ, we're the joke of the world with this clown in charge. If he doesn't epitomize what this country has come to, I don't know what does."

The next question pertained to a gathering movement among Southern states to ban homosexuality. He answered, "My administration fully supports states that have forbidden same sex marriages. It's this sort of abomination that caused the turmoil this country is facing down—"

Tessa, fuming, turned off the radio. Gritting her teeth, she said, "Sure, it was the gays! It had nothing to do with Washington's twenty-five trillion dollar debt or the two-hundred trillion dollar Medicare/social security debt or what they let the bankers get away with or—"

"Calm down," said Kevin. "You're sounding disturbingly like my father. Want to get rid of some of your tension by helping me bump off a few Mexicans? They're Catholics."

"So am I—though not a practicing one. I just hate the way the President perverts religion."

"Religion is *the* perversion, Tess." He got out of the car and said, "Back up to the fence so I can manage the barbwire, then park around the corner up the street in case someone official happens by."

"Be careful climbing that tower," she said as she backed to the fence.

"I'll show those fucking Mexicans I won't forget the ... the ... What the hell was it? Starts with an M, I think."

"The Malamo?"

"That's it."

With Tessa shaking her head, he clambered onto the roof, jumped over the fence, and ran off with his prized rifle and a rope fitted with a hook on the end.

*

Lighting a match to cast a bit of light, he threw the hook up to the lowest rung of the ladder on the water tower; he climbed the rope to it and started up.

This was dangerous enough in daylight. At night it was treacherous; he could hardly see a thing, so he took his time getting to the top. Once there, he sat on a hatch at the top to catch his breath. Taking the rifle from his shoulder, he set it up and looked through the scope at the mansion. Every window he could see was shuttered. He waited.

After fifteen minutes, a limousine pulled up to the front entrance of the mansion. Kevin peered through the night scope, hoping it was Alfredo Alvarez. He sighed to see it wasn't his target. Then a Mercedes pulled up and another man got out. Again, not Alvarez. "Shit," said Kevin. Next, a Lexus pulled up, but another man unknown to Kevin got out. "Shit!" *Maybe Alvarez would come out to greet his guests*, thought Kevin. The men went inside. *Meeting of drug kingpins*, Kevin told himself.

An interminable two hours and twelve minutes later, the three cars were brought to the front of the house. Kevin, his ass long since asleep, looked through the scope. Almost before thinking, he squeezed the trigger. Alvarez and one of his guests were just inside the front door embracing. The bullet went through both men. The second bullet hit the man just to their left. He shot at the third guest, who was bolting, but the distance, perch, and sleeping ass, along with a moving target, proved too much to overcome. The bullet missed.

He scanned back to the front door. Three men were down on the floor motionless. He looked around and saw men already scrambling and getting on motorcycles and in cars. *Motorcycles!*

As he went down the ladder, he saw two motorcycles coming his way through the gravel pit. *Shit!* Hurrying now, he missed a rung and started falling; he grabbed a rung at the last second. Cursing a blue streak, he made it to the last rung, hung down, and fell the last ten feet. With the motorcycles closing in, he decided to leave the rope behind. He sprinted down the paved path toward the fence.

As he neared the fence, a light shined on him; a motorcycle had burst through the trees eighty yards behind him. The man on it commenced shooting, but was wildly inaccurate. Kevin turned, replaced the magazine, and aimed at the fast-moving target. The man was getting close, and the bullets he was sending Kevin's way were getting even closer. Kevin fired; the man fell off and the motorcycle went down and skidded along. Kevin had to jump aside to avoid it as it sparked its way past him.

He ran to the fence. Another motorcycle came around the bend forty meters back and closing fast. That driver, too, began firing a handgun from a hopeless distance. Kevin knelt, aimed, and took out the rider.

Kevin climbed the fence and, of course, got caught up on the barbwire. He tore his shirt and scratched his stomach. More expletives. Freeing himself, he took one step toward the Toyota when a car came speeding around the curve two hundred meters west. A man with a machine gun was leaning out the passenger window firing. Looking through his scope, he fired at the windshield, and the car went off the road into a telephone pole, then into a tree.

As he reached the corner, another car sped around the distant bend. "Shit!" He aimed, but heard something from behind him. Startled, he turned fast, ready to shoot, but saw it was the Toyota backing up to him.

The Toyota reached him with Tessa screaming, "Get in!"

But Kevin determined he had the advantage standing still sniping at the fast-approaching car, which now featured flashes coming from a machine gun oriented his way. But his advantage turned to dust upon pulling the trigger and having nothing happen. No more bullets! He never miscounted: Chan had shortchanged him a bullet. Muttering, "Fucking Chan! I wish I hadn't killed him, so I could kill him," Kevin threw his gun into the SUV and jumped through the open back seat window. Tessa floored it, but its acceleration left much to be desired, at least under the context of a hail of bullets. The pursuing car turned the corner with the Toyota only fifty feet ahead. A man hung out the passenger window, shooting.

The road was only about 700 feet long, and Tessa, fast closing in on a stop sign, said, "Left or right?"

"I don't fucking know!" he answered while peeking over the seat to the vehicle behind. She chose left and again floored it, the chase vehicle right on her bumper. Kevin scrambled over the back seat to the cargo area. He kept his head down while grabbing one of the Uzis, which was fortunate, for the back window disintegrated when bullets rocketed through it and out the front windshield, one of which grazed Tessa's ear. She yelped.

Kevin sat up and opened up on the chase vehicle, pouring fire into the driver's side windshield. The SUV went careening off the road, flattening a small tree before smashing into a parked car in a driveway.

Tessa, apparently still in panic mode, kept speeding. "Tessa, we're okay. Slow down. Tess!"

She finally heard and slackened her speed; the Toyota rolled up to a stop sign. She turned north on Albany Shaker Road. After a few moments, she said, "You just had to get this man—you *did* get him?"

"Yup, along with two drug kingpins."

"You say that with such pride, but you almost got us both killed."

She pulled into a small dirt lane just south of the airport and stopped. She got out and came around to open the back gate for him. Climbing out, he saw that she was crying. She punched him over and over on his chest and arms, yelling, "You had no right, Idle. You have three people's lives depending on you, and you risked not only your own life, but ours, too. You're out of fucking control!"

"Calm down, Tess. We're okay."

"That was blind luck, you stupid asshole! For God's sake, aren't things bad enough already? Did you really have to make things worse for us?"

She was still hitting him, but exhaustion was slowing her down. He tried to hug her, but she pushed him away. "I'm detecting a shade of hostility," he said.

"Shut up!"

"I'm sorry."

"I came so close to dying. A bullet nicked my ear."

"That's not really that close. Your ears stick way out."

"Oh! You asshole!" She folded her arms and tramped down the lane, crying.

Kevin looked at the damage to the back of the SUV. The rear window was gone, the back door pockmarked. The right, rear tire was flat, its wheel ruined. He dug out the full-sized spare.

He called Tessa back to hold a flashlight he'd found in the glove box and got to work changing the tire. Tessa taped an emergency blanket over the back window.

*

Back at the inn, Heather had waited up for Kevin. The four had earlier decided that the two females would room together and each man would have his own room. But Heather had other plans.

"Kev, I want to stay with you," said Heather.

"Out of the question. We have too many killers to count after us."

She hadn't meant staying with him after tonight, although she was going to broach that, too. "I'm not safe anywhere. You said it yourself: I'm worth a million dollars in China or Dubai. They'll track me down."

"Shave off your hair, wear an eye patch, dress down, develop a personality like Tessa's."

Tessa hit his shoulder.

Heather pulled Kevin into the room he'd taken, saying, "I have a better idea." He looked at her expectantly. "I wouldn't be worth their while if I weren't a virgin."

Tessa's and Kevin's eyes opened wide. "No, Heather, I can't."

"Why not?" said Heather. "I'm just about seventeen."

"So, you're not even legal. Sixteen's too young."

"Get real, Kev. I'm practically the only sixteen-year-old virgin I know. I'll be seventeen in four days."

"That's probably why they were desperate to kidnap you now; there's something timeless about a sixteen-year-old girl; you know, sweet sixteen and all that. I'm not up on the economics of kidnapped virginal beauties, but I'm guessing your value goes down next week."

"Still, being a virgin is too risky for me. I want to give it to you."

He shook his head. She started unbuttoning her shirt as he looked on.

Tessa, her eyes screaming, *No!*, came into his room and closed the door. Heather frowned at her, but took off her shirt, undid her bra, and removed it. Kevin looked with admiration at her perfect breasts. She smiled shyly.

"Idle, you're not going to do this, are you?" asked Tessa.

Heather unbuttoned her jeans and lowered the zipper.

"Idle, she's a child."

"She could pass for twenty, easy."

Heather pushed her pants to the floor and stepped out of them. Grasping the elastic of her white, frilly panties, she began to lower them.

Tessa said, "Heather, you don't have to do this. Don't let sick criminals dictate to you when to—"

"Go," said Heather to Tessa. "Forget the gang; I want him. I have for a long time." She took off her panties. "Natural blonde," she said to Kevin with a salacious smile. "Worth a million?"

Gazing at her with awe, he nodded.

"You can't be serious!" cried Tessa.

He replied, "I'm always in the mood for love after a good slaughter."

Tessa said, "God, Idle, here I respected you for a few hours after you rescued her, but you're no better than—"

"A little less put down and a lot more shut up," he returned. "Piss off, Red Bush."

Heather sauntered to him, embraced him, and kissed him. "Be gentle," she cooed.

*

Tessa, distressed, went to bed, which was a thin wall away from the action in the next room. When she heard Heather moaning, she turned on the TV.

It wasn't that she was jealous, she told herself; it was that that son of a bitch was taking advantage of a vulnerable young girl. "Damn pig!" she muttered. "She's only *sixteen*, for God's sake. I hate that pervert."

Tessa heard Heather giggle and exclaim, "Oh! Kevin! That feels so good. Oh, my God!" Then she heard their bodies slap together. Heather on top going wild, Tessa guessed, before covering her ears. Then the headboard in the next room hit the wall rhythmically, and Tessa guessed doggy style. When Heather said, "Lick me all over again," Tessa turned off the TV and put the pillow over her head.

*

The following morning in the breakfast nook, Tessa kept her glower on Kevin, who ignored her. Heather was hanging onto Kevin as if she were in love. Tessa couldn't help glowering at her, too. Heather didn't seem to notice.

Mort had no change of clothes, so he wore the same baggy pants and gaudy shirt. The women were outfitted in pants and sweaters, for it was a cool, wet morning. Kevin wore his old Navy Seal jacket with the black Seal patch above the U.S. Navy patch.

Breakfast turned out to be toast and jam with coffee and orange juice from concentrate. All four got seconds; Mort was denied thirds, but he asked Heather for some of her seconds, and she gave him a piece of toast. He then asked Tessa for some of her food. She cast her eyes up and gave him a piece of toast, as well. She shook her head at Kevin, but he said, "That's precisely why the phrase 'fuck off' was invented."

No sooner did Kevin say this than Mort asked him for a piece of his toast. Mort reached over to take it, but Kevin stabbed his hand with a fork. Mort cried out, glared at Kevin, and withdrew to the bathroom to wash out his cut. Heather and Tessa laughed.

The bill with taxes came to just under two hundred newbucks, which had Kevin cursing, even though Heather paid half.

The four hunted travelers went out to the SUV. Kevin had to explain to Heather and Mort what happened to the vehicle. Mort chastised him for risking all their lives. Ignoring him, Kevin turned on the radio to listen to the news. Kevin and Tessa sat in the front seats; Heather and Mort got into the back seat, out of the rain.

The reporter said, "Michael Warner, the Lieutenant Governor of New York, was shot dead last night at a prominent local businessman's Albany home. Also murdered were the businessman, Alfredo Alvarez, and Miguel Garcia, a Mexican national who made his home in New York City."

Tessa and Kevin stared at each other with gaping eyes and mouths.

"Albany Police and New York State Troopers are following a number of leads, but this reporter has learned that a person of interest in the case is a disgraced former Navy Seal, Kevin Idle."

"Shit!" yelped Kevin.

"Mr. Idle, who was kicked out of the Navy for using drugs—"

"That's wrong, and it was one joint, one fucking joint!"

"Shut up, I want to hear this," said Tessa.

"… a sniper who was apparently capable of shooting accurately from the water tower the shooter allegedly used, which was approximately half a mile from the Alvarez home. He was also said to hold some sort of grudge against Mr. Alvarez."

"Oh, for Christ's sake!"

"Shush!" said Tessa.

"… are seeking Mr. Idle for questioning. In national news, tens of thousands of gays and lesbians marched on Washington again yesterday. Four men were killed when they clashed with Christian fundamentalists—"

Kevin turned off the radio and said, "Some sort of grudge. Do you believe that? That goes way beyond the media's normal incompetence. The station must be in the pockets of the Mexican mob. Not once did she mention the apparently unimportant fact that Garcia was the head of the Mexican Mob in New York and that Alvarez was his upstate lieutenant. It must've slipped their mind to question why the Lieutenant Governor would be meeting with Mexican mob brass at their place."

"So now we not only have two mobs and who knows how many hit men, we have the police after us, too?" said Tessa. Kevin nodded.

"Great going, Idle," said Mort.

Kevin flourished his middle finger at Mort.

"He's right," said Tessa. "I understand your need for revenge, but you had no business exercising your grudge when you have to get three people to safety."

"Yes, you made that clear yesterday," Kevin said as he got out of the truck.

"Well, now you can update your resume: three more murders," said Tessa across the roof of the Toyota. He said nothing, so she continued, "So you got kicked out for using drugs?"

"I was an expert sharpshooter for almost two years. Long enough to go on dozens of incredibly risky missions to serve my country. I personally took out four of the President's Kill List targets that I know of; these were some of the most dangerous men on the planet. But get caught with one joint by some green asshole just out of Annapolis—"

"You'll never learn."

"Really, Sharp, fuck you. I'd just come back from a mission where my best friend got shot through the eye." He walked out into a weedy field.

"I'm sorry, Kev," said Tessa, accompanying him.

"I got busted down to Petty Officer First Class and got kicked out of the Seals. Shithead told me I was lucky I wasn't kicked right out of the Navy. That came two months later, when the massive layoffs started. With my record of dozens of successful death-defying missions and one joint, I was an easy choice in the first wave. The officers managed to protect their jobs for the most part, so the troops—the same ones who'd just fought two wars for the ungrateful fuck heads, the same ones who'll be needed but won't be there when we're attacked next—were fired."

"I'm sorry for you." She took his hand. "But I can't help thinking I'd be dead if you were still in the Navy."

*

A half hour later, they left for Ascutney. They took a direct route, which involved no highways, for the two-and-a-half-hour trip.

On the way, Heather asked Tessa, "So, um, how did you two meet?"

"I moved to the house next door to his the summer before grade six," answered Tessa. "My father got a professorship at Cornell. His father was a professor there, too ..." She asked Kevin, "Is he still a professor there?"

"Part time. They cut way back on the economics department—pretty well everyone hates economists now—and laid off my father. He raised a stink, saying he was the only one there who called the great crash before it came, yet the old guard, mostly Keynesians who had a hand in providing the advice that created this disaster, were keeping their jobs. They hushed him up by shipping him to the policy analysis department. He teaches three classes; makes just enough to get by."

"Anyway," Tessa continued, "our parents hit it off, so we got together as families a lot."

"He must've been really cute in sixth grade," said Heather.

"He was, yes. It was awkward for both of us because we were really attracted to each other, but too young to know how to handle it. He showed me he liked me by throwing me into his swimming pool, giving me noogies, pulling my ponytail. I hit him back, of course, but mainly I tried to ignore him."

"So you started dating?" asked Heather.

"No, my father wouldn't let me then. We were friends, best friends; inseparable for grades six, seven, and eight."

"But you fight all the time now. What happened?"

Kevin said, "She became the world's greatest cock tease. By high school, every boy in town was after her, and she delighted in making me jealous."

"That's true, I have to admit. It drove him nuts," she said with a grin.

"I do that to boys, too," bragged Heather.

"It's fun, isn't it?" said Tessa. Heather nodded with a bright smile. Tessa went on, "But to answer your question, Kevin changed. One day, he's this cute, funny, brilliant boy who I had visions of marrying. The next day, he's the school's biggest loser."

"Oh, come off it. There were cocaine and heroin addicts, retards, fat shits, assholes who beat up their girlfriends—"

"But they were just being their true selves, whereas you had everything going for you and you chose to use none of it. Choosing to be a loser is much worse than being a natural loser in my book. You became everything I despise: a pothead, a smoker, a petty thief, a boy with an A plus brain and a C minus average, a boy with no aspirations other than to get high or get laid, a boy with no respect for anyone, even himself." Turning to Heather, she added, "In the first month of grade twelve alone, he got suspended twice; the first time for dealing weed."

"Just to my friends."

"You were so lucky they didn't expel you and call the cops. The vice-principal made him sign a contract spelling out do's and don'ts and the penalties for breaking the rules. So what does he do? He gets suspended again the *next week*."

"Nowhere in that contract did it say I couldn't put a bearded dragon in the vice-principal's minivan."

"A big lizard? You did that?" asked Heather with a chuckle.

"Yup." Addressing Tessa, he went on, "Anyway, all that happened well after you ditched me. I wasn't all that bad when you left me."

"You were well on the way, and I had guys asking me out every day and didn't have to put up with you, so I didn't. No apology."

"Not looking for one. No second chances," said Kevin.

"Not looking for one."

"Here I thought that being unemployed, broke, disgraced, wanted for murder, and on the run for my life was fine, but now that you mention it, maybe I *am* a fuckup. Thank you for setting me straight!"

"Well, against all odds, you developed a skill set that somehow came to be key to survival nowadays."

"I developed that skill set as a direct result of my behavior back then."

"Good plan: spiral down until you have to choose between jail and military school. You were just a lazy shit. Period. 'Just give me some weed and some pussy and leave me the hell alone.' That was your entire belief system."

"Did you go to military school?" asked Heather.

"That's an interesting story, with Tessa here playing the central role. I'll let her tell it."

"Against my better judgment, I agreed to go to the junior prom with him. His parents were pushing for it, and I respected them; I think they were hoping I could straighten him out. He and his father hated each other by this time because Kevin was such a loser."

"Yes, you've mentioned that ten times already, Red Bush," said Kevin.

"Stop calling me that!"

"Why does he call …" started Heather before looking at Tessa's gorgeous auburn hair. "Oh." She giggled.

Tessa resumed, "As was entirely predictable, the date went sour. He opened our date by telling me, and I quote, 'You fucking look fucking nice.' Then he spit on the doorstep. He was already drunk. During the dance, he went outside and got stoned out of his mind, *of course*. He was gone for so long, I went looking for him. I found him in the hall; he'd thrown up all over the floor in front of my locker. I lost it."

"In front of all my friends, she screams, 'You're a freaking lowlife, you good for nothing piece of shit. I hate you! I hate you!' I'd never been more embarrassed."

"You deserved it. He shoved me, and I slipped on his puke and banged my head on the lockers. I started crying. A teacher saw it and asked if I wanted to press charges. I was so mad at him at the time—not so much for the shove as for getting too wasted to even dance—I said yes. From the time the police showed up, the whole thing spun out of control. I wanted to back down, but a female cop kept pushing me to proceed. My parents, too, told me not to back down; they were afraid he'd hurt me. And when it came out they found an ounce of weed in his backpack—which he always took everywhere because it held his drug paraphernalia—even his father pushed for charges."

"That ended any chance of peace between my father and me," said Kevin.

"He told me you were bound to end up in jail the way you were going; he wanted it to happen before you turned eighteen so it wouldn't ruin your future. He hoped getting arrested would turn you around."

"Did it?" asked Heather.

"No," answered Tessa. "He ended up being convicted of assault for something that really wasn't a big deal. And he got convicted of trafficking, too. He had to go to a juvenile boot camp. I felt awful."

"Not as awful as I felt."

"The boot camp made him worse. Afterwards, every time I saw him he'd look at me with this evil leer. I was never afraid of him, but my parents worried all the time. Things between him and his father deteriorated. I'd hear them screaming at each other. It came to a head one night when Kevin, high on cocaine, punched his father in the face. He kicked Kevin out of the house. That caused big trouble between his parents. Kevin was on the streets for a couple of weeks before his mother moved out of the house into an apartment so Kevin could move in with her. He did, but his behavior stayed the same. He got arrested for selling weed and cocaine possession that fall. His father staved off juvenile hall with the promise that he'd send him off to military school to finish high school. His father wouldn't let his mother move back in. They ended up divorced a year later."

"God, I don't blame you for hating him," said Heather.

"I don't hate him. I was just so disappointed. He could've been anything he chose to be, but he chose—"

Mort interrupted, "How about you stop nagging him and stop boring me? Let's have something to eat."

Kevin said, "Yeah, this romp down memory lane has depressed me enough to kill myself. If I don't, ask me sometime what *she* was like in high school, Heather."

# CHAPTER 7

"There," said Tessa, pointing to the road they were looking for.

Kevin shook his head at the Dead End sign and turned down a dirt road cut through a thick forest. The sun had found its way through the clouds, but the road was cast in deep shade.

After driving about a mile, he again shook his head, muttered, "No," and came to a stop.

"What's the matter?" asked Tessa.

"Something's not right." He looked around as she waited for an explanation. "If I were going to plan an ambush, I couldn't pick a better spot."

"Paranoia doesn't apply to every situation."

"Nowadays, it does, especially with half the known world gunning for us."

"But how could they possibly know about Heather's aunt?"

He whispered, "Maybe they got to her mother and forced her to talk. Or maybe her uncle decided to get rich—Heather's mother told him who was after her."

Kevin executed a three-point turn, which turned out to have five points because of the constricted space on the narrow road.

"Why are we turning around?" asked Heather while taking her earphones out. "What's wrong?"

Tessa fielded this one. "Kev's a bit paranoid after all we've been through. He just wants to make absolutely sure it's safe."

After completing the turn, Kevin kept the brake on and turned to ask Heather, "Do you like your aunt and uncle?"

"I love my aunt; she's just like mom. They *are* sisters, after all. My uncle is okay. It's just …"

"Just?" said Tessa with Heather hesitating to finish her thought.

"When I went there last summer, I didn't like the way he was looking at me. But then, Aunty Becky had just been diagnosed, and everyone was upset."

"Diagnosed with what?" asked Tessa.

"Lupus." Tessa and Kevin looked at each other. "It gets really bad sometimes, and that's why Chaban, Chaban and Epstein fired her. Aunty Becky's a lawyer."

"Does your uncle work?"

"Not since Sears went bankrupt. Mom sends them five hundred newbucks every month to get by."

Kevin glanced in his rearview mirror. He started back down the road. Rounding a curve, he spotted a plume of heavy dust ahead. "Shit!"

"Might be her aunt and uncle," said Tessa.

"And the one behind us?" Tessa looked back, as did Heather.

"People probably live down this road somewhere."

"I don't like it. Heather, Tess, get down."

Heather tried to get down, but Mort had beaten her to it, so she had to squeeze down as best she could. Tessa stayed up for the moment and asked, "What are you going to do?"

"Drive them off the road," he said as they saw the black sedan with dark windows closing in fast. "Triad," said Kevin. "They all drive those Geely pieces of shit."

"What if they don't move out of the way?" She glanced at the speedometer; it read seventy-seven.

"We're bigger; either way they move."

"But if we hit them at this speed …"

"If they trap us between them, we're dead," he said as the vehicles drew closer. "They all carry Heckler & Koch submachine guns. Plus, they'll hesitate to hit us because their bosses would kill them if they ruin the million dollar prize."

"You're not ramming me head-on, full-speed into another car!" exclaimed Mort from the back floor.

"Good idea," returned Kevin. "Climb on out to our front bumper. It'd be like a blimp bouncing off a skyscraper. Or, with all those beans he ate yesterday, the Hindenburg."

His voice was quavering. *He does feel fear*, mused Tessa as terror gripped her.

Mort sat up and leaned forward to grab the steering wheel. "Let fucking go!" hollered Kevin, as he struggled to hold the road. The right wheels teetered on the edge of the road. Beyond it was trees.

"Stop the car before you kill me!" screeched Mort.

With the cars now two hundred yards apart, Tessa put the Smith & Wesson to Mort's temple and yelled, "Let go!" Mort did so and ducked back down on Heather.

"You're crushing me!" said Heather.

As the vehicles hurtled toward an imminent collision, Kevin told Tessa to "Get down!" Her eyes fixed on the missile coming toward them, she froze in place. She did manage a lusty scream.

At the last second, both drivers hit the brakes and the Geely veered off the road. The driver tried to go between the Toyota and the trees, but once he left the road, he lost control and stopped dead when he hit a big enough tree. They heard the huge crash as Kevin accelerated.

"Kevin," said Tessa as the Stop sign loomed dead ahead. He had yet to slacken his speed. Beyond the stop sign was a dead end adorned with an assortment of large trees. "Kevin!" she repeated.

All at once, he jammed on the brakes and yanked the wheel. With all passengers screaming, the SUV came to a rocky halt on the gravel road and came within a hair of tipping over. With the other Geely speeding toward them, Kevin bounded out, ran to the back of the SUV, and got his rifle. He rushed to the side of Mountain View Drive, lay down, and took aim.

A man in the fast-approaching sedan leaned out the window with his machine gun and began shooting, but with the distance and speed, the bullets came nowhere close. As the car closed in on the stop sign, it slowed, and Kevin fired five times. Tessa saw the holes appear in the windshield in front of the driver. The car slowed more, but when it converged with the trees, it was forced to go to zero instantaneously. One tree suffered a deep gouge; the two men in the car suffered death.

As Tessa sat stunned, Kevin stood and returned to the back of the SUV. He changed magazines, put his rifle in, closed the back door, and got into the driver's seat.

"That was good thinking holding the gun to his head, Tess."

She nodded and said tongue in cheek, "I can't get over how well a Navy cook can shoot."

"You haven't tasted my cooking. I had to learn how to defend myself."

"Get off me, fatso," said Heather. Mort got up and looked at the smoking wreck. Heather sat up and gazed at the same scene. "Are they dead?" she asked in a shaky voice.

"No one could've survived that," said Tessa.

Kevin drove back toward the highway. After a few moments of silence as the four pondered what had just happened, Heather asked, "What does this mean? Did they get my mother?"

*She has her mother's brain*, thought Tessa. Figuring the other obvious possibilities were less frightening for the girl, she turned to Heather and said, "It's possible your step-father let the bad guys know about your aunt."

"But my mother told him I wasn't going there." Looking in Tessa's eyes, she said, "You think my uncle … That's why you were asking about him. He sold me out, didn't he?"

"We don't know; I hope not. But he's unemployed, and so is his wife, and they probably have steep medical bills. Extreme poverty makes people do desperate things." Heather began to cry. "Pull over," said Tessa.

Kevin pulled into a disused parking lot beside the highway. Tessa traded seats with Mort and embraced Heather.

With the morose girl still crying, Tessa asked Kevin, "Can she call her mom?"

"It's possible they have her phone tapped." The two females looked at him sadly. "Alright, but make it quick."

Heather turned on her phone and said, "Mom." The phone dialed. A moment later, the crying girl said, "Mom? Are you alright? I was so worried they got you." Heather conveyed the news to her mother and said, "She wants to talk to one of you."

Taking the phone, Tessa explained the situation and their suspicions to Janet. She refused to believe her sister or brother-in-law were involved. Asked if her husband believed that Kevin was taking Heather somewhere secret, Janet said yes. Janet could hazard no guess as to how else the Triad might have learned about the handoff. She decided to phone her sister.

Tessa turned off the phone and passed on what Janet had said, saying she would call back in ten minutes. They got out of the car to stretch.

The second phone call transmitted Janet's suspicion that her brother-in-law had indeed betrayed his niece. Crying, she said he wouldn't even let her speak to her sister. Asked if there were any other options for Heather, Janet said none she trusted. Tessa then asked Janet if she would trust her to bring Heather somewhere safe. Janet said yes, as long as she told her where. Tessa said not over the phone, but that they would be in touch soon. She handed the phone to Heather, so mother and daughter could cry their goodbyes.

"Oh, Kevin, should I have told Dr. Hope that you were selfless enough to render Heather only a tenth of her former value? Maybe she could've transmitted that news to the Triad and they would've backed off."

Kevin didn't reply, but Heather looked with surprise at Tessa. Then her face changed, and she said, "Oh, God, Tessa, I'm sorry; I didn't know."

"Didn't know what?" asked Kevin.

"Nothing!" said Tessa. "I know where to hide Heather: at my great aunt's in Canada."

"I'm wanted for murder. I can't cross the border."

"Well, maybe you can stay near the border while I drop her off."

"Which way?" Kevin asked Tessa.

"To the Thousand Islands Bridge at the top of Highway 81."

Kevin drove north along the Connecticut River on the New Hampshire side. Arguing they should do their driving at night to maximize their chances of evading everyone after them, he stopped at a shuttered house. There they ate lunch.

Afterward, Mort napped, Heather and Kevin strolled into the woods for some privacy, and Tessa strolled along the river, brooding. Returning to the house, she used the GPS to find a little-traveled route back west to Alexandria, NY. She, too, took a nap.

\*

Coming off the exit ramp from I-89 onto Route 4 west, Tessa hit the brakes. Kevin, who had wanted to drive shotgun in case immediate action with guns became necessary, at first didn't know what was going on. Daylight was fading fast and it was difficult to see. When he saw a little boy standing on the road ahead, he said, "Don't stop!"

"Am I supposed to run him over?"

"Go around him." She brought the truck to a halt. "Go!" yelled Kevin, taking his Colt 1911 out from under the seat.

"Shut up," requested Tessa as she opened her door to help the child.

Just then, four adults—two men and two women— emerged from the trees with guns leveled at Kevin, screaming for him to "Get the fuck out!"

Without looking at Mort, Kevin said, "I have only one bullet in my gun; hand me my rifle between the seats."

But Mort was too frightened to test the gunmen, and he got out of the truck with his hands raised. Heather and Tessa got out as well.

One of the men put his rifle against the window by Kevin's head and said, "Put the gun down on the floor. Do it!"

Kevin obeyed.

"Now get out. I don't want bloody brains all over my new front seat." He backed away, and Kevin opened the door and stepped out. "Back off."

Kevin stood his ground, assessing his chances.

"Now, or I blow you away!"

Kevin saw a tattoo on the man's forearm that indicated he'd been an Army Ranger; he knew how to handle himself. Kevin backed toward the woods, joining Tessa, Heather, and Mort.

The ex-Ranger picked up the gun in the SUV. "A Colt 1911 .45 ACP with suppressor. Nice."

The five strangers got into the truck. The ex-Ranger said, "Nice assortment of bullet holes in the windshield. Oh. Accuracy Rifle! Extra nice. Worth a mint. Special Forces?"

"Fuck you."

"You're kind of fucked without these fine weapons, aren't you? Mind if I take them?"

"Please do. Then you can inject yourself with HIV and fuck me up the ass."

The ex-Ranger roared at that, but the other man said, "I don't get it."

One of the women said, "We had no bullets, chumps!" with a hearty laugh as they drove away with darkness closing in.

With the news they had no bullets, Kevin dropped his head. He'd decided against the same strategy and had been beaten as a result.

Kevin turned his outraged face toward Tessa, who immediately lowered her eyes. "Okay, Mother Fucking Teresa, what now?" She had no answer, of course. "Not only do we have no food, we have no weapons, which is a slight problem with a bunch of assassins on our trail. And they got my fucking rifle. And it's nighttime, it's getting cold again, and we're out in the middle of nowhere." She said nothing, so he said sarcastically, "Oh, well, we've got our health."

"God, I hate people," she said.

"Good," said Kevin. "That's lesson number one in your new People's Studies practicum: desperate people will eagerly take every means you have of survival to save themselves."

"Shit. I'm hungry and cold," whined Mort. "We have to use Heather's phone to call the police to rescue us."

"First of all," answered Kevin, "I'm wanted for murder. Second, they won't respond to people lost in the woods. Third, even if they did, they take two days to come for murders, so they wouldn't be here until our carcasses were picked clean by animals. Fourth, they might pass our whereabouts on to paying assassins."

They started walking south along the road. Kevin told them to duck into the trees right away if a car came along. He then said to Tessa, "Lesson number two: never help anyone again. If a pack of wolves comes out of the woods"—here Mort's, Heather's, and Tessa's eyes grew bigger—"and drags me away screaming, 'Help! Please help me,' and they get me into the trees and you hear them ripping me apart, and my blood comes squirting through the branches, and you wince at my agonized screams—'Ah! Ah! Oh, shit there goes my arm! For the love of God, Tessa, help me!'—I want you to ignore it and walk on." He turned to Mort and added, "And you, don't eat any of my leftovers."

Tessa became sullen and silent as they walked along the road. Kevin teased, "Listen!" Again the six eyes around him, even Mort's beady eyes, got wide. "That's the sound of Tessa not talking. Isn't it wonderful?" Heather chuckled, but Tessa pouted.

"Cheer up, Tessa," said Heather. "We'll be alright. We have Kevin."

But Kevin was still angry at her and didn't want to let her off the hook yet. He said, "Yup, I'm here, alright. And I found something to improve our outlook." He picked up a stick.

"How will that help?" asked Tessa. He whipped her in the butt. "Kevin, cut it out!"

"There, my outlook has improved already," said Kevin as he tossed the stick and wiped his hands. Tessa hung her head. "Why so sulky, Red Bush? Sad because everyone is giving you the silent treatment? Okay, I'll make sure you get the attention a pretty girl figures is her due. I guarantee you the spotlight. I'll be your narrator! Tessa rolls her eyes in reaction to my suggestion. She walks past me, making sure her shoulder collides with mine to convey her anger, her snooty nose hovering in the air above her, as always. Her ass sloshes about in her sweat pants as she stomps away. She turns her head to cast me an irate look, thinking '*My* firm ass does *not* slosh!' but continues on her way, deciding to try ignoring me, hoping maybe I'll get bored or run out of things to say to piss her off.

"She looks toward the western horizon, painted a dark purple by the sun beneath it, but frowns to see the panorama obstructed with Mort. She clenches her jaw, trying to control her temper, and barely manages to beat down the impulse of attacking her narrator. Oh! Fuck … In an unforeseen development, the impulse triumphed and she kneed her narrator in the crotch … This has brought a bright smile to the maiden's lips as spasms of pain bounce from the base of my spine to the top of my head and back down to my hapless sack. Tessa chuckles at my evident discomfort. She doesn't suspect that I'm fixing to wring her neck as soon as I recover.

"Her smile disappears. She turns and runs; I follow, wincing in pain as my throbbing sack objects to the strain. I catch her."

"No, Kevin, let me go! I'm sorry."

"She screams, as I bend her in different directions, knowing something will eventually break."

"Kevin, you're hurting me."

"She exclaims, as she lavishes punches upon her narrator, even though I've decided to show what a considerate fellow I am by only breaking her left arm."

"Ow!"

Tessa started crying.

"Oh, shit, did I hurt you, Tess?" asked Kevin.

He tried to hug her, but she pushed him away, calling him, "Asshole!"

"Sorry, Tess. I really didn't mean to hurt you."

She walked away. Heather jogged to catch up and took her hand.

They resumed their trek as the road curved westward. With no moon to light the way, the darkness became all but impenetrable. They could see only a few feet before them. They crept along for perhaps fifteen minutes, hoping to come across civilization. As the temperature dropped, all four began to shiver. They came across what seemed to have been a built-up area, although they couldn't tell the extent of it; there were no lights, so it was clear whatever had been here was abandoned. This wasn't unusual nowadays; small settlements had disappeared all over the country. They walked along a crumbling sidewalk. Coming to a parking lot invaded by weeds, Kevin walked up to a ruined building, but it was too rundown to offer shelter.

They kept walking along the sidewalk. Kevin rejected two other ruined buildings as shelter. It was frustrating because they couldn't see anything. Maybe good shelter was just beyond them.

In the lead, Kevin came up to a guardrail. He proceeded, but then suddenly halted, saying "Whoa!"

Tessa, Heather, and Mort also came to a halt. The road had suddenly terminated. The four looked into the darkness, trying to make out the environs.

"There's supposed to be a bridge here," Tessa said just as Kevin drew the same conclusion. They crossed to the south side of the road and saw part of the railing hanging over a ravine. "This is incredibly dangerous," she said, just as a set of car lights appeared in the distance behind them.

"Into the trees!" ordered Kevin.

"No!" said Tessa. "We have to stop them before they drive over the cliff."

"Could be the cops or killers after us," said Kevin as he, Heather, and Mort stepped over the guardrail and headed to the trees. "Tessa, come on. Remember lesson two. We have nothing to defend ourselves if wolves are in the car."

She ran down the road and waved her arms, yelling, "Stop! The bridge is out. Stop!"

When the headlights shined on her, the driver sped up.

"No! Stop!" she screamed, but the car shot past her and disappeared over the precipice. Three seconds later they heard a crash from below.

Tessa crept to the cliff and looked down. The other three joined her. They saw the car. One taillight was still working. Shaking, Tessa asked, "Do you think anyone could survive that?"

"No way," said Mort. "It's at least a hundred feet."

"Half again that, I'd say," said Kevin. "I guess you were right, Tessa; he was no threat to us. Seems a bit extreme, plunging off a cliff to clear oneself of suspicion, but it's hard to refute."

Tessa said, "Not funny. Why didn't he stop?"

"He did," Kevin answered, pointing down.

"Kevin Robert Idle, there's nothing funny about this!"

"Okay, you're right. He didn't stop because either you wanted help, which would cost him some of his resources, or you were setting up a trap like the one you fell for, which would cost him everything. I wouldn't have stopped either."

"We have to call the police," insisted Tessa. "Drivers can't see this until it's too late. A lot more people could die."

"Ordinarily I'd agree, but that would put us at great risk. The only reason we're still alive is no one knows where we are. We use Heather's phone to call the cops and you can bet someone will track us."

"News flash, Mr. Idle; some of us are still human." Addressing Heather, she said, "Give me your phone." As she dialed 911, Kevin shook his head. It took twenty-seven rings before the emergency call was answered. "They put me on hold!"

"Every second you're on the phone makes it more likely they'll track us down," said Kevin.

"Who?" asked Heather.

"The police and anyone a corrupt cop sells the information to, including the Triad, the Mexicans, and the people after Tessa and Mort. Or the Triad might know your phone number by now."

As they awaited the 911 operator, they managed to find a few downed branches in the darkness and take them to the highway, hoping any drivers would perceive the barrier and stop. "If it were me," said Kevin, "I'd drive right through, thinking it was a trap."

"Maybe we can set it on fire," suggested Tessa. "Anyone have matches or a lighter?"

"I do—in the SUV," said Kevin. Tessa's shoulders slumped.

Finally, after almost seven minutes, the 911 call was answered, and Tessa explained the emergency and asked for help. She hung up and said, "Apparently this is, uh, was the bridge over Quechee Gorge. They said help might not arrive for at least a half hour."

A small fire had erupted from the car that had sped past Tessa into the abyss. The fire illuminated another vehicle that had met the same fate. Tessa said, "That's our truck, isn't it?"

Nodding, Kevin said, "Stay here while I check it out."

"Kevin, climbing down a steep hill in the dark to a car on fire isn't exactly safe."

"Neither is waiting for the cops when I'm wanted for murder, or for one or more groups of assassins," he said as he gingerly made his way down. "I at least need to get our guns. It's not too bad over this way, actually," he called up. "Maybe you three should follow. Getting caught up there is a bad idea."

"But—"

"Tessa! You came to me for protection, so stop arguing and get your ass down here."

Tessa and Heather started down. The fire below helped illuminate the way.

"I'm not climbing down there," protested Mort.

"Bye," said Kevin.

Mort cursed and followed the ladies down.

# CHAPTER 8

The four made their way down the hill in about ten minutes, Mort breathing hard and grousing the whole way. They stopped and looked at the wreckage: their Toyota, the Ford that had just joined it, and chunks of what was formerly a small bridge across a narrow chasm.

Kevin said, "You saved our lives, Tess. We'd have driven over the edge, too."

"If that's true, then I also killed them," she said despondently.

"Lesson three: stop feeling sorry for assholes who laughed about leaving you to die."

Tessa, Heather, and Mort looked on while Kevin climbed over the debris up to the Toyota and looked inside. He winced, shook his head, and waved at them to stay away. Making his way to the Ford, he again shook his head. "I wouldn't advise you to look," he said.

"Careful, Kevin, it's still burning a little; it could blow up," said Tessa.

He headed back to the Toyota. The engine compartment was obliterated, but the cabin was relatively intact. He opened the passenger side back door and reached in across a corpse to get his rifle.

As he climbed in, Tessa warned, "Another car can come hurtling down at any moment, Kevin. Come back here."

"Cars are few and far between out here. I need to get ammunition, food, and a few other supplies if we're going to survive."

So in he went as Tessa urged him to hurry while looking up with concern. He threw out the Colt and the Smith & Wesson, ammunition, several cans of food, his Seal jacket, backpack and suitcases, the C-4 kits, the flashlight, and a first aid kit. "Couldn't find the goddamn can opener," he said as he climbed out. "Let's get away from here." He put on his jacket, stuffed what he could into his backpack, and put it on; he pocketed the Colt and picked up the rifle.

He looked at Heather, who was on the phone, and darted his angry eyes to Tessa, who explained, "When her mother is told her SUV was found at the bottom of a ravine with bodies inside, she'll die. Heather has to tell her she's okay."

"Great. Now we've doubled our chances of being found."

After Heather hung up, Kevin took the phone, dropped it, and stepped on it. She and Tessa knew better not to object.

Heather and Tessa opened their suitcases to put on another sweater. Each carried her own suitcase and picked up a share of supplies. Mort pocketed four cans of soup and two of creamed corn. Kevin said nothing because there was no can opener.

The four waded across the shallow river and made their way up the opposite side of the ravine, three walking in silence, and

Mort bitching. With the fire below out, Tessa switched on the flashlight. Three-quarters of the way up the far side of the ravine they heard screeching tires and saw a small car plunging into the darkness. They heard the passengers scream until the harsh sound of crunching steel ended it.

Tessa, weeping and infuriated, said, "I called 911 at least a half-hour ago. People are dying out here. Where the hell are they?"

"Sitting on their asses," answered Kevin. "If it's like Syracuse, they asked the police union to accept a fifty percent wage and benefit cut. They refused, so they laid off half of them—and not the burnt out, old half; the gung ho, young half."

"That's terrible," said Heather, who was also crying.

"Yup, they'd hired so many city workers, paid them so much, and gave them such generous retirement packages that when the tax money started drying up because people were losing their homes and investors wouldn't touch their toxic bonds, they had to get rid of half the cops, teachers, fire fighters, and so on. So next time you need the police because of some minor thing like kidnapping or cars driving off collapsed bridges—which collapsed because the state and federal governments ran out of money for inspection and maintenance—comfort yourself with the knowledge that some fifty-year-old cop is making eighty grand hunkering down in the station where he's safe from the insanity, some thirty-year old laid off cop is working security for minimum wage at Costco, and some ninety-eight-year-old retired cop is getting his hip replaced in the hospital at a cost of a hundred grand courtesy of you."

"My legs are killing me," said Mort. "I need to rest. Let's stop and eat."

Kevin, who was also shaken by the sight and sound of people plummeting to their death and what that implied about what his country had come to, kept on walking and talking because he didn't want to start crying. "We get no city services anymore, yet taxes go up. Mom was panicking last month because she got a warning that if she didn't pay her property tax bill—which was almost seven thousand new dollars!—they would seize the property. I'd be surprised if the house was worth that anymore. She didn't have a hope of paying it because they'd laid her off three years back. She was a teacher," he said to Heather. "Twenty-two years and she gets booted out with nothing. Then they bill her seven thousand newbucks. For nothing! Not even garbage gets collected anymore.

"And the kicker? After she died and I tried to collect on her hundred thousand dollar life insurance policy, I got a letter explaining that the insurance company can't pay because it's in deep financial trouble, probably because the idiots were deep into derivatives. Fuckers! She'd paid them premiums for decades and they were still taking them, having no intention of paying benefits. They held out hope that I might eventually get a thousand bucks. I tried to explain this to the city, and they told me, 'Yes, times are tough, but you still owe us seven grand.' They renewed the seizure threat if I didn't come up with the money by the end of the month. Well, the assholes can have whatever's left after the barbarians finish stripping it of everything that's worth more than a cent!"

They crested the hill, walked to the road, and saw that the bridge jutted out about twenty feet on this side of the ravine before giving way to thin air. No police at either end yet.

They walked along the south side of the road for a few more minutes until they saw another set of headlights coming. "Oh, no!" said Heather.

"Maybe it's finally the police," said Tessa.

"And if it is?" said Kevin. "I can't get caught. And it's too dangerous for you three. Everyone in the trees." Once again, Tessa stayed on the road. "Tessa!"

"If it's the police, I'll just tell them I live nearby and walk away."

He readied his rifle. She waved her arms. This time the vehicle slowed.

The 2016 Ford Escape came to a halt, and a man got out of the passenger seat. Tessa said loud enough for her three friends to hear, "Finally, the police."

"Stay put," ordered Kevin, who was on his stomach aiming at the man's head. Heather, who lay beside Kevin, listened; Mort didn't. He walked out to join Tessa.

The man still in the Escape said something and the one next to Tessa grabbed her, putting his arm around her neck to restrain her, and pulled out a revolver.

Mort put up his hands and started begging for his life, adding, "She's the one who knows about the battery."

Turning toward the woods where Mort had been, the man yelled, "You in the woods, come out, hands in the air, or these two die." He pointed his gun at Tessa's temple.

"What should—" Heather began.

"Shh! Keep your head down," whispered Kevin.

The rear passenger side window glided down and the driver hollered, "Just kill them and let's get the fuck out of here."

"That fucking Navy Seal might be in the woods," he replied. Turning back to the woods, he said, "You have two sec—" before a bullet between the eyes cut him off. Tessa shrieked as the man fell; his dead weight dragged her down. Frantically, she wiped her face to get the man's blood and brains off. Mort fell down and covered his head.

Tessa was then showered with shattered glass as the passenger side front window exploded with a shot from within the Escape toward the woods and one from the opposite direction. A blaring horn drowned out Tessa's screaming.

Kevin walked out, followed by Heather, whose legs were shaking so much she fell to her knees. Tessa was still screaming.

Kevin heaved the body out of the driver's seat and dragged both bodies into the trees. If they were found too soon, the police might start looking for their vehicle.

He then knelt beside Tessa and tried to calm her down, but she was hysterical. He ended up covering her mouth with his hand, then holding her tight against him. Eventually she settled down. She collapsed into Kevin's arms and sobbed.

A few minutes afterward, with all four in the truck, Kevin did a U-turn and drove northwest. They drove in silence. There would be no chastisement of Tessa this time; she knew well she'd been victimized yet again and was paying a heavy enough emotional price.

\*

They saw headlights in the distance. "We're not stopping," warned Kevin.

Tessa had made up her mind to say nothing, but when a school bus drove by, she turned immediately and saw children on it. "Kevin!"

"Tessa!"

"They're children!"

"Kevin?" said Heather.

"Ah, shit." He braked, turned around, and floored it. "What the hell would a school bus be doing out here?" asked Kevin. "They've closed half the schools in the country. I would've figured any money for field trips dried up years ago."

"Not for some sports teams," yelled Heather from the floor of the back. She and Mort had to deal with the hurricane blowing in through the open front-side window that had been shattered. Everyone had to shout to be heard. "Parents at my friends' school pitch in for trips when the championships are being played."

"Son of a bitch is moving at quite a clip," said Kevin. "I don't know if we can catch him in time."

"Oh, God!" said Tessa. "Go faster." She looked at the speed: 102 miles per hour.

"Have to stay on the road," he said as he slowed for a curve in the road.

"Flash your lights!" suggested Tessa.

He followed her advice, but the bus driver paid no heed. "Idiot!" screamed Kevin.

"How far to the bridge?" asked Tessa.

"I think this curve is maybe a half-mile or so out," he said, pulling out to pass the bus as the long curve continued. She could hear his voice tremble again.

"A half mile!" hollered Mort. "Stop! Stop!"

They pulled in front of the bus and Kevin braked. The bus drove right up to his bumper. "He's driving up our ass!" said Kevin.

"I think I see the sign for the gorge ahead!" screamed Tessa.

"Pull out of his way and stop!" shrieked Mort who had sat up. He went to grab the wheel, but Tessa, expecting this, pointed the Smith & Wesson at his head. He withdrew.

Kevin applied the brakes. The school bus pulled into the other lane and surged ahead. Kevin floored the Escape, pulled out in front of the bus again, and put on the brakes again.

"Kevin! That's the parking lot just before the bridge. The cliff is right there!" screamed Tessa. Heather shut her eyes. Mort screamed.

Blaring his horn, the bus driver braked hard to avoid an accident. The Escape bumped along with the tires and brakes smoking, coming to a stop on the last bit of the road hanging over the chasm. When Mort stopped screaming, they heard loud creaking. "Kevin, it's going to go down!" said Tessa.

Putting the truck in reverse, Kevin gunned it as the last piece of the bridge began to disintegrate underneath them. The front wheels bounced hard upon hitting the cliff's edge because the rest of the bridge had just disappeared. They heard the crash below. Kevin backed up more and put the Escape in park. He rested his head on the steering wheel, took a deep breath, and got out.

The bus driver, still unaware of the lack of a bridge not thirty feet from the bus, got out screaming at Kevin. Kevin said nothing, but did punch the man in the face. He staggered back. Evidently wondering what was going on, several young men and three parents of the students left the bus, some looking intent on teaching this maniac driver a lesson. One father grabbed Kevin, but Tessa stepped out of the truck and yelled, "Leave him alone; he just saved your lives."

They looked to her. One student said, "Holy shit, the bridge is out!"

Tessa came over and asked the stunned driver, "Why didn't you stop when we flashed our lights?"

A father said, "He's a know-it-all, and he said cops never flash their lights like that. He thought you were just an asshole in a rush."

Another father asked the bus driver, "Do you want to sue this man for striking you? I'd be happy to represent you." Kevin grasped his collar and lifted him. "This is assault! I'm suing you!" the man said.

"No, counselor," said Kevin, "until I'm judged guilty by a jury of my peers, I'm only allegedly assaulting you." Kevin lugged him toward the gorge.

"You're all witnesses!" screeched the man.

Tessa said, "Kevin, what are you doing?"

"I saved his life, and that gives me the right to unsave it. I'm going to allegedly throw him over the cliff."

"Kevin, let him go," she said.

Having made his point, he let the man go.

"I'm still suing! My neck is hurt."

"Oh, shut up, Feldstein," said one of the other fathers. "He's just another desperate, out-of-work lawyer." He shook Kevin's hand and said, "Thank you, mister. What's your name, anyway? You saved all our lives: we'll shout your name from the rooftops."

Kevin answered, "Well, then, good sir, you may go to your rooftop and shout the name Dillard Blifil."

"Bbbfffff!" was merely the first syllable of a gargantuan guffaw loosed by Tessa that startled the assembled. The deep stress she was under had transformed a silly comeback into the funniest joke ever uttered by mankind. After laughing for about a minute, she said, "Let the world resound with the name, Dillard the Chucklehead," then laughed some more.

Kevin chuckled and walked with Tessa to the Escape. With the bus crowd gawping at them, they turned and drove away.

Tessa took the front seat; she clutched Kevin's hand and expressed her thanks. Heather reached forward, put both arms over the seat and around his shoulders, saying, "You're amazing!" She kissed his cheek.

Three more minutes on, a police car sped by with lights flashing. "There's the cavalry, right on time," said Kevin.

A short while later, Kevin said, "I have no idea how those assassins got here so quickly. They were obviously in the area, so they somehow knew we were out this way. Maybe when Heather called her mother the first time, or maybe Heather's uncle found out about the price on your heads. We know for sure one of the phone calls you two made tonight enabled them to pinpoint us."

Heather said, "Hey, there's a laptop back here."

Tessa said, "Pass it forward." Heather did so. "It has a portable Internet stick. I'll see what we can learn from the history." She opened the laptop and powered it up. A minute later, she said, "The hit men went to a website that required a password."

"So we can't learn anything?" said Heather.

Kevin responded, "Tessa's tremendous at anything to do with computers. She can hack into pretty well anything. I used to bug her to use it to our advantage but Ms. Goody Two-shoes never would. She'll break in."

After nine minutes, Tessa gasped.

"What?" said Heather and Kevin simultaneously.

Her voice shaking, she replied, "It doesn't say it outright, but knowing what we know and reading between the lines, I'm pretty sure there's a reward of ten million new dollars on our heads. And flashing at the top of the screen is Quechee Gorge, Vermont."

"Shit. Right up to date. We'd better take a few turns."

"What they call 'the reward' has been doubled to ten million new dollars because an ex-Navy Seal is babysitting."

"Someone might shoot back, in other words. Who's offering the money?"

"Doesn't say."

"How would killers collect?" said Kevin.

"It has an email address. They'd send pictures of our corpses, I guess."

"Can you find the computer that put up the webpage?"

She worked on it for a few minutes. She then looked at Kevin and said, "The computer belongs to the Islamic Center of Washington, DC. I'll look it up." A couple of minutes later she said, "It's funded by Saudi Arabia."

"So the Saudis are putting up ten million newbucks to stop a technology that could dry up its money fountain. Makes sense." He shook his head. "This confirms you two have freelancers after you. That's why some are idiots and some are professionals. They're coming out of the woodwork for a chance at the big bucks."

"God, Kev, what should … how can we possibly survive?"

"Make your battery and sell it fast. Once it's out there, no sense killing the inventors, unless they're just pissed at you."

"What about the FBI or CIA? Surely to God a foreign power can't just put up money to murder Americans in nearly plain view like this, not even in today's world."

"They not only can, they did. But maybe the feds don't know. They've probably been cut to the bone, too. You can try asking them to step in, but I wouldn't hold my breath."

Tessa sent emails to the FBI, CIA, and a few other lettered agencies, attaching the link and password, and letting them know who was behind it and what might potentially be at stake: a technology that just might help the country wean itself from Mideast oil; a technology that could earn Americans billions of dollars.

Since the computer battery was low and they could find no power cord in the car, Tessa turned off the computer. On their way to Canada, she turned it on a few times to check the website for updates. It continued to show Quechee Gorge as their last-known location.

They drove through Vermont and upstate New York, across the Adirondacks. Mort and Heather slept in the back. Tessa stayed awake, unable to sleep sitting up in a car, especially with the racket from the wind through her missing window.

The two discussed Tessa's plan to take Heather to her great aunt. Kevin said, "I can't cross the border with the cops after me, which would leave you three unprotected. It's too dangerous."

"But we need to get Heather to safety."

"How safe is it? The Saudis might find out about your aunt and have people waiting there, too."

Tessa threw her hands up and said, "Well, why didn't you bring that up before?"

"Why didn't you? I can't think of everything, and I didn't know the extent of this."

Tessa said, "What would you think of getting my aunt to come down here? She lives with her sister-in-law near Kingston, Ontario. But her sister-in-law has a nice cottage on Keuka Lake. I went there last summer."

"Might be ideal, but chances are a cottage will be occupied or chopped up and carted away if the owner is away for long periods."

"I don't think so. The cottage is on a crescent that skirts the lake. Most of the people live there year-round. The street got together to pay a caretaker—a man who lives a few doors down—to watch all the houses. He's pretty serious about it. He's a retired Marine or something. Anyway, I'll Skype my aunt and ask about it in the morning."

"She must be ancient. She's into Skype?"

"As a young woman, she was the first female professor of computer science at the University of Toronto. She taught me a lot of what I know on computers."

\*

Heather and Mort awoke as they drove up Route 12 toward Watertown. She yawned and said, "Kev, you promised to tell me what Tessa was like in high school."

"Snootiest bitch on the planet."

"Come on, Kevin. Be nice. Now tell me," insisted Heather.

"As she told you, she ditched me just before high school. What she didn't say was how much she enjoyed it. She got a charge out of my agony. She did the same thing to, what, a dozen other guys in high school?" Tessa shrugged. "But she reserved her worst for me. With every new boyfriend she got, she'd march him next door and introduce him to me."

"I did that maybe twice," said Tessa.

"It was a lot more often than that. In eleventh grade, she started bringing Cornell men by."

"Once, Kevin."

"The worst was the night of the Christmas dance in eleventh grade, and it illustrates perfectly the kind of person she is. Tessa knocked on my window at one in the morning. I opened it; she climbed in like she used to when we were friends and sat on my bed, then looked in my eyes as she told me, 'I just gave my virginity to Everett Whittingham.' She sat there staring intently at me, enjoying the effect her news had on me. I was so shocked, mad, and jealous, I couldn't say a thing. I swear she sat there staring with this malicious smile for at least five minutes."

"It was maybe half a minute."

"It was much longer. She went on to tell me the details. How she got him so horny he couldn't hold back—"

At this point, Mort interrupted with, "I know what that's like. I had a sixteen-year-old dick once."

"When? Last week?" said Kevin.

That shut Mort up. Kevin thought back to the incident that had made him realize he still loved her, because it had shattered him. Tessa had said, "I expected it to hurt when he broke my hymen, because he's so big, but he was so gentle I felt only a momentary pang as he slowly slid inside me." She stopped to enjoy his misery, then continued, "God, Kev, he felt so good so deep inside me. He flipped me on top and grabbed my ass. I could feel him tense up as his thrusts came faster and harder until he gushed inside me. He was moaning and breathing so hard that I got more excited than I've ever been and I came, too." Breathlessly she said, "Oh! Oh! Oh!" as she pretended to climax. He felt sick to his stomach to think of another man doing this to her. It devastated him, and she could tell.

Savoring his devastation, she put her hand on his leg close to his crotch, squeezed his thigh, and leaned over to whisper, "Don't tell anyone, but I didn't make him wear a rubber. I felt him squirt inside me. It was so exciting, I was actually quivering!" She finished by saying, "Hope I don't get pregnant; I'd have to marry him. Not that I'd mind. I think he's the one, Kev. God, I need him right now! I'm sneaking back to his place to fuck him again. Good night." Then she kissed his cheek and climbed out the window, smiling with the knowledge that she had destroyed him.

He said to Heather, "She knew she was torturing me, and she reveled in it."

"Well, you'd been diddling your way through all the sluts in the school, including Kim Menninger for months. He told me he loved her. The tramp all the guys in school bopped; after boarding her, the next stop was the clinic. It was payback, that's all."

"Where is good old Whittingham, anyway?" Kevin asked Tessa.

"No idea."

"Poor Tess; he was the city's best catch, but you made an error. You put out far too fast. You were just another slut on the way up to the school's only jaw dropper, Cathy Jorgenson."

She tried slapping him, but he blocked it.

"Stop hitting him," rebuked Heather. "You're so mean to him."

"He deserves it," she said, taken aback at Heather's reproof.

"You always excuse your shitty behavior by pinning responsibility on the other person," said Kevin. "When my parents split up and I told you, do you remember what you said to me?" With her head lowered, she shrugged. "I can see you do." He turned to Heather and said, "She told me it was my fault."

"Their fights *were* mainly about the trouble you were causing."

"I know that; I knew it then, and I feel worse about that than anything else in my shitty life. But at that point I needed consolation, and you gave me only grief. That's pretty much all you've ever given me."

"Kevin, that's not really what you believe, is it?"

"Let a man wallow in self-pity, will you?"

Heather leaned forward, kissed his cheek, and whispered, "I'll give you the opposite of grief later."

Tessa turned to look out the window.

*

By the time they approached Watertown, the trials of the day had caught up with Kevin and Tessa. They could hardly keep their eyes open, so they began to look for abandoned farm houses. They soon found one. Kevin took his Colt and checked it out. Declaring it safe, he motioned the three others in. There was no food, electricity, or running water, but there were a few rundown beds, albeit without blankets.

Heather was quick to claim the best one for her and Kevin. Tessa, who was careful to pick a room down the hall, noticed that Heather knelt next to the bed to pray when she passed her room on the way downstairs.

Mort was sitting in the corner of the living room eating Maling peas. Kevin had opened it with his Swiss Army knife.

Before going to bed, Tessa and Kevin decided to have a bite to eat, too. They opened two cans of chunky soup and one of beans, and ate with spoons they'd pilfered from the bed and breakfast inn.

Tessa said, "Did you see Heather praying?" He nodded. "I know you have no use for God now, but did you pray when you were younger?"

"Sure, right before I beat off."

"Wouldn't that kind of invalidate the prayer?"

"Don't think so; Dear Lord, please make Cathy Jorgenson fuck me. Amen. He never granted that, which made me suspect He was a crock of shit. Everything since has only confirmed it."

"Every guy in the school wanted her. I hated her at first, but later we became friends."

"Rumor had it that Jorgenson and you made it big in Las Vegas as ten-grand-a-night call girls."

"What? Who the hell told you that?"

"Heard it from Connors and McNamara."

"And you believed them, I suppose."

"Not for an instant. I told them Jorgenson maybe, but Tessa Sharp would never—"

"You're damn right I would never—"

"You didn't let me finish. I told them Sharp would never fetch ten grand a night. I wouldn't pay a rotten tomato for her."

"For your information, asshole, when Cathy and I went there right after high school, we *were* approached by someone from an escort agency and told we could earn two grand every hour, and we'd get to keep half. She took it; I didn't. She made a career of it, last I heard."

"Whereas you just screwed yourself with two hundred grand in loans for a worthless degree. You should've taken the offer."

"Are you out of your mind? Do you actually see me working as an escort? With my brain?"

"No, with your twat. Just screw some rich dudes for, say, twenty-five hours a week, and you could make twenty-five grand a week for lying on your back. What's that a year?"

"One-point-three million dollars," she said immediately and with not a little trace of lament in her voice.

"Tax free. Sounds like a dream come true."

"For a man, maybe."

"Hell, yeah. If women were stupid enough to pay top dollar for sex, I'd be on the next flight to Vegas."

"Even if women *were* that stupid, you wouldn't fetch more than a can of Spam a week." He smiled. She went on. "It's not a simple calculation for a woman, and you know it. Prostitution is not only degrading, it's dangerous. And what quality guy would ever be interested in a prostitute?"

Kevin said, "In the time it took you to earn your degree, you could've earned six and a half mill. Then hang up your red bush, move back to Canada, and marry a nice Canadian man who would never know how deliciously naughty you were."

"And worry every day that he would find out and leave me."

"So what? You'd never need a man."

"But I want one. I want a husband and children, and I want a career that I can be proud of."

"Yeah, you're right. Here you are facing a quick death from assassination or a slow one from starvation. Meanwhile, Jorgenson has millions and probably ended up with one of her super-rich sugar daddies living on their own island in the Caribbean. Any regrets?"

"Shut up."

Heather sauntered up to Kevin and took his hand. "Come on," she said as she pulled him toward the stairs.

Tessa looked at her as if to say, *hey!*

But Heather said, "You said you didn't want a second chance, right?" Tessa nodded slowly. Heather snatched two more cans of soup and led Kevin upstairs. Tessa kept looking at the stairs. She was upset, but wasn't sure why. She hated him, didn't she?

From the other room, Mort said, "I'll keep you warm tonight."

"Dream on, blubber boy," she said as she made her way to her room. She opened her suitcase and put on another layer of clothes. She curled up on her bare, lumpy mattress. Dog tired, she soon fell asleep.

# CHAPTER 9

With Kevin by her side, Tessa Skyped her great-aunt mid-morning and communicated the situation. She felt she couldn't hold back telling of the dangers they faced, because her aunt could be putting herself in the line of fire. "Aunty Evelyn," as Tessa called her, didn't hesitate before agreeing to help. She and her sister-in-law, Bell, would meet them at the defunct 1000 Islands Campground at the junction of Highways 180 and 12 about three miles southwest of the Thousand Islands Bridge, which connected Canada and the United States, and proceed to the cottage.

Kevin, worried that Evelyn was under surveillance, worked out a plan to check for and clear any tail that the old ladies had on them. Given the circumstances and vulnerabilities of the people involved, the plan had to be basic. The old ladies were to make sure they left no clue behind of their destination. They were to stop by a store in Canada to purchase groceries and two disposable cell phones, then cross the Thousand Islands Bridge and proceed down Route 12.

Kevin presumed that if the ladies were being followed, the pursuer would do so via electronic means. It would be too risky to tail by sight, especially if the ladies crossed the border, which always had its unpredictability. Since the depression hit, American borders had been tightened considerably to keep those job-stealing Mexicans and Canadians at bay. But two old ladies probably wouldn't have much trouble crossing.

Kevin hoped the necessity to cross the border would give them the advantage they needed to escape from any pursuers. As soon as the old ladies crossed the border, the women were to travel at high speed to the parking lot of an abandoned motel at the junction of 180 and 12.

The timing was critical. Any killers would likely not be more than a minute or two behind, unless the border delayed them. Kevin wanted the meeting to take place at dusk; enough light to give him time to check the aunt's car for bugs, but with the imminent cover of darkness to help them make their getaway. It had to be fast.

The four had ten hours to kill before the 8:30 PM meeting. Heather said, "Let's go back to bed, Kev." Tessa narrowed her eyes.

Kevin took her up on that offer. Tessa was left to breakfast with Mort. Only her control of the Swiss Army Knife kept Mort from polishing off most of the food they had left. They had cash to get more, but it would be risky lining up to buy more just now.

At mid afternoon, Heather and Kevin emerged from their room. Tessa once more glared at them. The two lovers examined the available food. Kevin looked askance at Mort as he opened the last can of CCS and one of wax beans.

Heather continued a conversation she'd begun in their room, pushing to let her stay with them, but he was adamant in his refusals, saying it was far too dangerous. It was an argument Heather couldn't win, and she reluctantly accepted it.

Tessa helped by telling Heather, "Aunty Evelyn took me in after my mother killed herself. She helped me through the hardest period in my life and gave me hope for the future simply by showing me love. She's a wonderful person."

"So, this great aunt of yours managed to beat the pandemic, did she? How old is she?" asked Kevin as he frowned at the taste of cold wax beans.

"Mid-eighties, I think. Yeah, she made it, but one of my grandmothers died from the Owl Flu, and the other was over eighty when she got cancer, so Medicare wouldn't pay for treatment, so she died. My grandfathers had died before all this. What about yours?"

"I had only one grandparent left before the pandemic, but it got her."

"My mother's parents died before I was born," said Heather. "I don't know about my father's parents. My mom kicked my father out when I was two; I don't even remember him. She told me last year that he couldn't keep it in his pants."

"I know someone just like that," said Tessa with an eye on Kevin.

"Mom said women were always throwing themselves at him because he was so handsome."

"Oh, wait, maybe I don't," said Tessa. Kevin gave her a look that said, *ha!*

"I was sick for a month," put in Mort. "I should've been in the hospital, but the old fogeys clogged them up. I lost a lot of weight."

"I'm pretty sure you found it again," said Kevin.

Heather said, "My mom's a doctor, so she saw a lot of people die from the flu. She said it happened because the government ran out of money."

"Yup, the few things they were actually needed for went by the wayside," said Kevin. "The damn Chinese covered it up for God knows how long before it burst out of control and spread around the world unchecked for another God knows how long. Advanced nations ran out of money to monitor these things, so nobody who could do anything about it noticed until it was too late to stop it."

Mort said, "It's no secret that governments around the world collaborated to design a bug that would get rid of the most expensive, least productive members in society. Unfunded liabilities of a million bucks per taxpayer? Just get rid of most of the old and sick. Health, social security, and pension costs dive. Problem solved. Good public policy."

"It's no secret that you're an idiot," responded Tessa. "Flu bugs usually pick off the weak and elderly. This one was just particularly virulent."

Kevin surmised, "The governments' crime was more passive: standing by while the influenza spread and wiped out the costly old coots who just wouldn't die on their own, not before costing us trillions anyway. Hell, if the government didn't do this, it should have."

"That's an awful thing to think, let alone say," said Tessa.

"So what? These are the assholes who looted our generation to get the things they wanted but were too cheap to pay for. They lived off us before we were even born, for Christ's sake. What goddamn audacity! They caused this nightmare we're living through now. So, wipe them out now and maybe we can wake up sooner."

"Remember what I said about being too callous, Kevin Idle," said Tessa. "Throw away your humanity and you're lost forever."

\*

Tessa stood on the shoulder of Route 12 looking through the scope of Kevin's rifle. Kevin and Heather sat on the hood of the Escape they'd acquired from the hit men; Mort snoozed in the truck.

"I think I see her car," said Tessa. Her aunt drove a dark green 2006 Nissan Maxima. "Yeah, it's them," she confirmed a few seconds later.

Kevin and Heather hopped down from the hood. "Okay, let's do this fast."

Tessa was to keep watch on the highway to warn them of approaching vehicles, while Kevin and Heather checked the Maxima for an electronic tracking device. If they found one, Kevin would lead the pursuers astray. If not, he would take the Maxima, while everyone else would take the aptly named Ford Escape, just in case people were following.

The Maxima pulled into the parking lot and came to a stop. "Stay in the car," said Kevin by way of hello.

Kevin and Heather immediately went down to their knees and checked. Almost right away, Heather said, "I think I found it," holding it up to Kevin. It was about the size of a matchbox, the kind that could be tracked with a smart phone. He took it and patted her on the shoulder for a job well-done.

She smiled and ran over to take spotting duty from Tessa, as earlier arranged. Tessa ran over to greet her aunt. After kissing her through the window and thanking her for coming, she asked if they'd brought the phones.

Aunt Evelyn held them out to Tessa, saying, "I've set them up. All either caller has to do is turn the phone on and hit star one." Tessa handed one to Kevin.

"There's a car coming!" hollered Heather.

"Hurry!" said Kevin. "Everyone in the car now!"

Mort, still sleeping, had to be roused by Tessa. "Get up, you lazy son of a bitch!" she screamed to him. He slowly opened his eyes.

"It's almost here!" said Heather. She ran back toward Kevin.

"Tessa, Heather, get in the car now. Forget that fat bastard," said Kevin. He looked up and saw the car within three hundred yards and realized there was no time for the ladies to get away. He sprinted to the Escape, where he'd left his rifle loaded and ready to go. He only had time to raise it when the car, an old Chevrolet Cruze, passed by. When a yawning Mort finally got out of the Ford, Kevin pointed his rifle at him.

"Kevin!" warned Tessa from the driver's seat of the Maxima. Evelyn, her sister-in-law, and Heather had taken the back seat.

He lowered his weapon and said, "Get in the car, you useless piece of shit."

"What are you mad at me for?" he asked as he got into the front passenger seat.

Looking through the scope, which he'd just affixed to his rifle, Kevin said, "Another car maybe a mile and a half out and closing fast. Move out. Make sure their phones are off."

"Be careful, Kev," said Tessa. As arranged, she proceeded southeast on 180.

Dashing to the Escape, bug in hand, he drove northwest on County Road 195 toward Fisher's Landing. At the first road, about two hundred yards from Route 12, he turned right and waited to see if the vehicle he'd spotted turned on 195. It did. Kevin floored the SUV and took the next right, a dirt road back to Highway 12. There he waited to make sure the vehicle was following. It was. He hurried to Route 12, turned left, and sped back toward Highway 81 as daylight faded.

Kevin stopped under the Highway 81 overpass. Turning off the Escape's lights, he exited, dashed up the hill, and stationed himself beside the southbound lanes waiting for a semi-trailer. Border traffic was thin these days, and he cursed as he waited, knowing the hunter would be along any minute. He saw headlights approaching from the west—probably the bad guys, he thought—but nothing but a couple of cars driving south on 81. He cursed. "What a shitty plan!" he said aloud to no one. With the headlights from the west now creeping along—likely the hit man determining the prey was motionless just ahead—a mid-sized truck came off the Thousand Islands Bridge. It would have to do. As it drove by, Kevin tossed the magnetic tracker. It landed on the side of the rig and stuck.

The headlights now came on fast. A dark sedan raced around the entrance loop onto the highway. Kevin smiled and sprinted down the hill to the Escape, did a U-turn, and took off to catch up to Tessa.

Five minutes later, his phone rang. He answered. "He's following us, Kevin!" cried Tessa.

"What? No, I just saw him go by."

"He's definitely after us. I sped up, and he's staying with us."

Flooring his car, he said, "Shit! There must be another bug on or in your aunt's car. You're still on 180?"

"Yes. We passed a place called La Fargeville a couple of minutes ago. What should we do? Oh, God, he's coming closer."

"Keep going. Try not to let him stop you, but if he does, let him get out of his car and get close, then shoot him. But remember what the black hit man did; if he has a rifle or machine gun, start shooting at him right away."

"Oh, God!"

Mort could be heard in the background, saying, "We'll never survive this without Idle. Oh, shit, we're all dead!"

"I'll get there as soon as I can," promised Kevin.

"Hurry, Kevin! He's closing in fast."

\*

Tessa had the gas pedal on the floor, but her aunt's car couldn't outrun the hit man's. He bumped up against their rear bumper, which almost threw her car out of control. The passenger side tires went onto the soft shoulder, but Tessa managed to get them back on the asphalt. Her natural reaction was to brake hard when she started losing control. Taking advantage of this, the hit man pulled up alongside. Tessa looked over and saw him pointing a gun. She screeched and stood on the brakes as a bullet shattered the window to her left and exited through the right front edge of the windshield. Everyone but Bell screamed at that. She'd been sleeping in the back seat, but awoke and said, "Put up your window, dear, it's cold."

The hit man's car had surged ahead when Tessa hit the brakes. Now in front of her, he hit the brakes. She yanked the wheel hard and barely clipped the rear bumper of the hit man's car. This made her car fishtail and caused more screaming, but again she regained control.

Once more, the hit man drove up alongside, but this time he turned his wheel right to force her off the road. She responded by turning her wheel to the left. It was a standoff for a few moments, until she saw him raise his gun again. She again braked, which pushed the sideward pressure from the other car toward the front of her car, throwing her car into a clockwise spin. Mort's scream outdid the combined screams of the four women as the car travelled two revolutions before rocking to a halt on the shoulder.

After a few seconds of gathering her wits, she put the car in reverse, but the engine had died. She tried to start it, but it wouldn't catch. "God dammit!" she yelled.

The man got out of his car, pistol in hand, and walked leisurely toward his victims. Tessa opened the center console and grasped the Smith & Wesson handgun. She checked her mirror, but saw no headlights; no rescue at hand.

When the man got close, he said, "No Navy Seal, I see. Easy pickings." He brought his gun to bear.

Tessa quickly lifted the gun and shot. The man went down! Good thing, for she dropped the gun after it went off. But then the man got up! Cursing loudly, with a hand to the lower left part of his torso, where a red spot was slowly expanding, he shuffled toward the car.

"Oh, God, he's going to kill me!" hollered Mort. There was no escape.

What happened next seemed to unfold in slow motion. The man's furious eyes were focused on her as he pointed his gun at Tessa's head. Then he turned his head and his eyes opened wide. She blinked and he was gone. Only when the vehicle had already sped past did she realize what it was. She looked forward and saw brake lights, then backup lights. The car rolled back and stopped just in front of theirs, and a man got out and walked to her.

"You alright, Tess?" asked Kevin.

She got out of the car and threw her arms around him.

"I looked for your headlights, but I didn't see them," she said.

"I turned them off as soon as I came around the bend back there and saw what was happening here. I was worried he'd hurry if he saw lights coming. When he pointed his gun at you, I turned my lights on to distract him. He didn't have time to react." She hugged him again. "That thoughtless bastard fucked up my windshield, so we'll have to borrow his car."

"Watch your mouth, young man," said Evelyn.

To Tessa's shock, he gave her aunt a respectful nod and said, "Yes, ma'am."

Mort and the ladies got out of the Maxima as Kevin moved equipment and supplies from the Explorer to the 2018 Kia Sorenta, a mid-size SUV.

Tessa embraced her aunt and said, "I'm so sorry, Aunty. I shouldn't have involved you in this."

"Well, I can't remember ever having been so frightened, but now that it's over I feel absolutely rejuvenated. I'm an eighty-six-year-old woman who thought all the excitement in the world had passed her by. I've lived more in the last half-hour than I had in the last six decades. And, anyway, of course you should have involved me. If we can't rely on our family to help, we might as well all give up."

Tessa hugged her aunt once more. As she commenced with the introductions, Kevin said, "Save that for later. We need to get off the road and find a place to stay for the night." Gesturing to the Maxima, he said, "Tess, you drive that behind us, and take whale boy with you."

She told him she hadn't been able to get it started. She got in and tried again. It caught after a few attempts. Kevin checked the Maxima for bugs with his hands. Finding one in the back left wheel well, he held it up to show the group and shook his head. "Sorry, folks," he said, "it never occurred to me there might be two." He tossed it aside.

"Might there be a third?" asked Tessa.

"Shit … uh, I mean, pooh. We better leave this car behind, too. We'll have to squish into that," he said, pointing to the Kia. "We'll have to tie Mort to the roof."

"I've had my car for almost fifteen years," protested Evelyn.

"I'm sorry, Aunty," said Tessa. "It's too dangerous to keep it. If we get our battery to work, I'll buy you ten new cars."

"Nine will do, honey. I've never been greedy."

Mort had to take the Kia's front passenger seat, or there was no hope of fitting the people and their gear on board. Heather had to sit in the cargo area amidst suitcases, military backpack, food, and equipment. Other supplies were jammed in wherever there was a spare inch. After stashing the body behind some bushes, Kevin pulled the Escape off the road and left it to whomever came upon it first. Tessa followed the Kia in the Maxima until Kevin pointed to a small grove. She pulled the car in behind the trees, then climbed into the back seat of the Sorenta.

They drove about twenty-five miles and started looking for abandoned farm houses; they came across a few, but not until the fourth did they deem one acceptable. This one had a foreclosure sign on it. It had been abandoned so recently, it had yet to be stripped of everything of value. It even had electricity, although the water had been shut off, and there were no appliances or furniture.

They brought in what they needed. Kevin checked everything the old ladies had with them to preclude another surprise. He found nothing that could lead killers to their position. Even so, he stayed outside to make sure they weren't followed, while the others got settled and prepared a meal.

Inside, Tessa said, "Aunty, I'd like to introduce you to Heather."

They shook hands. Aunt Evelyn, able to see the girl in the light, said, "So this is our million dollar baby? My, you *are* beautiful. What a shame it's being so cruelly used against you. They'll get you over my dead body."

Next, Tessa yelled, "Bell, this is Heather."

"If you like, dear, but be careful not to catch yourself a cold."

"She's deaf, but she's never admitted it," explained Tessa to Heather and Mort. "She thinks she can read lips, but she always gets it wrong. It's comical and sad at the same time."

Bell looked at Heather and said, "Bet you have all the boys after you. Flaunt it while you got it, dear. It's gone before you know it, and soon only the ugly ones will bother with you."

Tessa introduced her aunt to Mort, saying he'd built the breakthrough battery. They shook hands, with Evelyn furrowing her brow, evidently trying to picture this man as an ingenious inventor.

Tessa yelled to Bell, "This is Mort."

"I think it's a Buick. Why do you ask?" She shook her head at Tessa and said, "So who's this? I sure hope he's rich because he's not much to look at. Or rather, he's too much to look at. With your looks I think you can do a lot better, dear."

"She's become embarrassingly blunt in her old age," said Tessa.

"That hadn't escaped my notice," Mort said.

"She knows she can get away with it, and I think she enjoys it." Addressing everyone, she said, "We should get something to eat."

Evelyn and Bell had brought plastic plates and flatware, along with sliced bread, cold cuts, Miracle Whip, baby carrots, bananas, and milk. It seemed like a feast. The ladies prepared sandwiches and put them on a plate on the kitchen counter. Mort helped himself to all three sandwiches they'd prepared thus far, along with most of the carrots, and a liter of milk.

"Hey, save some for someone else," said Heather.

Evelyn said, "Since my glaring at you has failed to halt your slobbering and swilling, I'll put it in words: Listen, trencherman …"

"Trencherman?" asked Mort, looking at Tessa.

"Gluttonous pig," she said.

"Honest to God, did you grow up around pigs? Stop shoveling and come up for a breath," said Evelyn.

Tessa handed the next one directly to Heather.

Kevin came in at that point, and Tessa introduced him as she handed him the next sandwich. Bell said, "Oh, now he's more like it. He'd do nicely in the back of a fifty-five Chevy. And look at the way she's looking at him." Heather blushed and lowered her eyes. "He's a bit too old for you, dear. But he's perfect for Tessa." Tessa also lowered her eyes. Turning to Kevin, Bell asked, "So what do you do for a living?"

"Right now I'm fleeing."

"Is there much call for that? I didn't even know they made them anymore."

He showed his confusion, so Tessa explained the issue with her hearing. He nodded.

Bell went on, "Where do you live?"

He answered, "I'm currently between addresses."

"Oh, that's a dump. I'm disappointed. What did you say you do for a living?"

"Despoiling virgins."

"Hasn't all that gone to China? I'm afraid you're not good enough for our Tessa. She deserves better."

"Too bad the pandemic spared you," said Kevin.

"Have more respect, young man," scolded Evelyn. "Allow for her age."

"Yes, ma'am," said Kevin. Facing Bell, he said, "Sorry I spoke ill of you, Bell. I'm a bad person, a mere turd, swirling around, lost in the flush of time, and needless to say, yak milk costs so damn much."

Evelyn watched her grand-niece gazing and grinning at Kevin. She said in a low voice, "Don't make it too obvious, dear."

"What?" said Tessa as she took a bite of her sandwich.

"You look at him with love in your eyes."

"I do not!" she insisted.

"Careful lest ye protest too much," said her aunt with a smile.

The women finished making sandwiches, and the group stood around the kitchen eating and talking.

Naturally, Evelyn was curious about the source of the threat facing her niece.

Tessa filled her aunt in on the details she'd glossed over during their conversation over Skype.

Kevin said, "It's all these damn foreigners."

Tessa objected to that assessment. "Since the depression began, Americans have had it in for immigrants. I've had all sorts of people tell me to go back to Canada. Apparently it's my fault they're unemployed, homeless, starving, ugly; you name it."

"Everyone knows the depression is Canada's fault," said Kevin.

"The worse the economy gets, the more people hate immigrants. They already deported hundreds of thousands of illegal Mexicans two years back—"

"Leaving the upstanding Mexican mobsters behind," said Kevin.

Tessa continued, "And I heard rumors that everyone with a green card might soon be deported. I've lived in this country for fourteen years!"

"That'll never happen," said Kevin. "The government laid off anyone capable of carrying out something like that. Same reason these foreign gangs do whatever they please with impunity."

"What about you, Mr. Idle?" asked Evelyn. "What do you think of immigrants?"

"The worst thing I can say about immigration is that it brought Tessa here." That got no reaction, so he added, "Today's a bad day to ask what I think of immigrants. We're running from Chinese, Mexicans, Saudis, and two or three of those assho … assassins after Tessa and Mort had thick accents of some kind. Take foreigners out of the equation, and I'm as safe as a baby at its mother's tit."

"Your family must have immigrated here at some point, too," said Evelyn.

"Sure, but we've been here for hundreds of years. I was told that my great-great-and-a-bunch-more-greats-grandfather was involved in the siege of Boston at the outset of the Revolutionary War. He apparently distinguished himself as a drunken swine, then died of dysentery before exchanging even one bullet with the enemy."

"Amazing how faulty genes can survive through so many generations," said Tessa. Her aunt laughed.

Bell laughed, too, saying, "If I found a bone in the Jello, I'd certainly wonder about the chef. I can assure you I wouldn't leave a tip."

That got everyone laughing.

Evelyn whispered to Tessa, "You have to get away from him as soon as you have your battery. It's too dangerous; *he's* too dangerous."

Tessa lowered her head and murmured, "I know."

People shifted to find suitable sleeping quarters. Off to claim her own space, Tessa encountered Kevin in the front hall. She said, "You're not sleeping with her again, are you?"

"I'll be in the truck on the lookout for bad guys overnight."

"Good."

"With Heather."

"God, Kevin, she's sixteen. *Sixteen.*"

"She's a lot safer because of what I did."

"That's how you justify taking advantage of a vulnerable girl? You're a pig."

"Actually, I'm closer to a roué. So shut up and let me be what I am."

"You're supposed to be protecting her."

"I am."

"By boning her all night?"

"By systematically bumping off her kidnappers and removing the incentive to send more kidnappers. Who knew mixing murder and sex could be so noble?"

"Oh! I hope you drown in your own turpitude."

"Is that like turpentine with attitude?"

"Not even close to funny."

"You *are* jealous, aren't you?"

"Over you? Don't make me laugh."

"Then what's it to you if I bone her?"

"She's a child!"

"Weren't you sixteen when Whittingham 'slowly slid inside' you?" he asked, using finger quotes to repeat what she'd told him in eleventh grade.

She blushed and said, "He wasn't a twenty-five-year-old man."

"So, is it my age or hers that you're worried about?"

"Both. Your respective ages are what makes it *statutory rape.*"

"Leaving aside the irony of the heinous crimes we've seen perpetrated over the last few days without any hint of law enforcement, contrasted with the thought of the police rushing in to arrest me because I had sex, I'll point out that the particular law we're talking about is so arbitrary and unnatural, it invites defiance. She's what, ninety-nine-point-nine percent of the way to seventeen? I screw her Tuesday, I'm okay. Monday, I'm in jail for years. A couple of hundred miles south at the Pennsylvania border, she's legal at sixteen. So, if I screw her one inch south of the border, I'm okay; move one inch north of the border—jail for years. How insane is that?"

"Didn't I read that Pennsylvania is raising its age of consent to seventeen as of July 1?" asked Tessa, arms folded.

"Hadn't heard that, but that would mean I screw her Monday, I'm okay. Tuesday, I'm in jail for years. If I pull out of her at one second to midnight June 30th, I'm fine. One second later, jail for years. Some states have the age of consent at eighteen. So a seventeen-year-old girl there can join the army, go to war, crush the enemy's head and scoop out his brains, but she can't do the most natural act that humans do.

"A boy can screw at any age, but a girl has to wait until seventeen, even if she's given her permission. Who is the goddamn government to dictate that? Just puritanical, patriarchal, hypocritical, sexist men worried about protecting their daughters. Nature perfected her by age sixteen, and she *is* perfect. Every straight man in the world would screw her if given the chance. She's giving me that chance, and I accept."

"Do you know what my aunt and Bell would say if they found out?"

"Your aunt would give me shit. Bell would tell me that salmon aren't running at this time of year."

"How can you live with yourself?"

"In my imagination I'm perfect; it's only reality that's letting me down."

"I'm so disappointed in you."

"What else is new, Red Bush?" Kevin turned to leave and took a couple of steps before turning back to her and saying, "I saw your aunt whispering to you and how you looked at me. I never expected you to stay with me, and I wouldn't want you to; it's too dangerous. So, you see, you can't possibly disappoint me, because I expect nothing of you. Even if I wasn't in this horrible situation, you'd leave me behind anyway. I know you, Tess. You use people. Once I'm no longer of use, I'm history."

"No, Kevin; that's just wrong."

"Don't bother, Sharp. You mean nothing to me either."

She turned and rushed to her room.

\*

Kevin and Heather went outside, shared a joint, got into the Kia, out of their clothes, and under a blanket.

# CHAPTER 10

Early the following morning, the ladies and Kevin stood in the kitchen eating Rice Krispies with lukewarm milk and bananas.

"Want sugar in your cereal?" Tessa yelled to Bell as she handed her a bowl.

"Thank you, dear," said Bell, accepting the cereal. "But let's not talk about diarrhea at breakfast."

Kevin said, "That's crazy talk, Bell. You can't stir your coffee with a submarine." Speaking to Tessa and her aunt, he said, "I didn't think I'd ever say that."

Mort had yet to emerge from the room he'd taken. Kevin was chuckling at Mort's missing out on breakfast when they heard a rumbling down the hall.

"What's that racket?" asked Evelyn.

"That's Mort," said Kevin. "I'd recognize the clip-clop of those cloven hooves anywhere."

He appeared and said in an angry tone, "You're having breakfast, and you didn't call me?"

Kevin laughed and said, "I've never seen a less smiley face."

Mort dug in and would have dispatched the whole consignment were it not for an old lady beating him back with a cane.

Tessa checked the computer. The webpage was flashing *Quechee Gorge. Heading west.*

"These guys are competing with each other, so they're withholding information," concluded Kevin. "Otherwise, one of the two tracking your aunt would have reported that she crossed the border."

He had a decision to make concerning the Kia. Checking the glove box, they'd determined that it was a rental from Ontario. If he removed the GPS tracking device, the rental company would likely contact the police soon thereafter. Not that he expected the police to hop to it, but if a police cruiser happened upon them, it could be trouble. On the other hand, leaving it in could give the police or the killers a link to them, presuming the bodies were found and someone determined they had rented the vehicle. After discussing the matter with Tessa, he decided to leave it in for now, but remove it before they got close to their destination, where Heather was to hide out indefinitely with the old ladies.

They packed up, piled in, and left the farm, bound for Pulteney on Keuka Lake. "Not a bad car," said Kevin. "Can't get these things anymore." No foreign-owned automobile companies could sell cars in the U.S. since 2018, when a trade embargo went into effect. The only way around the embargo was not only to assemble it in the U.S., but to build all components in the U.S. as well. Few products qualified. Other countries followed suit, and it made the depression much worse everywhere. Smoot-Hawley revisited.

Kevin decided it was probably safe to use the highway, so they proceeded to 81 and drove south to Route 20, where Kevin turned east. When Bell said her cottage was the other way, Evelyn got across to her that they were trying to confuse anyone following them.

At Cazenovia, Kevin stopped and disabled the GPS tracking device. Tessa checked the computer. The webpage was now flashing *La Fargeville, NY*. The computer's battery went dead.

Kevin turned back, and they went west on 20.

They made the two hour and fifteen minute trip to Pulteney, NY. No one complained that the trip was without the excitement they'd come to expect, though Mort was displeased at being too confined.

Driving into Stone Point, Kevin followed Bell's directions and pulled up to a modest cabin. The two-story structure had white plastic siding and a grey roof. It was situated on a quarter-acre lakefront lot. The property looked well-kept. "The cottage is just a little younger than me," said Bell, "though it's not showing its age as much. Bill and I bought it in 1972 for about a hundred thousand. Can you believe it reached pretty near half a million in assessed value before the crash? I doubt it's worth what we paid for it anymore. Oh, well, I'll be dead soon and it'll be my son's problem."

The six got out of the SUV and began to unpack. As Bell unlocked the front door, a man—sixtyish, over six feet, broad-shouldered, bald, and mean-looking—toting a shotgun marched up to them. He eyed Kevin, perhaps thinking him a potential troublemaker. Recognizing Bell and Evelyn, he greeted them. Evelyn said, "Hi, Tom, nice to see you. You remember Tessa, my niece. This is her younger sister Heather, her brother Kevin, and Kevin's friend Mort."

They shook hands. Tom told them he'd had to chase a few punks away from the property over the winter. In other words, the hundred fifty newbucks per month that Bell was paying him was well-spent. As Tom went on his way, the others brought suitcases, the backpack, food, blankets, weapons, and other supplies into the house.

Bell and Evelyn had their own bedrooms; the other was assigned to Heather. Tessa would room with Heather, Kevin and Mort would sleep in the family room; they planned to stay only one night.

The four took overdue showers and changed. Tessa did a load of laundry, including Mort's only clothes, which were rancid by the time she dropped them into the washer holding her breath. Mort had to wear a beach towel until they were cleaned and dried. He was a sight and a half.

While the ladies unpacked and prepared lunch, Kevin mowed the lawn, and Mort slept on the couch.

After lunch, Tessa cleaned up while Heather and Kevin went into town to line up for gas and food. They needed to buy a lot of food because the ladies wouldn't have access to a car for the foreseeable future.

They were back well before Tessa expected them. "The lineups were short," said Heather as she and Kevin put the first load of groceries on the kitchen counter. "Only fifteen minutes at Price Chopper and maybe ten at Gulf."

"Oh, then why did it take you two hours to get back?" asked Tessa. Heather's blush served as all the explanation Tessa needed. Heather went out to the SUV for more groceries, leaving Tessa glaring at Kevin.

He told her to mind her own business. Looking around for something to hit him with, she settled on an ugly portrait hanging on the hall wall. She walked over to it and said, "How would you like to be up to your neck in picture frame?" as she took it off the wall.

"You wouldn't dare."

She walked over to him and deposited it over his head. He didn't try to stop her because he never thought she'd do it. It didn't hurt, but it was a surprise.

Tessa said, "Hm. The portrait has taken on a three-dimensional look, and it really brings out its ugliness."

Bell walked by and said, "Why did you ruin that painting? Wait, you were framed!" She guffawed at her wit as she continued on her way.

Lifting off the portrait, he said, "Feel better?"

Tessa smiled and followed Bell.

They finished bringing in the groceries, then relaxed for the rest of the day.

In bed that evening, Heather asked Tessa to leave her room for a little while. "It's our last night together."

"If my aunt or Bell catch you, you'll have a miserable stay here. They're old-fashioned."

"Is that really the problem? Isn't it really that you're in love with him?"

"No!"

"Then why do you care so much that he's sleeping with me?"

"Because you're too young."

"I'm young, Tessa, but I'm not stupid. Good night!"

Tessa woke up at 2:37 AM. Heather wasn't there. She had a good mind to get up and drag that little tart back to bed, but rejected the idea. When Heather snuck in just before dawn, Tessa was still awake, but didn't let on.

\*

The next morning, Tessa got up early and bumped into Kevin leaving the bathroom. She gave him the now-familiar glare. Playing along, he looked in the mirror at himself and said, "Hey I recognize that pervert. Watch out for him; he's big trouble."

Bell emerged from her room and saw the two at the bathroom mirror. "Spend the night together?" she asked Tessa with a wink. Tessa shook her head. "I would if I were your age. I was a looker, too, when I was young. You believe me, young man?"

He nodded and said, "You must've been something else when the Magna Carta was enshrined, you ancient ruin you."

"Aren't you sweet?" she said as she walked down the stairs.

After breakfast, Kevin took Tessa aside and said their next step was to get Mort somewhere to build his battery. He asked what that involved and where they had to go.

Tessa said, "He can't just build a battery. He'd need all sorts of highly specialized prototype cell testing and formation equipment, a multi-channel electrochemical test station and impedance analyzer—"

"Stop. He needs big machines."

"And expensive facilities, like a wet chemistry lab to characterize raw materials, a process R&D lab with clean room to produce the electrodes, a cell production facility with a dry room, a cell testing lab—"

"This is all Greek. Where can we get access to all that?"

"Cornell, if they haven't sold or mothballed the equipment, but it's not as simple as getting access to a cell fabrication facility. You need to understand that it's a complicated and dynamic process. These labs are simultaneously testing lots of different possibilities for electrolytes, anodes, and especially cathodes. It begins at the molecular stage—finding a candidate molecule, then producing and testing it, and scaling it up. Molecules that pass certain standards move along to the next stage. The great majority don't make it out of the lab.

"An ideal battery not only has to produce a lot of power at a low cost, it has to last a long time both on each charge and over the years, it should have short recharge times, it can't explode or leak toxic fumes … Yeah, I know, you get that it's complicated. The point is, my father already went through all this for the prototype Mort produced. It was the culmination of years of work. It's unrealistic to think we can do all this work over again. It takes too long and costs too much."

"So Mort has to remember what he did for the prototype."

"Yeah, but remembering what he did for this particular cell when he was at different stages on probably dozens of different cells, isn't so easy. It was just a code number to him. Not until this one passed all the tests did Mort realize he had a winner."

"Does he remember the code number?"

"Not at the moment. And even if he did, we'd need my father's master list that linked the code to the formulation."

"I understand; it's hopeless."

"Maybe not. I did this for over three years, and I learned from the best in the business. My father was systematic. He literally went in the order spit out by my software. If Mort can remember certain, uh, parameters, I can maybe use my software to zero in on the winning formulation."

"Didn't the bad guys delete the software?"

"Not at Cornell. It's probably still on the supercomputer there."

"Lots of ifs and maybes." She shrugged. "Okay, at least we finally have a destination."

*

Midmorning, the gang liberated Bell's motorboat, a 2011 Larson LX 850, from the garage, and put it in the lake.

Kevin decided to take it out for a spin and invited Heather for a "legal cruise," for today she was seventeen. Tessa and Mort invited themselves along on that sunny, warm May morning.

The ladies went into the cottage to change into their bathing suits. Five minutes later, they emerged.

Tessa was a fine-looking woman, even beautiful when she took the trouble to look her best, but that was rare; she got too much attention from men looking for action as it was. She was wearing a turquoise one-piece bathing suit that Kevin might have described as frumpy had he been able to tear his eyes away from Heather. The breathtaking creature stood smiling at Kevin in her skimpy red bikini. Mort stood staring at the young maiden, his mouth agape.

Heather trotted to Kevin, took his hand, and led him to the boat. Kevin in the driver's seat, Tessa seated to his left, Mort covering the rear bench seat, and Heather sitting at the bow looking back at Kevin, the sleek boat zipped out into the lake.

After zooming up and down the lake for thirty-five minutes at speeds up to fifty-miles-per-hour, all four taking a turn at the helm, they found a deserted place on the lake and docked at a ramshackle pier. Kevin had brought his rifle and the Smith & Wesson along to teach Tessa and Mort how to shoot, just in case the need arose. Mort declined, but Tessa was all for it.

Kevin gave her the basics. Tessa knelt on her left knee leaning into a fallen log with her right elbow resting against her right knee, aiming the rifle as Kevin had taught. He said, "I've zeroed it and set the scope power for you already. Remember, there'll be a little kickback. You have to be ready for it or it can hurt you. Treat it with respect, or it'll mess you up. It's a lot like you, in that way."

"Funny," she said, aiming at a tree two hundred meters away.

"Control your breathing, focus on the target, and slowly squeeze the trigger."

She shot and saw splinters shoot out from the left side of the tree. "I got it!" she said with glee.

He taught her how to shoot the handgun, and they went through a couple of potential emergency situations where she had only a second to react. Walking along the shore, he'd say, "That tree has a gun!" At first she'd try to aim, and he'd say, "Never mind, you're dead." Next time she'd shoot quickly and miss. After a while, she got better; good enough to defend herself in an emergency, judged Kevin.

They got back into the boat and rocketed up the northwestern branch of the lake. They moored about a hundred feet from the eastern shore at what used to be Keuka Lake State Park. Tessa turned on the stereo system and broke out a small birthday cake and Keuka Spring Chardonnay. While the four ate and drank, Kevin pulled a joint out of his pocket and lit it.

Tessa frowned and said, "Why do you need that if you already have wine?"

"I don't need it; I want it. Want some?"

"You know I don't do drugs," said Tessa.

"You're doing a liquid drug. In my book, that's worse than grass."

"Then you're illiterate."

"Lighten up," suggested Heather as she took a drag. Mort was finishing off the cake.

"Tessa Sharp," said Kevin. "It's 2020. We've been through a horrible depression for the last few years. We're unemployed and broke. We're *marked for death*. Just once, let go."

She took the joint, sucked in some smoke, and coughed. The others laughed.

"Try again and hold it in your lungs if you can," said Kevin.

She did and coughed again. She tried once more and managed to hold the smoke inside for a few seconds before coughing again. "I don't feel anything," she said as she passed it on to Heather.

Heather took a final toke and handed it to Kevin. Sauntering to the back of the boat, she circumambulated Mort and lay down on the sun deck just behind him. "Kev, maybe you should sunscreen me," she said.

Kevin handed the end of the joint to Tessa, joined Heather, and slowly worked the sunscreen into her skin. Kevin took his shirt off, and Heather rubbed sunscreen on his back and chest.

Tessa gazed with undisguised desire at his pecks and abs; she inhaled once more and tossed the joint overboard. By now, the combination of alcohol and cannabis was working on her brain. She didn't like the feeling; she hated to lose control of herself. And what was controlling her now was jealousy; full-on jealousy.

Heather stood on the swim platform at the backmost end of the boat. She smiled at Kevin, turned, and dived into the water. "Oh, it's freezing!" she said. She swam toward the shore. About halfway there, she stopped and said to Kevin. "Come in."

"It's too cold," he said.

"Come on, Mr. Navy Seal Pussy. I'll warm you up behind the trees." She resumed her swim to the shore as Kevin prepared to dive.

"Kevin … Please don't. Don't go to her," said Tessa.

"We've had this conversation a few times already. She's a child, and I'm a pig. We've established it."

"Dammit, Kevin, I don't want … I just don't want you with her."

"What's with you?" He dived in and followed Heather to shore.

Tessa watched the two go into the bushes together. All at once, she jumped into the water. Gasping at the temperature upon surfacing, she swam to shore.

Tessa lay on her stomach and pulled aside the branches. Kevin was lying on his back and Heather was sitting on him.

His bathing suit was pulled down to his lower legs; she had pulled aside her bikini bottom and was slowly lowering herself on him. *He's not even wearing a rubber!* Tessa said to herself.

Tessa was prepared to be appalled, but in her intoxicated state, other emotions predominated: envy and arousal. With all her being, she wanted to charge out, knock that little blonde bitch off him, and take her place.

Heather pulled her bikini top down, and Kevin lifted his head to nibble and suck on her nipples.

She put her hands on his shoulders, dug in her fingers, and grinded back and forth on him. She appeared desperate for him as she pressed her heels into the ground for support and thrust her hips back and forth almost frantically. She moved her hands down to his chest as her thrusting accelerated and her moaning started. Her breathing got deeper and faster. As she climaxed, she collapsed on him and buried her tongue in his mouth.

A minute later, with Tessa still looking on, Heather sat up again, brought her feet forward, and propped them flat on the ground beside his hips. She put her hands behind her just above his knees and began pumping up and down on him. She was so aggressive that Tessa was sure anyone within a mile could hear their bodies slapping together. This brought Kevin to climax. She lay down flat on him and kissed again.

"Getting a good show over there?" asked Kevin.

Tessa immediately let the branches go and ducked down; she could still see parts of them through the vegetation.

"Come and join us, Tess," invited Kevin.

"No, Kevin," said Heather.

"Or join us and come." He laughed. "I want to be frank with you, Tess, honey. Actually, no, I want to be Kevin with you." He guffawed; the marijuana was busy making nonsense funny. "Come on, beautiful Tessa. Why else would God have given me a dick and a tongue if not for two-perfect-girl situations like this?" Another laugh. "Get over here, my luscious Tessa. I've already tasted vanilla; can't wait to taste strawberry. I'll stay away from the chocolate." Here he laughed so hard he shook Heather off him.

"Kevin!" said Heather. She climbed back onto him and cast toward Tessa a *get lost!* scowl.

Thoroughly embarrassed, Tessa ran back to the water and swam to the boat, where Mort was napping.

The two lovers joined them presently and they were off to the cabin. No one spoke during the ten-minute ride.

After lunch, Tessa and Kevin packed the Kia. Besides their meager belongings, they took food and beer, and a sleeping bag Bell offered. Tessa still wasn't speaking to him.

In mid-afternoon, people said their goodbyes. Heather hugged Kevin while crying. Tessa embraced and kissed both elderly ladies; she gave Heather a cold smile and got one in return. Mort shook hands. Kevin thanked Evelyn with a hug, saying Tessa was lucky to have such a fine aunt. Kissing Bell's hand, he said, "I love the way those leathery bags dangling underneath your bloodshot eyes flap in the breeze."

"What a gentleman," said Bell, with a warm smile.

Heather laughed, but the other two women rolled their eyes. Tessa, Kevin, and Mort headed out for Cornell University in Ithaca.

Deciding to put her jealousy behind her, Tessa spoke up about fifteen minutes into the journey. "We might run into your father at Cornell. Have you had any contact with him recently?"

"Oh, she speaks. I called to tell him mom had been killed. After letting me know I failed to protect her, he suggested I bring her body out to his hobby farm to bury her, so I did. First time we'd met in almost seven years. We said practically nothing to each other of a personal nature, but he went on and on about the economy, the government, and how all the greedy morons got us into this mess. He got so worked up about it, he practically ended up crying."

He parodied his father. "One generation; that's all it took. That's all it took to ruin the greatest nation on earth. And we did it to ourselves with our refusal to pay for everything we wanted, driving ourselves into a debt spiral that we never even tried to get out of until it was too late. Giving up manufacturing for a bunch of useless Mcjobs and make-work government jobs that paid a hundred grand or more a year and produced nothing but regulations that held everyone else back. One awful generation. The moral decay, hubris, irresponsibility, laziness, and willful blindness that enabled it are still everywhere."

Tittering, Tessa said, "You sound just like him. Did your brother and sister come for the burial?"

"No. Carmen's down in New Zealand; Jeff's in Denver. Wasn't worth their time or money to come, I guess."

"So in the end, only the black sheep of the family was there for her."

"Not when she most needed me."

"You can't blame yourself for that. You can't protect anyone twenty-four hours a day. It was mean of your father to blame you. What did you say to him?"

He chuckled and said, "I repeated what the cops told me about parricide being the third leading class of murders nowadays and told him I understood why. He didn't laugh."

"Well, I'll tell him when I see him it was really unfair—"

Tessa stopped talking because Kevin had slammed on the brakes and turned the wheel so abruptly that it took her breath away. The Kia spun around about five-hundred-twenty degrees, almost a circle and a half. With Mort screeching in the back seat, Tessa gaped at Kevin and saw blood dripping down the side of his forehead. Before she could calm down enough to figure out what was happening, Kevin yelled, "Get down!" and floored the gas pedal. They were at the junction of 54A and County Road 76 on the outskirts of Hammondsport. Kevin went up the hill on 76.

As they gained speed, she heard pings off the rear of the SUV. Just as she was about to speak, he veered left at another Y junction. About twenty seconds later, he hit the brakes and turned west on a gravel road.

All this was such a shock that she only then noticed the noise level in the vehicle had increased dramatically. She sat up, looked back, and saw that the back window was gone, as was the left side window beside the cargo compartment; small pieces of glass covered the cargo area. Turning her head forward, she noticed something in the windshield: a hole—a bullet hole.

"Are you alright?"

"The bullet took out a chunk of my scalp, but I'll live."

"How did they find us?" she asked.

"How the fuck should I know?" He looked in the mirror.

She, too, looked back and saw a car just turning onto the road where they had entered. She gasped and said, "Does this mean they found my aunt, Heather, and Bell?"

"I don't know. Let me think for a minute." He slowed a bit and followed the road as it curved north. Mort screamed at this sudden maneuver, too.

"Maybe if we could figure out which group found us—"

"Simple, Ms. CSI. Just check the bullet hole, and that'll tell us everything we need to know."

He slowed slightly at a stop sign and took a left. The truck fishtailed on the gravel, but he regained control and again floored it. That road ended fifteen seconds later. Again he went left. Twenty seconds on, he abruptly turned right and proceeded up Glenbrook Road. This road went up an incline that enabled both predator and prey to spot each other. "Shit!" yelped Kevin, looking in the mirror. The pursuers were maybe half a minute behind. They crested a hill. Kevin quickly pulled over, dashed to the back, and got out his sniper rifle.

Tessa watched as he went down on his left knee and took aim. Unlike the sniper who'd shot at him, he wouldn't miss, Tessa knew. The black truck came over the ridge about two hundred meters in the distance. It slowed as the driver spotted their SUV. She heard a pop. The truck veered off the road into the trees. She heard a loud crash.

Kevin got back into the Kia. They sped along until they came to another intersection. Kevin glanced in the mirror and stopped. He turned south, drove for about a minute, then turned west on a dirt road. While they were driving, Tessa took out the disposable phone to call her aunt. As she dialed, Kevin said, "Stop!"

"Why? I have to make sure they're okay."

"Turn it off. Now!"

She followed his command.

He said, "I've been trying to work this out, and my guess is they only had a general idea of where we were; otherwise, they would have killed the works of us last night. If they knew, somehow, that we were somewhere around Keuka Lake—"

"Then they'd post people on the main roads around the lake," concluded Tessa.

"Especially at key junctions like the one we were at when they shot. The idiot shot too early; allowed us to get too far ahead of him in case he missed."

Kevin pulled over. "That phone wasn't on, was it?" Tessa answered in the negative.

He looked at Mort, who said, "What?"

"Tess, does that phone have last number dialed?" asked Kevin as he looked closely at Mort.

"No, it's really basic. It does have redial … Oh."

"What?" asked Kevin.

"I kind of pushed a couple of numbers before you told me to stop." His glare shifted to her. "I'm sorry."

Glower relocated to Mort, Kevin said, "Who did you call, ass driller?"

"Me? No one!"

Tessa said, "But I've had the phone the whole … Except when you and Heather—"

"And you swam ashore to play peeping Tess on us."

Kevin took the Colt 1911 out of the glove box, got out of the Kia, opened the back door, put the gun to Mort's head, and hollered, "Lie to me and I swear to God I'll blow what little brains you have over the back of this truck. *Do you understand?*"

"Yes! Yes!"

"Who did you call? I saw it in your eyes when I asked Tessa if the phone had last number dialed."

"My, my mother. I swear! Just to tell her I'm okay. She worries, you know?"

"How long were you on the phone?"

"I don't know; maybe a couple of minutes."

"Did you tell her where you were?"

"I, I, uh, sort of said I was sitting on Keuka Lake. I didn't tell her anything about any of this."

"And it never crossed your mind that the killers would be monitoring any calls to your mother?" Mort shook his head and lowered his eyes.

By Kevin's face, Tessa could tell he was ruminating about shooting Mort. She said, "Kevin, shooting him would definitely be murder, and we still need him." He gritted his teeth and pulled back the gun.

Kevin drove another couple of hundred yards and, spotting a shady glen next to a stream, pulled in behind some shrubs, and parked. He said, "I'm tired, and I have a headache."

"Because you haven't gotten much sleep with your activities during the last three nights," said Tessa.

Kevin didn't react to that.

"I'm hungry," said Mort.

He reacted to that. "That fat twit gets nothing! Get out of this truck, Wood."

Mort didn't argue, but did request that Kevin not leave him behind.

Checking Kevin's wound, Tessa pronounced it a scratch and cleaned it with supplies from the emergency kit. He opened his window and asked Tessa to open hers; a nice, fresh breeze refreshed them. He reclined his seat and closed his eyes. Tessa didn't feel tired, but she reclined her seat and eventually closed her eyes as well.

# CHAPTER 11

Tessa, sound asleep, heard something that brought her closer to consciousness. *What was that?* Settling back to sleep, she heard it again; an exhaled snort, the kind that comes from the back of one's nose when one is trying to suppress a laugh. She opened her eyes. Kevin was looking outside. He snorted once more, then burst out laughing. "What's so funny?" asked Tessa, sitting up.

"That," answered Kevin, pointing at a black bear sniffing Mort, who was sound asleep sitting against a tree.

"Oh, my God!"

"The bear must be thinking, 'I've hit the jackpot; this thing could tide me over for a year!'" The bear continued to sniff Mort, but seemed to turn its nose up. "'But it smells like shit!'" Kevin was by now laughing hard.

"Do something."

"Let's just let nature take its course."

"We still need him, Kevin."

"Don't sell Mort short. I wouldn't put it past him to kill it, fry it, and eat it." He continued to laugh. "Shit, I wish I had a camera."

"Remember I told you how callous you are? This is a perfect example. He's a human being in desperate danger."

"Spoil sport," he said as he leaned on the horn.

The bear looked lazily at the car, but Mort leaned forward, startled. He looked at the bear, but didn't seem to believe what he was seeing at first. He put his hand out to touch it.

This reduced Kevin to tears.

Then Mort shrieked so loudly, his voice broke; he sounded like a panicked little girl. At this, Kevin guffawed so hard he involuntarily lurched forward and knocked his forehead on the steering wheel. That got Tessa laughing. Mort rolled over to get up; the bear pawed him, knocking him back down.

Still hooting, Kevin said, "He suspected trouble when he felt its claws on his ass."

That made Tessa laugh harder. Part of her was horrified, but Kevin's laughter was so infectious, and the predicament was certainly humorous as long as Mort was still in one piece, so she couldn't help herself.

Mort screamed something to his two companions.

"What did he say?" asked Tessa.

"I couldn't quite make it out, but I think it might've been, 'Could you spare a moment? A bear is eating me.'" Now Tessa's tears commenced.

Mort got to his feet and ran toward the car. The bear, seeming more amused than hungry, followed at a leisurely pace, eliciting another girly scream from Mort.

"I never knew how enjoyable a good chase from a bear was; it's most invigorating," said Kevin, finally calming down.

Mort got to the car. Tessa saw Kevin's hand on the electric lock button.

"Don't," she said, though her laughter lightened the gravity of her command.

Mort opened the door, climbed in, and closed the door. The bear walked around the SUV. It stuck its head in the vacant back window and sniffed around. Then it walked along the passenger side.

"I've never seen you move so fast, Mort," said Kevin, whose laughing spell was spent; not Tessa's, however.

"What the hell are you laughing at?" hollered an enraged Mort at Tessa. "I was almost killed."

"She's so damn callous. She really does get off on suffering," said Kevin.

"Oh, you asshole!" said Tessa.

"What's that smell?" asked Kevin. They turned and looked at Mort. They saw the front of his pants was wet, but the smell indicated something else. "You piss *and* shit yourself!" said Kevin, which reignited his laughter and revitalized Tessa's.

"This is *not* funny!" bellowed Mort.

"No it's not, but it certainly is stinky. You smell like you've been dead for a week. Get the hell out of the truck."

"Are you out of your mind? The bear wants to eat me."

"If it wanted to eat you, you'd be partly digested by now … but you wouldn't smell any worse. Get the hell out."

"No!"

"You better get rid of it," Tessa said.

"I'm trying to."

"No," she said, snickering, "the bear."

"Ah, shit." Kevin got out of the car and shot into the air. The bear trotted toward him. "Shit!" said Kevin. He shot again. The bear got closer. "Shit!" cried Kevin, scrambling onto the hood. He looked through the windshield at Tessa, who looked scared, but was nevertheless laughing. "Not funny," he yelled at her. The next shot went into the bear's left front paw. It yelped and ran off.

Then Tessa let out a loud peal of laughter. Lowering her window, she asked, "Feel invigorated?"

Kevin hopped down and opened the back door, telling Mort to "Get out." He looked around and exited the car.

Tessa said to Kevin as her laughter subsided, "I wouldn't have suggested you go out there if I'd known. I thought you knew what you were doing."

"So much for your thought. You could have gotten me killed, you idiot."

And again, she chortled.

They made Mort clean himself in the stream before they would readmit him to the Kia. As Mort was doing this, Tessa and Kevin sat on the hood and discussed their next move. They decided that going to Cornell was still the best plan. Tessa called out to Mort to ask if he mentioned this to his mother. He was adamant he'd said nothing about Cornell.

Tessa then said, "Do you smell gas?"

Kevin sniffed, his face showed confusion, then his eyes bulged. He ran to the back of the Kia and got down on his knees. "Shit!" he cried. "One of the bullets hit the gas tank." Sprinting to the dirt road, he saw a trail of gasoline dotting the road. He turned and yelled to Mort, "Get in the truck now!

We'll have company any time." Addressing Tessa, he said, "You drive."

She knew what that meant.

Mort was standing there bottomless—a sight both Tessa and Kevin would long try to forget—wringing out his pants; he had yet to deal with his boxers. As he bent over to pick up his boxers, Tessa started the SUV and rolled out. That got Mort moving and he traipsed to the vehicle as fast as he could.

"Won't we continue to leave a trail?" asked Tessa.

"As long as the level in the gas tank is above the hole, yes, and of course, the hole is practically at the bottom of the tank." They both looked at the gas gauge. Their previously full tank was now well under a quarter.

"We have to get to the hardtop," said Tessa. Kevin nodded. They looked in their side mirrors and saw a dust cloud come around the bend. "Kevin—"

"I see it."

The road ended at County Road 13. They went south. The first available turn went west, but Tessa, mindful of the fuel situation, wanted to head toward their destination. She took the next road east, but that few hundred feet enabled the car behind to see their vehicle.

Then another surprise from behind: red flashing lights.

"Shit!" said Tessa as she almost went off the road taking a right onto a short dirt road that returned them to 13. She went south again as the police car turned onto the dirt road behind them.

Tessa accelerated to ninety. The police car was closing ground.

"Faster!" said Kevin. With the back windows out, he had to yell.

"It's too dangerous to go faster on this road!" said Tessa.

Kevin climbed over the seat and made his way past a cringing Mort to the cargo area. Tessa saw him preparing his rifle.

"Kevin, if you shoot a cop—"

"I'll shoot at the engine area to try and stop the car," he said from the back. He raised his rifle and aimed it.

All at once the police car braked hard and rolled over, ending up back on its wheels just off the road in a field.

Tessa said, "What did you do?" as she pulled over.

"Nothing. I think she saw the gun and panicked. Why are you stopping?"

"She might be hurt," said Tessa.

"Well, Doctor Sharp, what the hell are you going to do about it? Other cops are on the way for sure."

She took her foot off the brake, but stopped again and said, "The car's on fire!"

"Help will be here anytime. Move it!"

She sprang out and ran to the police car. She tried to open the driver's door, but couldn't. "Help me, Kevin! She'll burn to death!"

Shaking his head, Kevin tried the passenger door, but it was locked. He came around to the driver's side and couldn't open the dented door. The officer, a fortyish woman, was unconscious. "Turn away," he said. He smashed the glass with the butt of his rifle. Flames had by this time engulfed the back of the car. "It's going to explode any second."

Tessa looked at him with gloomy eyes.

"Ah, shit. You won't shake that altruistic bug you've caught until it kills us." Coughing in the smoke, he reached in and tried to undo the officer's seatbelt. "Shit! It's stuck." He pushed himself farther into the car.

Tessa held his legs so he wouldn't get stuck in the car. Over the officer's phone, which was on the back seat, they heard, "Are you still on them? What happened? Hello?"

Kevin finally got the belt unbuckled. He and Tessa pulled the officer out and dragged her away from the car. Kevin's clothes were smoking, and he was still coughing as they lowered the woman to the ground. Tessa checked on her and said, "She's alive," just as the car exploded. Kevin covered Tessa, but nothing came their way.

"We need to leave right now. Uh! No argument. There's nothing more we can do for her. She's working with the hit men anyway. Cops use radios to communicate with each other, not phones."

They made their way east toward Ithaca, keeping to paved country roads as much as possible. Approaching Birdseye Hollow State Forest, they were running on empty, and Tessa pulled into an abandoned farm.

"Why are we stopping?" asked Mort.

"We don't want to run out of gas on the road," answered Kevin. "We'll stay here for the night and try to figure out what to do next."

They brought their food and supplies into the dilapidated farmhouse. After finishing off their sandwiches for dinner, Mort fell asleep, and Tessa and Kevin walked down the road into the forest. They discussed their predicament and could come up with no satisfactory solution. They dared not call

Kevin's father for the same reason Mort shouldn't have called his mother. Using their telephone for any reason was out since it was now compromised. That left driving as far as the gas would take them toward Ithaca, then walking the rest of the way. They thought they were maybe forty miles from Cornell.

They returned to the farmhouse.

Kevin thought Tessa might be open to replacing Heather tonight. He hinted such; she told him to go to hell. They slept apart.

\*

The next morning she told him he had some nerve thinking he could just take up with her where he left off with Heather.

"I wouldn't have considered sleeping with you for my own benefit. It was only to make up with you," he claimed.

She laughed. "It was to make *out* with me. You've wanted me since puberty."

"Once upon a time I did, but I have better taste now."

"Oh? So if I were to, say, take off my shirt, you wouldn't bat an eye?"

"If you did I'd probably puke."

"Well, let's test that, shall we?" She lifted her shirt over her head and looked at him with a coy smile.

He shrugged.

"And if I were to, maybe, take off my bra, you'd simply yawn?"

"I'd probably skip the yawn and fall fast asleep."

She undid her bra, pulled the ends around, and slowly pulled the bra away from her breasts. Apart from wider eyes, there was no reaction. "Not asleep, I see." He forced a yawn, but was obviously having a hard time averting his eyes from her breasts. "What are you looking at?" she asked.

"A couple of pimples," he answered.

"Pimples? You always drool when you see pimples?"

"My mouth is a desert." With great effort he turned away and forced another yawn.

"Still bored, eh? You wouldn't care if I took my pants off, would you?"

"Just like being in the boys' locker room. Wouldn't even notice."

She undid the button and unzipped the zipper. For the life of him, he couldn't help but turn back to stare. She smiled and let her pants fall to the floor. Then she said, "You told me once I had the perfect bum." She turned around and looked back at him over her left shoulder. "Still perfect?"

"Uh, no ... Looks like a deflated basketball."

Her coy smile turned distinctly naughty as she slowly lowered her panties. His jaw dropped in unison. She glanced down to see a noticeable bulge. "Worth two thousand bucks an hour?"

"Maybe a bottle cap and a rubber band," he said, as if in a trance.

To finish off his faux apathy, she turned to him and gave him the most sultry don't-you-want-me? pout a woman ever beamed. His breathing was now fast and deep, his eyes and mouth gaping, his bulge trying to burst out of his pants. She could tell he was aching to have her. "It is kind of red, isn't it?" she said, as she slowly ran her fingers through her pubic hair. He was so mesmerized, he couldn't answer. He stepped toward her. She stepped back. He took another, larger step. She again stepped away. Losing control, he dashed at her and took her in his arms, one hand on her right breast, the other caressing her rear. "Stop it!" she yelled. He didn't; he couldn't. "I said stop!" she screamed as she slapped him hard across his cheek.

He let go and looked at her, blinking and breathing fast. She picked up her clothes and ran out of the room.

Five minutes later, she came out of the house and saw him throw his backpack into the truck.

"Packing already? Mort's just waking up," she said.

Making no response, he got in.

Tessa ran to the passenger door. It was locked. "Kev?"

He started the truck. She knocked on the window. "Kevin, open the door." He shifted into drive. "I'm sorry. Please don't leave us!" she hollered. He took his foot off the brake. "Kevin, stop. Please stop!" she screamed as he drove off. "They'll kill us for sure! Kevin!" But he was gone.

Mort ran out and said, "Where's he going?"

"He left us," she said with tears in her eyes.

"Oh, shit, we're dead, we're dead," moaned Mort. He glowered at Tessa and resumed, "What the hell happened? What did you say to him?"

She didn't answer.

"This is your fault!" said Mort. "You're not happy unless you're teasing him or humiliating him. Congratulations, genius; you just killed us." With Tessa still standing in silent shock, mouth agape staring at the dust the truck kicked up, Mort went on, "You seem determined to look down on him. You're so desperate to put him in his place, I have to wonder if you think he really is better than you."

"In this crazy, topsy-turvy world we're in now, he's better than anyone I ever met. I don't look down on him. I … I think I still love him. But he left me; left me to die."

She broke down crying.

\*

Tessa felt she had no choice but to follow the plan she and Kevin had discussed the evening before. She and Mort, carrying their few supplies, including her suitcase and the Smith & Wesson Kevin had given her, left the house and proceeded east along County Road 16.

After they had walked about half a mile, she looked back and saw dust rising near the farmhouse they'd just left. At first she thought it was Kevin returning for them and almost cried for joy. But she then noticed two vehicles; her heart fell, along with her stomach.

She pointed the vehicles out to Mort, who began to belabor his bad luck. They hastened to the trees north of the road and continued trotting east. A few minutes later, they crossed a dirt road and made their way up a hill. Mort had to stop to rest continually. Tessa stood beside a tree, looking down at the county road, and saw one of the trucks had stopped near where they had left the road, and two people got out.

Tessa said, "They're tracking us. We're obviously leaving a trail; probably your footprints driven deep into the earth. We have to cross that river," she said, pointing south. Maybe we can lose them. Come on. Hurry!"

Mort hurtled down the hill like a stop sign.

"God, it's like you're standing still," groused Tessa as she slowed for him to catch up. "When was the last time you ran?"

"Sixth grade. Fifty yard dash. Still haven't finished," he said, gasping.

Tessa decided she had to abandon her suitcase. She dropped it in the woods before coming to the river.

"Uh, I can't swim," mentioned Mort when they reached the river.

"Of course you can't! But we have no choice. I don't think it's deep," she said.

He put his foot in and quickly pulled it out. "It's freezing."

"Listen: if they catch you, you're dead! Stay here if you want. I'm crossing."

She walked resolutely into the river, keeping her grimacing face away from him. The water *was* freezing.

He cursed and followed. The water was shallow, except for some dips, one of which Mort found. Tessa learned that Mort wasn't lying about his inability to swim. He swam exactly like stones don't. He managed to bounce off the bottom and gulp enough air to stay alive.

"You'd think all that fat would make you more buoyant," noted Tessa as she grabbed his hand and pulled him toward the far bank.

"It makes me more heavy," he said, breathing hard. As they reached the shore, he collapsed to the ground. "I'm not accustomed to drowning."

"Well, you got the hang of it pretty quickly. We can't stay here," she said, shivering. "Let's get going."

"Not yet; I'm too exhausted and too cold. Do you have any matches?"

"No."

"Shit! We don't have to worry about getting shot; we're going to die of exposure." His shivering was shaking the ground around him.

"Keep whining, Wood. That'll just complete my day … Oh, no!"

The two people who'd been following them suddenly emerged from the woods on the other side of the river. They ran up to the river.

One was a woman who yelled, "I'll give you a moment to pray to whatever god you believe in."

Tessa slowly extricated the handgun from her sweater pocket, but the woman said, "Drop it!" She did.

"Don't shoot me!" shrieked Mort. "I can build a battery that can make you all rich!"

"Good bet that's what our clients are worried about," said the woman. The man lifted his rifle and took aim.

"No! She's the one who knows how to make the battery," said Mort.

"You son of a bitch," Tessa said, kicking him. He yelped.

"Where's the other man?" asked the hit woman.

"Aiming at your head right now," answered Tessa, hoping this last ditch gambit might spare her.

The man looked around in fear, but the woman just laughed.

"We're not stupid. Unlike you, we made sure we weren't being followed." She said to her colleague, "Finish them. I want to collect our fee and eat a huge dinner to celebrate."

Mort started crying and stood. Tessa thought he was getting set to run, but she knew running was hopeless, since cover was a good seventy feet away. She was taken by surprise when Mort pulled her in front of him to use her as a shield. "Oh! You pantywaist," she screamed. Gaping across the river at the rifles pointing her way, she told herself, *Oh, God, this is it!*

But within two seconds both killers fell dead, blood seeping from the back of their heads.

Mort took a few seconds to realize his deliverance was at hand. He let Tessa go. She turned and socked him in the jaw. "Ow! That hurt," he yelped.

Sitting on the ground flexing her sore hand, she remembered she was freezing. She pulled her knees up to her chest, rocked back and forth, and breathed down her shirt. A few minutes later, Kevin walked out of the woods, carrying his rifle and backpack. Tessa stood, charged into the river, swam and jogged to the other side, then ran to Kevin and threw her arms around him, crying.

"Jesus, you're soaking me," he protested.

He tried to push her away, but she held on tight. She couldn't let go. "Thank you for my life," she said and planted a passionate kiss on his lips. "You came back." Another kiss. "Thank you." Another kiss.

"I never left; I just had to get away from you for a while. I went to high ground to check for anyone following us. I watched the chase unfold, but I couldn't get back faster because I ran out of gas. When I got to the hill over there and saw them about to shoot, I nearly shat myself."

"I realized something after you left us."

"You're fucked on your own?"

"I've known that all along. I realized I'm, uh, getting really attached to you."

"How halfhearted of you. I'm somewhat attached to you, too, and I'm getting wet and cold." He knelt to check the bodies for booty. They had nothing other than their guns and keys, which Kevin took.

"Do you have matches?" asked Mort, who had managed to cross back over.

"Nope."

"Well, then we're doomed," said Mort.

"Come on, Mort, do I need to point out the insulation value of all that blubber? I saw you pull Tessa in front of you, you miserable mountain of shit. Even your imaginary friends must despise you." Turning to Tessa, he went on, "We need to get out of here right away."

"Why not take their truck?" asked Tessa.

"Yeah, we'd better chance it. We can't keep it long, though, because they'll be checking for it soon."

Tessa retrieved her suitcase. While they walked toward the pickup, Kevin said, "One of the vehicles at the farmhouse was a state police car. Might be another crooked cop, but it's possible the assassins told the police the Lieutenant Governor's killer is in the area."

Tessa said, "Get the police to find us, take you away, and leave Mort and me exposed."

"Now you're thinking like a killer. They would've put an APB out for me. Someone must have seen us driving this way yesterday, so they were probably checking all the abandoned houses around here. We got out just in time."

When they reached the edge of the forest near the truck, Kevin said, "The cop is lurking close by, but the coast looks clear. Mort, for once in your life, don't take fifty times longer than it should take to do something. Pretend there's a bear chasing you. Ready? Move!"

Tessa and Kevin sprinted and Mort waddled to the black Ford F-150. He gunned it and turned south on Myers Road. Tessa asked why.

"Because they'll be focusing on that road back there in their search. We also have to worry about tipping them off that we're heading toward Cornell. If we get too close, they might use the same logic you did and ambush us there. We need to lead them astray."

Tessa nodded.

Kevin took NY-226 south. He sped for a couple of miles and took a right on a crumbling road in search of an abandoned house. They soon found one near the tiny Round Lake.

Despite Tessa's objections, Kevin left her and Mort there with all their belongings, but for the Colt 1911, which he pocketed. He raced down 226 to the small town of Savona and left the truck running on the onramp to I-84 East. Without waiting to see how long it took someone to steal the truck, he dashed back to the tree line along 226, then jogged the three miles north back to the house.

There the three relaxed and napped until dark.

# CHAPTER 12

The three fugitives left the house and walked north beside 226, dashing to the trees whenever they saw a set of car lights. Since they had a long trek by foot ahead of them, they had decided Tessa should leave her suitcase behind. Kevin had tossed some of his clothes out to make room for some of Tessa's in his backpack. She carried the sleeping bag packed in a plastic garbage bag, the flashlight, and the small handgun. Mort carried some food, but Kevin kept the can opener.

Traffic wasn't heavy, but Mort was, so he was slow getting to the trees; a few drivers couldn't have missed seeing him. Kevin decided to take a less-traveled road.

After about four and a half hours of walking, with Mort carping about his sore feet, it began to rain. Sugar Hill Road had been a good choice, for there were few cars, but there was also little civilization. They wanted to get out of the rain, but couldn't find shelter.

"I'm absolutely frozen," said Tessa. She had her only sweater on, which was now soaked.

"Too bad you don't have a coat like this. I'm toasty warm," said Kevin.

"God, you can be an ass."

He laughed, took off his coat, and held it out to Tessa.

"Never mind," she said. He shrugged and put it back on. "Hey! You're supposed to insist I take it."

"You had your chance, babe," he said as he buttoned his coat and led the way down the road.

"Oh!" she barked.

A few minutes later she said, "Let's talk about something to take our minds off the cold. What should we talk about?"

"Ice cream?"

"Come on."

"Women?"

"Okay. What qualities do you admire most in a woman?"

"Beauty and promiscuity."

"Just the kind of answer I'd expect from Mr. Shallow."

"Don't worry, you're halfway there."

She smiled.

He went on, "Hm, I didn't think you'd smile at that. Let's go to bed."

Her smile vanished, and she punched his chest.

"What'd I say?" he asked as she picked up her pace to put some distance between them. "Oh, I bet this ends up with us not having sex again tonight. How long's it been now? My whole life!"

She slowed and tried again. "How about sports?"

"Hate sports."

"You used to love hockey and baseball."

"That was before the Sabres folded, along with half the rest of the league, and the baseball players went on strike for a whole season. Half the country is literally starving and they go on strike because a salary cap of eight million newbucks per player wasn't enough for the greedy bastards. It was so great when a bunch of teams went bust and so many of those overpaid assholes ended up in minimum wage jobs."

They noticed a light in the distance. As the three bedraggled travelers approached the house, a gunshot shattered the silence. Kevin and Tessa halted; Mort turned and shuffled away. Kevin called out, "We're no threat to you, Sir or Ma'am. Just looking for a place out of the rain." The next bullet hit the ground a few feet in front of him. "That would be a no," determined Kevin.

"Let's go, Kev," suggested Tessa.

Kevin took a bottle out of his backpack and shouted, "I have this fine quart bottle of Canadian beer stolen from a Canuck foolish enough to take a vacation in these parts. I mean, what's she doing on vacation? Canada's almost as bad off as we are, so she must've been rich, so she deserved to have her beer stolen, right? It's Molson Canadian; goes down smooth; good for whatever ails you. Tessa here is Canadian and can vouch for—"

The next bullet hit a foot in front of Tessa. She screeched and ran off.

"I don't care for foreigners either. Uh, I wonder if you'd consider letting us stay in your barn there for this bottle—"

A bullet took out the bottle in his hand. That angered Kevin enough that he put his right hand up to grab the rifle on his shoulder. Three more bullets came his way, one of which winged his left arm. He put out his hands to signal *stop*.

"Okay, I'll be leaving now. You have a wonderful way of getting your point across non-verbally, though you went a bit far killing my beer. Uncalled for, if you ask me." Another shot missed his foot by an inch. "Right. You didn't ask. Okay, well, you gave us everything we asked for except for the only thing we asked for, so I guess we can't have ... everything. Fuck you for your hospitality."

He turned and walked back to the road, where Tessa and Mort were waiting.

"Why did you have to tell him I'm Canadian?" she said, shoving him.

"The bugger killed my beer," he said, sucking a drop or two out of his sleeve. "I could've bought a case of KD for that."

The rain picked up. "We have to find cover. Let's keep walking down this road; there'll be other farmhouses.

They walked a few more minutes, crossed over a stream, and spotted a house looming in the gloom. They hurried toward it. This house was dark. All the windows were broken, the shingles were gone, the porch dismantled and carted away. The front door was missing.

"Hey, Mort, go on up to the house and see if there's a crazy farmer with a rifle."

"Me? No way. You're the hired muscle."

"But you're the excess fat," Kevin returned as he walked to the house. He looked inside and shined in the flashlight. "Oh, shit!" he cried as he turned and took off. Seeing this, Tessa and Mort also turned and ran.

"Who was ... Oh! Pew."

"God dammit!" said Kevin. He removed his backpack and his coat, which had caught the brunt of the skunk spray. "So much for these," he said as he tossed aside the coat. "I've had this backpack since basic training. Fuck! And things were going so well."

"If you'd been a gentleman, we'd still have your coat," pointed out Tessa.

"Amazing how women can figure out how to blame every goddamn thing that goes wrong on the nearest man," he said as he dumped the contents of the backpack onto the ground. He spread out the ammunition, the C-4 kits, the first aid kit, clothes, the bag of marijuana, and sundry small items such as Swiss Army knife, string, fish hooks, compass, and batteries. He fit what he could into his pockets. Tessa stuffed one change of clothes each into the plastic bag with the sleeping bag, after sniffing them to make sure they escaped the skunk spray.

"You still stink," she said. He hugged her. "Get away from me!"

"I guess some must've got on my pants," he said, shivering. "Should I go bottomless, Tess?"

He emptied his pockets, removed his pants, and tossed them aside. "Hey Tess, did you know it's fucking freezing?" he said as he held his hand out for a change of pants and underpants.

"Your pants must've been in the back part of your backpack. Both pairs stink."

"Fuck, anyway! What about boxers?"

"Just these," she said as she handed them to him.

She averted her head as he replaced his boxers. She turned back to him and chuckled.

"Yes, these are my Tasmanian Devil boxers. What about it?"

"Cute."

He put his boots back on and picked up his stuff. "Let's check out that barn." The three walked to the barn and stood on the ready to flee as Kevin pointed the flashlight inside. It was clear; they went in. Rain poured in through holes in the roof, but there was a corner that was dry.

Tessa and Mort went there, but Kevin went to the opposite corner and kicked the wall. "Shit!" he yelled.

"What're you doing?" asked Tessa.

"Seeing how hard I have to kick a wall to break my ankle; I've always been curious … I'm trying to get us some fire wood, but I found the only solid board in this whole dump." He tried another spot with his other foot. It went right through the rotted wall and he got stuck. "Shit!" he repeated as he tried to withdraw his foot. Tessa came over to help. After freeing his foot, she picked up the splintered boards. Kevin broke more of the wall, and the two brought the wood to the dry corner, gathered a bit of old hay, and lit a fire.

The three sat around the fire, warming up and drying out.

"They'll find us, won't they?"

"When they didn't hear from the latest two corpses, another bunch will have shown up to follow our trail. Leaving their truck on the highway might throw them off for a while, but good trackers will probably find us." She sighed. "And given the trouble they've had so far, I think the next posse will be bigger."

They lapsed into silence. Soon, Mort lay down and fell asleep next to the fire. Tessa took the sleeping bag out of the green plastic and set it out on the opposite side of the fire. She got in, pulled the sleeping bag closed, reached down, took off her wet sweater and pants, put them next to the fire, and looked at Kevin. "I'm still freezing," she said. He nodded. "Do I have to engrave an invitation for you, dummy?" she said. She opened the bag and said, "Get in here, for God's sake." He smiled and joined her. "Behave!" she ordered.

He lay on his back, and she turned to him and put her arm across his stomach and her leg across his legs. As she warmed up, she moved her leg up to his crotch. He immediately hardened. "You're not behaving," she whispered.

"If you drape your perfect thigh across my dick, you have to expect my behavior to deteriorate."

"I can move it if you want."

"Back and forth would be nice." She grinned and did as he suggested. Then she put her hand down his boxers and grabbed his penis. "Oh, Christ, your hand is cold," he said.

"I can move it back and forth if you want," she cooed.

He nodded, and after a minute said, "My balls are nice and warm." She laughed and warmed her hand there.

"Oh, they *are* nice and warm." He put his hand down her panties and clutched her butt. "Oh, it's freezing," she said as goose bumps jumped up on her backside and thighs. He moved it down between her legs and she gasped. She closed her legs on his hand and said, "Let it warm up a bit." After a minute, she opened her legs and said, "I'm really hot inside." He smiled and warmed his fingers so thoroughly, she climaxed.

She pulled her panties and his boxers down, climbed on top of him, and guided him inside her. "I've dreamt of this since sixth grade," he said breathlessly.

"You want to know a secret? So have I."

Having his number one fantasy come true after all this time was almost too much to bear; he lasted only a minute. "Well," she teased with a titter, "two thousand dollars an hour times one-sixtieth of an hour is thirty-three dollars and thirty-three cents."

"Just wait another thirty-three-thirty-three and I'll see you earn the rest of the two grand." She chuckled. Slightly embarrassed, he explained, "I just got so excited thinking of myself actually in your perfect red bush that I've dreamed of a thousand times. I think I did well lasting as long as I did."

But, apparently, she wanted to hear something a bit more romantic than how stimulating her vagina was. "You're supposed to tell me how much more special I am than any other woman you've ever been with."

"You want me to lie?"

She tapped his chest and said, "The unvarnished truth."

"Okay. Of the countless women I've been with, you're definitely not at the bottom."

She hit him again and said, "Say something nice about me, or you may have to wait a long time before the next time."

"You make me want to be a better hit man."

"Kevin!"

"Tessa, as I told you, I've been dying to make love to you forever. I wanted you more than all the rest of the women on earth combined. You had to be perfect to live up to my expectations. You were."

"That was beautiful."

"I know. All the women fall for it."

"Kevin! Why did you have to ruin the moment?"

"Tessa Sharp. You know damn well you cast a spell over me the day we met. I fell in love with you within days. When you ditched me, I wanted to die. And every time I think I'm over you, you show up and I'm a goner again. I fought so hard this time because I'm too dangerous to be around. But fighting is hopeless. I love you too much. I always will."

With tears in her eyes, she said, "I love you, too, Kev." She kissed him hard and clutched his balls. He was ready to go again in no time. The second time he lasted about five minutes. He looked at her contritely.

"Don't be embarrassed. Having you so excited over me, you can't contain yourself, is exhilarating. I love driving you wild. Why do you think I undressed in front of you yesterday? It wasn't to make a fool of you; it was the thrill I get when I see the longing in your eyes for me. No man makes me feel more desirable than you do."

"This time I was thinking of those irresistibly cute freckles on your cheeks and nose. And contrasting your sweet, innocent face with what your fabulous body was doing to me—that was it."

"That'll be another one-hundred-sixty-six-sixty-seven." She again grabbed him and said, "See if you can make it to five hundred this time."

*

Sound asleep four hours later, Tessa and Kevin awoke to the sound of a distant gunshot. They put on their underwear and got up. Their fire had expired, but the rain had ceased and the temperature had climbed. Still, the air was chilly. Tessa put on a dry set of clothes, including both shirts she had left. More gunfire erupted. That woke up Mort.

"The posse must be talking back to our belligerent farmer," said Kevin. "Sounds like several guns. We need to get out of here now; they're obviously not letting the night slow them down."

"Do you think we can outrun them?" asked Tessa.

"Not with sumo Mort here dragging along."

"What can we do? Maybe use the C-4?"

"I have no idea how many of them there are. It's unlikely we'd be lucky enough to get all of them, then the survivors would surround us pretty quickly. The smartest thing we can do is run fast and leave him behind."

"No!" said Mort. "I … I think I know what I did; I think I can make the battery. We'll all be billionaires."

"Odds are much better we'll all be dead." To Tessa, Kevin went on, "Is this whole thing really worth your life? Because if we continue to let him give us away and slow us down, we're done."

Tessa said, "As I told you the day we came to you, the battery is far more important than any of us; it means a brighter future for our country and the world. So, what can we do to escape?"

"Double back on the bastards."

"How will that work, if they've had such an easy time tracking us this far?"

"We make for the creek, walk in the water, come out on a paved road, and find our way back to the gun-happy farmer, where we'll hide for a while."

"He'll just shoot at us again," said Mort.

"The gunfire has stopped, which means he's dead."

"It's our fault," said Tessa.

"No, it's the fault of the murderers who killed him, or even of the mute farmer who was stupid enough to greet a bunch of crazed killers with gunfire."

He walked outside; the others followed. The moon had just risen; it was only a crescent, but it shed enough light to see a good thirty feet.

Seeing Tessa was carrying the sleeping bag, he said, "We need to travel light. Let's put the key supplies into the garbage bag and leave everything else." They put the ammunition, the C-4 kits, and the other small items into the bag. He put his last shirt and Tessa's last pair of pants into the bag, mostly to reduce the rattling. Kevin hoisted it over his shoulder. "I hope when the bad guys see my Tasmanian Devil boxers, they laugh long enough for me to take them out. Let's go." Tessa carried the flashlight and Smith & Wesson handgun. Mort carried a few cans of food.

They made their way a few hundred yards west until they came to the bridge they'd crossed a few hours ago. Tessa shined the flashlight down into the ravine, and down the hill they went. They stepped into the shallow water and walked north, Mort grumbling about his cold feet.

After following the meandering brook for about two-thirds of a mile, all three stopped simultaneously as they heard a disturbing thumping in the distance. A minute later, their fears were confirmed. They saw a search light in the sky maybe two hundred meters ahead.

Kevin said, "Oh, a helicopter is just not fair. Good guess some are on foot behind us, too."

"What now?" asked Mort.

"I don't really know, Mort, old buddy. You think I have a manual that tells me how to handle every disaster that comes our way? Oh, wait, I do." He pretended to thumb through a manual and stopped at an imaginary page. "When stuck in a river in your underpants trying to protect a hippo with a dozen killers on your tail and a helicopter closing in, you should run and leave the hippo behind."

He looked at Mort and added, "I'm improvising as we go. Maybe one of you can come up with something for a change; you're the frigging geniuses. Hey! I have it, Tess. Maybe you could bore them to death with a lecture on women's studies. Bitch to them about female circumcision or the glass ceiling or men's double standard on sex. They're bound to kill themselves before long."

"Hilarious. You ever consider a career in standup?"

"You ever consider a career in lie down?"

"We already had that discussion. You're a sniper; shoot the copter down."

"Much easier said than done." But no one had a better idea, so he eventually said, "You two hide behind the trees, and I'll find a place to snipe the pilot and maybe a few of our pursuers. If they find you, Tess, leave this son of a bitch behind. Don't get into a gunfight with them. Use the handgun only if it's your last resort; it's pretty hopeless against a rifle in the hands of a pro. I'll try to meet you back here. If not, try to make it back to the dead farmer's house."

"Kev ... Be careful," said Tessa.

He nodded and dashed up the east bank to the trees and up the hill out of sight.

*

The helicopter hovered above the water a hundred meters upriver, proceeding south slowly with its searchlight scanning back and forth. "Shit, they'll see us for sure," said Tessa. They were standing in a narrow band of trees to the west of the stream.

"Well, we can't stay here," said Mort.

"Try, for once in your life, not to panic. Just give Kevin a couple more minutes to find a good vantage point."

The helicopter got closer and closer. Mort panicked and ran for a thicker stand of trees farther west. The pilot must have noticed because the helicopter picked up speed. Tessa fell to the ground as the searchlight passed near her. Suddenly the aircraft veered off to the right and crashed into the trees about a hundred feet east of Tessa's position. There was a small explosion, and a fireball engulfed the downed helicopter.

Lifting her head, she noticed movement to the south; she saw two men running along the east bank toward her with guns leveled. One took aim at her, the other at Mort, who had only just got to the trees. But both men fell dead to the ground before they could shoot. Audible pops echoed in the distance almost simultaneously.

Tessa called Mort back. He returned to the river and resumed complaining about running for his life. She tuned him out, but then she heard a voice. "Shut up!" she whispered vociferously. The voice was coming from one of the dead men's radios. She ran to get the radio and heard, "Charlie? Zombie, come in? Shit, they must be down. Charlie? Zombie?

Fuck! I'm telling the client we want another ten million and they pay for the helo, or we walk. You two get after the fat one and the bitch; the rest of you with me to get that fucking sniper. Now! Go silent; assume they'll pick up a radio off a corpse."

Tessa took the body armor off the man, picked up his M4 Carbine, and walked back into the river. "Get his vest and follow me," she said to Mort as she donned the bullet-proof vest and slung the M4 over her shoulder. He did as asked, and the two retraced their steps back to the bridge. The vest didn't fit Mort, so he left it open in front.

As the two neared the bridge several minutes later, Tessa felt a searing pain in the middle of her chest and heard a loud bang. The impact threw her back so hard, she flipped over and landed on her front on the ground just beside the river. Then she heard another blast and Mort, who had turned to run, cried out and went down behind her. Mort writhed in pain and wept; Tessa, despite the pain and the trouble she was having getting her next breath, stayed perfectly still. She saw out of the corner of her eye two men walk out of the darkness; evidently they had been standing on the bridge.

One pointed a flashlight at Mort and said, "The fat one's still alive. He's got a flak jacket on."

"Blow his brains out," said his cohort.

As they lifted their rifles, Tessa quickly brought the carbine to bear and fired several shots. Both men went down; one shot in the head, the other in both legs. Tessa ran out, holding the carbine on the stricken man and breathing hard. She stared at the man she killed, aghast. The injured man reached over for his rifle, but she screamed, "Don't!"

"Fuck you, bitch," served as his next and his last words. As he lunged to get his weapon, she shot him through the side of his head. Then she dropped the gun and sat down to cry.

After a few minutes, she said to Mort, "This is the worst feeling I've ever had; I've killed two human beings."

"My back is killing me," said Mort in commiseration.

A truck stopped on the bridge. Tessa picked up and pointed the carbine toward the road. A man emerged from the truck. As she was squeezing the trigger, she heard, "Tess?"

The gun went off.

"Jesus Christ!" hollered Kevin. "Hold your fucking fire!" He walked down to the river.

"Kevin! I'm sorry. Did I hit you?" she said, running to him.

"I think it went right between my legs; my balls are currently hiding behind my spleen," he said. She hugged him. He looked at the dead men. "You're a quick study."

Weeping, she said, "I feel awful."

"Why? It was self defense. Plus, they were monsters. I'm proud of you." He returned the hug, a little too tight for her comfort.

She winced and said, "I got shot in the chest; it hurts like hell."

"Good thinking taking the vest." He followed her lead and stooped to take a vest off one of Tessa's victims; he also grabbed both M4 carbines and two ammunition magazines. "Let's get going. The bad guys'll be around in a few minutes, and they might be pissed that I borrowed their pickup without asking."

"Not because you killed a bunch of their men?" He shrugged. "And ruined their helicopter?"

"I am a troublemaker," he said.

She grinned and said, "What're those?" pointing to something on his head.

"Night vision goggles. Borrowed them, too, off a guy who had no further use for them. That's how I saw you down here. Here, try them out climbing up to our new wheels." She put them on and walked up the hill. Turning to Mort, Kevin said, "Come on, hurry."

They got to the F-150, and Kevin said to Tessa, "Leave the lights off. Drive with the goggles on." He took the passenger seat, rifle on the ready. Mort got into the back seat.

They headed east.

# CHAPTER 13

Driving through Watkins Glen, NY, Tessa looked at something on the dashboard. "This truck has satellite tracking. They'll shut down the engine."

Kevin said, "What they'll probably do is get people surrounding us before they do that. Pull over."

Tessa parked at the curb. She glanced back and saw that Mort was snoozing.

Kevin continued, "We have to make sure they don't start thinking of Cornell. Since they're tracking us, we can throw them off by heading north."

She took her foot off the brake, but he halted her again. "I think maybe you and Mort should take a cab to Cornell from here while I lead the fuckers north."

Tessa objected to that. "They might have already thought of Cornell. We'd be walking into a trap without you to help us."

"Whoever's in this truck is definitely driving into a trap. It's safer to—"

"We're safer with you. We're staying." She headed up 414, which skirted the east side of Seneca Lake. A few minutes later, she said, "What if we get to Cayuga Lake and borrow a boat?" Ithaca was situated at the southern tip of Cayuga Lake.

"Good idea."

Tessa sped north about halfway up the length of Seneca Lake before turning east. In the small village of Interlaken, she turned north. She took the next road east, but it wound through an abandoned neighborhood. She made her way out to a county road where she turned toward Cayuga Lake.

They'd seen few cars during the twenty-six minutes since leaving Watkins Glen, but suddenly two sets of headlights appeared behind them.

"Mort, wake up. Now!" said Kevin.

"How come they don't shut us down?" said Tessa.

"Waiting to box us in. Both of you be ready to get out and run. Take the left coming up. And go faster. Mort, wake the fuck up!"

Mort sat up.

Both sets of lights turned behind them.

"You and Mort run for the lake; we're within a mile, I'm sure. I'll try to lead them away before they shut down the engine."

"You can't leave us."

"No arguments! Take your rifle. Stay in the woods; use the goggles to find your way."

"How will we find each other?"

"Get to the lake and walk north along the shore; I'll find you."

The road veered eastward and dipped, cutting them off from the line of sight of the vehicles behind. Another set of headlights appeared about a mile ahead. "Stop now!" screamed Kevin. "Get out into those trees; hurry!" He turned, pointed his 1911 at Mort, and said, "Move faster than you ever have."

The two got to the woods as Kevin took the wheel and took off. He'd driven about three hundred yards when the engine shut off. Four vehicles closed in. He braked hard, grabbed his rifle, one of the carbines, and the garbage bag, and ran fast southwest through a fallow field toward a line of trees.

\*

Tessa jogged through a brook with Mort trailing, whimpering that he was getting scratched and cold. Constantly looking back for any pursuers, she led him through the narrow valley.

Gunshots echoed nearby. Tessa's heart sped up. *Kevin!*

"They're shooting at us!" exclaimed Mort.

"Keep it down!" Tessa said. "It's Kevin they're shooting at."

The gunfire got more distant. *He's leading them away from us.* With every gunshot, she cringed, wondering whether Kevin had taken a bullet, but as long as it continued, he was alive.

After about fifteen minutes, she heard no more gunfire. She started crying.

\*

Kevin had made it to the trees, but cursed upon realizing it was only a narrow band in the middle of a large field. He made a brief stand, picking off two pursuers with his Accuracy Rifle, but knew he'd be surrounded there. He ran west along the trees, then south when the tree line took that direction. But the trees petered out. Stopping to look through his infrared scope, he saw three men coming toward him. There had been eight initially. Where were the other three? Maybe circling in from behind? He scanned the woods to the south but saw no one. *Following Tessa!*

Turning his rifle back toward the three men following him, he shot one through the head. The other two immediately ducked behind trees. That was also the last bullet for his Accuracy Rifle. He was still a great shot with the M4, but not quite as deadly.

The two men were using the standard army procedure of popping up, shooting a short burst, and getting down. While one shot at him, the other bounded toward his position.

Kevin timed them and poured fire at the next burst of flashes. The man fell backward, but soon hauled himself up; his vest had saved him. Kevin lay down and the next time the man popped up, he shot him in the head.

He changed magazines and sprinted to the next tree, about fifty meters south. He was just about there before he was felled with a bullet to the upper back. His vest saved him, but the energy from the bullet threw him head over heels. He lay sprawled on the ground a few feet from the cover of the tree. He scrambled to the tree, managing to drag the M4 with him, but he had dropped his prized rifle.

Scanning back and forth with the scope, he couldn't see the shooter. He was typically patient as a sniper, but the disadvantage in this standoff was his, not only because reinforcements might arrive at any time, but because of the group he supposed was trailing Tessa. *Maybe this guy's instructions are to pin me down while they find her.*

He darted to the woods, about thirty yards south. This time one bullet grazed his head in almost the exact spot he'd earlier been clipped, starting a free flow of blood. Another took out a small chunk of his left triceps. Cursing, he dropped to the ground.

Lying on his back, he quickly took the first aid kit out of the garbage bag, took out the gauze, and wound it tightly around his arm. There being nothing in the kit to help with his head wound, he tilted up and removed his vest and shirt. He bunched up the shirt and pushed it hard against the laceration on his head—if he lost too much blood, it would be over for him, Tessa, and Mort—then put the vest back on. He rolled to his stomach and looked again for the shooter, still pressing his shirt on his head wound. He told himself he'd give it five minutes before running to help Tessa.

The sky was lightening in the east. At about the three-minute mark, he saw slight movement of branches in the trees across the field. He focused on it. A man's head poked out. Kevin put a bullet between his eyes.

After running out to get his rifle, he proceeded east along the stream that Tessa and Mort had followed.

*

"Don't make a peep!" whispered Tessa. She and Mort had hidden in the bushes to the north of the rivulet when they heard voices from behind.

"Shit. They must've got Idle. We're dead," muttered Mort.

"Shut up!" she whispered with bared teeth. She saw two men approaching through her night-vision goggles. She took them off and looked through the infrared scope on the carbine. As they got closer, she could feel Mort shaking. She aimed at one man's head.

She shot a burst of bullets, one of which found its target, who fell dead. Mort took off. The other man dived behind the trees. He sent a hail of metal her way. Shaking with fear, she tried pressing herself into the ground. The man dashed to find a better position. Tessa felt helpless in this battle against a professional killer. Out of her mind with fear and grief over Kevin's probable loss, she began crying. *My only chance is to run*, she told herself, as she prepared to take off.

*

Kevin had heard the shots ahead. He raced toward them. Seeing a man shifting to get the advantage over someone behind the bushes ahead, he knelt and fired continuously until the man dropped.

He stood and called, "Tessa?" but there was no response. All at once, a volley of fire came from a dirt road just east of his position, two of which smashed into his vest in the chest area, hurling him back into the stream. He struggled to sit up and gasped for breath. He'd lost his weapon.

A large, middle-aged man, who looked to be another ex-soldier, walked down from the road and smiled. "I got here just in time to see her take off that-a-way when you were shooting Jason. Couldn't get a clear shot at her, but I'll get her and the fat one in a minute. First I need to deal with their bodyguard. You've been a great deal of trouble, son. You made us earn the twenty million."

"Twenty?"

"Yup. They doubled it twice because of you. Thank you, son. And I guess I don't have to split it up much after you got through with us. You're a credit to the Seals."

He took aim at Kevin's head. Kevin shut his eyes. He heard a bang and jumped, but felt nothing. He opened his eyes and saw the man sprawled on the ground next to the stream. Behind him stood Tessa with a smoking M4. Kevin got to his feet, tottered to her, and hugged her, saying, "Thank you, Tess. You're amazing."

*

Along the western shore of Cayuga Lake was an almost uninterrupted series of docks. Most had no boats, both because it was still early in the season and because most people who had had boats were forced to turn them into cash, or lost them to repossession or thieves during the depression. But there were a few still available for the pilfering.

A sweet felon rang the bell of a fancy old house on Interlaken Beach Road. The elderly man who answered looked surprised at the pretty woman's getup, which was wet and torn in spots. She had goggles sitting on top of her head. He appeared further taken aback when she pulled a gun and said, "I'm really sorry, but we need to borrow your boat."

Kevin and Mort stepped into the light emanating from the house. The old man gawked at Kevin, who had a bloody bandage wrapped around his upper left arm and dried blood caked on his forehead; he wore two rifles that went with the vest, but clashed with the cartoon underwear.

Mort had his typical disheveled look.

Tessa said, "I promise we won't do any damage, but we're absolutely desperate. We'll leave it at the marina at Cayuga."

"Marina's gone bust," said the man.

"Oh. We'll leave it there anyway."

"And we'll have to tie you up for a little while," added Kevin, "so you won't tell on us until we can get away."

"Who is it, Darren?" asked a woman from the back of the house.

"Boat thieves," said the man.

"What?" said the woman, coming into the hall.

She screamed upon seeing the three strangers, the female pointing a gun, one male looking like a desperado in underpants, the other like a beach ball with legs. "Don't be afraid," said Tessa. Putting away the gun, she repeated what she'd said to the man.

"The whole world has gone to hell," said the lady as Kevin tied her to a chair. "How are we supposed to get loose? No one bothers to check on us. We could die here."

Tessa looked at Kevin, who shrugged.

She said, "Can we borrow a phone, too, and call your neighbor after we dock? We'll leave the phone on the boat."

"Even if I believed you'll leave our boat at the marina, someone else like you will steal it before we can get to it."

"I'm really sorry. I promise we'll make this right … eventually."

"Stop apologizing," said Kevin as he tied the man to another chair. Addressing the man, he said, "The key?"

The man said nothing.

"Lady?"

She said nothing.

"You see what comes of being a nice robber? They don't believe we're serious enough to hurt them." He clamped the man's face in his hand and said, "She's a pussy cat, but I'm a goddamn wolf. Tell me or I'll tear off your fucking head!"

"Kevin!"

"Why don't you tell them my name, *Tessa*?"

He turned his fierce eyes on the lady who said, "On a hook in the kitchen!"

He went to collect the boat key and a cell phone. Tessa got the phone number of a neighbor.

They asked for the location of tape for gags. So the two could breathe through their mouths if they had to, Tessa cut a small hole in the tape.

Tessa washed her face, changed pants, and took her outer shirt off. She took a sweater from the woman's closet.

Kevin washed dried blood off his face and hair, put his last shirt on—he struggled to get the long sleeve over the bandage, but managed—and absconded with the longest pair of pants he could find from the man's selection of clothes. The pants were too short and too wide. Tessa sized up his look with a guffaw.

On the way out, Kevin noticed an old bicycle in the hall. He snatched it.

Kevin unmoored the 2010 Bayliner 195, and the three stepped aboard as the sun rose. He started it and puttered it away from shore, then he gunned it and zoomed down to Ithaca.

Tessa and Mort got out at a dock at Stewart Park. Ahead of them they had a three-mile hike to the university. She took the Smith & Wesson revolver.

Kevin's next task was to hide the arsenal, except for his Colt 1911, which he kept in his pocket. This lake was Tessa's and Kevin's stomping ground, so they knew it well. His parents used to have a cottage thirty miles north of Ithaca on the eastern shore of Cayuga Lake. He tied the boat to a broken-down jetty in a forested area just north of his old cabin—which he noticed was demolished—and walked into the woods to stash the weapons, NVGs, and vests under a bush near the spot where, at age thirteen, he first kissed a girl: Tessa. Comparing those happy days to these horrid ones, he shook his head and trod back to the stolen boat.

He then continued to the northern tip of the lake. There, he called the neighbor of the boat owners as Tessa had promised. He wasn't sure the lady who answered believed him, but he tried his best to convince her. It was important the old people were found, not only for their sake, but so they would report the theft and the names of the thieves, and thereby draw the assassins away from Cornell.

Leaving the boat tied to a private pier just south of the former Lockview Marina, he made his way unseen—he hoped—between two small cabins to Route 90 and got on the old bike for a ride down south to his father's hobby farm located about twelve miles north of Ithaca.

*

Tessa and Mort walked to the Uris Library, which used to be open twenty-four hours, but was now closed 11 PM to 8 AM. They had to wait outside for forty-five minutes. Her plan was to check the webpage tracking her and Mort to determine if they might be at risk approaching the engineering quad.

She sat next to the library looking around and getting misty-eyed thinking back to her time here. She'd been so happy before the disaster with her parents. She'd excelled academically. On the social side, she had her pick of the men in engineering, sciences—well, anyone she came across. Life was wonderful.

Tessa's work at Cornell had involved several different aspects of battery engineering, including nanotechnology, computer engineering, chemistry and chemical biology, and materials sciences. She worked on her father's research project involving lithium air cells. They had access to world class laboratories and researchers, including research scientists in private industry.

She did most of her research work at the Cornell Energy Materials Center, which was where she was planning to head after determining it was safe. She had a few contacts at the center who could potentially help her, but she planned to focus on a young Materials Science and Engineering professor who had shown a great deal of interest in her, both academically and biologically. Unbeknownst to her father, they had been lovers for a few months in her third year, but she broke it off when he began to get too serious; he had a lot going for him, but he had no sense of humor, so anything permanent was out of the question. She hoped he would give her access to Energy Materials Center facilities for old time's sake.

When the library opened, she went to a computer and brought up the Islamic Center webpage. It was flashing *Interlaken, NY. Heading north*. She confirmed the reward was now twenty million dollars, which sent another pang of panic reeling through her.

She led Mort to the Energy Materials Center. Few people were there yet but a professor of chemical biology, who'd taught her, welcomed her and Mort into the lab. Professor Wagner, her former lover, was expected within the hour. In the meantime, she checked the website again. It was now flashing *Lockview Marina, Cayuga, NY. Heading north*; a small measure of comfort.

*

Tom Wagner stopped at the entrance to the lab when he saw Tessa. She'd broken his heart when she set him free three years earlier. He blamed it on all the upheaval in her life, what with her father's drinking and cheating and her parents' impending divorce. It couldn't have been him; all the girls wanted him.

Though he'd met another and was recently married, seeing Tessa was both upsetting and thrilling. The flame hadn't died. She looked tousled, but otherwise her beauty was undiminished. But it was her amazing brain that really attracted him. *What a woman!* He wanted her.

*

Tessa felt a twinge of attraction as well, along with a sadness that was more the result of a longing for the felicity she'd enjoyed during the time she was with him than for the man himself.

"Tessa, what are you doing back here?"

She stepped up and hugged him. "I need your help, Tom." He looked at her for an explanation.

Tessa told him the story, leaving out most of the gore of the last week so as not to scare him off, and leaving the impression that the battery was promising and not the breakthrough her father had been seeking, and finished by asking for access to the lab for a couple of days.

Tom said the equipment was still there, but hadn't been used in almost three years. The university had tried to sell it, but everybody was cutting back at that point and there were no buyers at a reasonable price. It would take some work to get the machines going again. She said Mort would do it.

"Still, it's a lot to ask, Tess," said Tom, with that suggestive inflection.

She'd seen his ring finger. She took his arm and pulled him away from Mort. "But you're married."

"I've missed you so much."

"But, your wife—"

"Is five months pregnant. Come on. We've done it plenty of times before."

"You weren't married!"

"Just wait till you're married and only have the prospect of humping one man for the rest of your life. You've had him a thousand times already. How can the thousandth and first be anything to you? Then Adonis comes along and offers, but you can't. Why? Because society imposes monogamy on us. It's bullshit!"

"The thousandth and first will be special if I love him."

"How idealistic you are. You'll change your tune when you're married. I know you suffered when your dad cheated, but it's because you didn't understand how stultifying marriage is when it comes to sex. It didn't mean he didn't love your mother. Because everyone overreacted to your father getting a bit on the side, it ruined four lives, including mine. It changed everything between us, and I lost you."

"It wasn't …" She thought the better of finishing that point. "Your office?"

He nodded with a smile.

She told Mort, "Get the machines ready to go. I'll be back in ten min—"

"A half hour," said Tom.

Tom was a devilishly handsome man, so the prospect of sex with him wasn't abhorrent. Still, it was humiliating paying for something with sex. He was treating her as a prostitute. And she detested cheaters.

In his office, he unbuttoned and unzipped his pants, and dropped them to the floor. He took off his underpants and pushed down on her shoulders, getting her to kneel.

She hated performing fellatio, which he knew. This was going to be more humiliating than she thought. After sucking and gagging for a few minutes, she put her hand up just in time to intercept the stream.

She hoped that was it, but he pulled down her pants and panties.

"Not without a rubber," she said.

"Ah, come on, Tess. You didn't make me wear one when we were a couple."

"I was on the pill; I'm not now. You don't want two women pregnant at the same time, do you?"

He took one out of his drawer, but insisted she put it on him.

He bent her over his desk. This wasn't exciting for her, so she was dry when he forced himself into her. It hurt for the first minute or so as he aggressively thrust. Finally, after maybe ten minutes he stopped. He sat on the desk and pulled her on top of him. Facing him, she lowered herself on him, but did nothing.

"Come on, Tess. Move." She glared at him, but did as he asked. She moved faster and faster to get it over with quickly. He opened her shirt and pulled down her bra to play with her breasts.

After he finished, she got off him and dressed. She walked out of his office without looking at him. Tears overflowed. Bad enough what she did; she was in love with another man. In a sense, she, too, had cheated.

# CHAPTER 14

Kevin used back roads to bike his way down to his father's house. It took close to three hours.

He ditched the bike a couple of hundred yards from the house and sneaked through the woods that surrounded the property. Through the trees, he looked at the house from every angle. The police or any of the three groups of outlaws after him could be watching. For all he knew, his father was already dead. The purpose of this visit was to take his father away from a potentially fatal situation; and to borrow his car. His Honda Accord wasn't there at present, probably because he was at work.

After reconnoitering for half an hour, he dashed to the back door. He checked under a decorative rock his father dragged with him wherever he lived. There he found a spare key. Unlocking the door, he looked through the window beside it to see if anyone moved. Seeing nothing, he walked inside. His father's weimaraner barked, but eased to growling when it recognized him. He got a piece of bologna for it out of the fridge to settle it down.

Kevin checked every room, but no one was home. He then checked for bugs; he found one connected to the phone line as it entered the house. He left it in place.

He opened a beer and had three bowls of Frosted Flakes. At 10:54 AM, he lay on the couch for a nap.

\*

A tap on the shoulder not only woke him, it launched him off the couch, his hand going for the gun in his pocket.

"Whoa," said Tessa, laughing. She, Mort, and his father stood looking at him. "You were so sound asleep, you slept through the dog barking and me calling you."

"What time is it?"

"Six-twenty," said his father.

Tessa said, "I remembered you said your dad worked in the policy analysis department, so we went there and found him. He offered us a place to stay for the night."

Kevin asked her, "Did you tell—"

"He knows everything," Tessa said.

"Including your killing of the lieutenant governor," said Richard Idle. "The police were here two days ago asking for your whereabouts."

"Warner was on the take."

"So Tessa tells me. I knew you were an executioner, but I didn't know you graduated to judge and jury, too."

"Nice to see you, too, Dad."

"What the hell are you going to do? You're the subject of a manhunt; if they catch you, you'll get the death penalty."

"For doing something the entire legal establishment was too stupid or scared to do. Warner was almost certainly the main reason the Mexican mob has gotten away with so much in this state."

"Yeah, the *New York Times* speculated as much in yesterday's paper. But, even if it's true, the state can't let citizens get away with taking justice in their own hands."

"If they won't do it, someone has to. He and those other two assholes I killed were the main people responsible for mom's murder. I got justice for her."

His father nodded, which pleased Kevin.

Kevin went on, "By the way, someone has bugged your phone line, probably one of the groups after me or Tessa. The police would just get the phone company to hand over digital copies of the phone calls you get or make; I'd be flabbergasted if they're not monitoring your phones and computers. And the feds are likely using their point-and-click surveillance system."

Richard's expression evinced surprise, then anger. He strode toward the phone, but Kevin said, "No, Dad. It's outside the house. Leave it on for now. They can't hear us unless you turn on the phone, but if you destroy it, whoever it is might come out here. And there's nothing you can do about the police and FBI wiretapping anyway."

Richard stood fuming for a moment, muttering, "Goddamn government," then went to the kitchen for a Friday evening beer.

Tessa held Kevin back for a moment, said, "I missed you," and planted an open-mouthed kiss on him.

As the four drank beer, they continued their discussion. Tessa held Kevin's hand under the table.

Richard told his son, "I'm glad you're protecting Tessa and that young blonde. She tells me you've killed half the state this past week."

"Yes, she has a big mouth. Listen, Dad, this mess has already shown up at your door. It could get very dangerous. You have to get out."

"I've talked to Tessa about this. I'm not leaving my house."

"I'm shocked," Kevin said sarcastically. "The people after Tessa will kill you for information; the people after me will kill you for revenge or simply for pleasure."

"I have a job; I have a life."

"Stay and you might not have either. Please, Dad, just tempor—"

"No. Subject closed. Let's barbeque some chicken breasts for dinner."

As Richard cooked the meat, Tessa and Kevin updated each other. Mort had set up the machinery and Tessa had found her software on the computer, and both were ready to work the full weekend.

"I'm surprised everything worked out so well," said Kevin. "Not only that the facilities are still there, but that they gave you access."

"Well, uh, I still have friends there," said Tessa. She kissed him again.

"Banging her old boyfriend sealed the deal," said Mort.

Kevin looked at her in shock. Her expression evidently confirmed what Mort had revealed, because he turned and marched out the front door, red with anger.

Tessa said, "Asshole!" to Mort, and cried, "Kevin!" She ran after him and clutched his arm to stop him. He yanked his arm away from her.

"I had no choice if we wanted to use his lab."

"It's none of my business. Ram whoever you want. I don't care."

"Then why are you so mad?"

"I couldn't care less," he said with tears in his eyes.

"It hurts because you're in love with me. I hurt every time you were with Heather."

"Is that why you did it?"

"No! It was his condition for using his lab." She took his hands. "I didn't want to; I cried afterward because I knew it would hurt you."

"Is this why you're so clingy?" She nodded. "Well, what did you do with him?"

"Kevin, don't ask me that."

"Everything?"

"Kevin …"

"You didn't blow him?" She lowered her eyes. "Oh! And you were French-kissing me!" He jerked his hands away from her and spit. "Oh, fuck, I taste scrotum." He spit again.

She laughed.

"This isn't fucking funny!" He spit once more.

"I hated it! It was humiliating and disgusting, but I had no choice."

"Just stay the hell away from me."

"I made him use a rubber."

He shook his head, turned, and walked down the road with his hands in his pockets.

"Kevin, wait!" He stopped but didn't turn to face her. "I can't regret that I did it, because otherwise everything we've gone through would've been for naught. But I'm sorry I hurt you."

He resumed walking, brushing a tear away.

"I love you," she called to him.

Tessa let him go. She would have much preferred he never found out, but since he had, she wasn't displeased with his emotional reaction. It went beyond jealousy and anger; it was sorrow. It showed his love for her was deep. A perverse part of her still enjoyed the power she had to do this to a man, especially this man, but now she felt the danger; the danger of losing him.

\*

Kevin joined the other three in the middle of dinner.

"Nice of you to join us," said Richard. "It was all I could do to keep Mort from eating your piece of chicken. Take it now before he manages to prong it."

He glared at Tessa. She returned a friendly smile. He sat across from her and took the chicken and a helping of rice and kernel corn.

Earlier, Kevin had told her, "Whatever you do, don't get my father talking about the economy."

Wanting to reduce the tension between them and show a little playfulness, Tessa kicked Kevin's shin, gave him an arch smile, and said to his father, "You're an expert in economics. I've wanted to ask you …"

Kevin shook his head, put down his fork, waved both hands, and mouthed *No!*

"... how things got this bad?" continued Tessa.

Kevin rolled his eyes, and Tessa grinned brightly at him.

Richard answered, "Feckless politicians, corrupt and rapacious bankers, voters too stupid and unprincipled to hold them to account. They all ignored the unsustainable debt levels, the demographic time bomb with millions of retiring baby boomers forced to retrench and too few workers to support them, and the derivatives mess created by a criminally greedy and incompetent financial system. But in the end it was just ... us. We never questioned for an instant that we were entitled to live beyond our means, to steal from our children and grandchildren to have everything we wanted today without working for it. Such delusions are a common feature of all dying empires. Anyone who bothered to read a bit of history would have known this, but we're too ignorant to read history and too arrogant to believe it would apply to us anyway."

"Yeah, I'd heard warnings for years about unsustainable government debt," said Tessa with a smirk at Kevin. "But how did that lead to people losing their houses?"

"Besides tens of trillions of government debt, there were tens of trillions more in private debt, most of it linked to a huge housing bubble we created with the connivance of government, bankers, investors, and borrowers. Millions of people who had no business buying a house got huge mortgages. As if this wasn't bad enough, people took out two and a half trillion dollars in equity from their homes, only it wasn't really equity; it was debt. They felt rich because house prices were going up and up, so they spent up a storm. Then, inevitably, the party came to a sudden end. Millions found themselves with mortgages of four hundred grand on a house worth maybe a third of that. The only logical choice for most was to walk away."

"Bankrupt with no place to live," Tessa said.

"Exactly. Debt to the average dolt in this country was just monthly carrying charges. 'If I can pay my mortgage and credit card bill every month, who cares that I owe, what is it? Uh, seven hundred grand. I mean, I make ten bucks an hour as a shift supervisor at McDonald's, and it's enough to pay my bills. In fact, I can extract fifty grand from my home equity, add it to my mortgage, and invest it in a vacation home, and another ten grand to go to Europe for a month, and still squeak by!' Imbeciles."

"What set it all off?" asked Tessa. She again grinned at Kevin, who put his finger to his temple and pretended to pull the trigger.

"A confluence of factors created a cascading disaster. Tokyo earthquake, the de facto collapse of the EU, an uptick in inflation and interest rates that started investors panicking, international loss of confidence in America, but primarily the implosion of the derivatives bubble, which was as high as one and a half quadrillion dollars. That was twenty times the size of the world economy! All the governments on earth could do nothing when it crashed. The market got so big, the destabilization factor was almost beyond imagining. What astonishing recklessness! The greed, the hubris—"

"Alright, Dad," said Kevin.

"Bondholders stopped buying our bonds, and the government was forced to take a machete to everything it did, including underwriting the stock market, which collapsed. There went the private sector. Bloated governments at every level started jettisoning scads of workers, which snowballed and added to the woes the private sector was already experiencing; companies everywhere shed workers.

"With so much unemployment, so much debt, so much uncertainty, and so many people retiring, spending cratered and prices dived on everything; deflation took hold. Millions defaulted on their loans, which destroyed so much money, deflation accelerated. The bad conditions made people more hesitant to buy anything, either because they couldn't afford it, or because things would be even cheaper soon; that, too, propelled deflation. Mix it all together and we get depression."

Tessa put her left elbow on the table, rested her chin on her cupped hand, and gazed at Kevin with the same impish smile as Richard continued his disquisition. Kevin couldn't help but chuckle.

"Everyone called on the government to 'Do something!' But it was beyond anyone's control once the inevitable avalanche finally began. And they had no money to do anything anyway; no New Deal make-work projects this time around. Politicians, of course, lied to everyone at first. 'Everything's under control; markets are already turning around. No need to panic. Blah, blah, blah.' A lot of talk. No action until they were forced to, when lenders ran away and tax revenues dried up. So raise tax rates and take an ax to everything: no social security until seventy and rates cut in half; no more prescription drug coverage; no Medicare until seventy and palliative care only over eighty; and on and on.

"When they could no longer deny that deflation was rampant, they, of course, panicked and put the money-creation machine into hyper-drive. The Fed just created bookkeeping entries out of thin air, and banks used fractional reserve rules to multiply the magic money by ten. And the same gang that brought us a collapsed, hopelessly leveraged economy with destabilizing deflation then gave us ruinous inflation, and that was the final nail.

"You can't keep printing money, backed by nothing and producing nothing of value and not expect the entire house of cards to collapse. Prices zoomed up because the dollar had become all but worthless, and gradually the mindset changed, and people moved to spend their cash before it became as worthwhile as toilet paper. At that point bartering became the main way of doing business. Other nations devalued their currencies before they became uncompetitive, Congress passed the foolish made in America policy, and trade wars began."

Tessa, still having fun goading Kevin, said to his father, "Will it ever get better?"

"Of course. It's already getting better. Inflation is under control. Introducing a new currency helped people believe things were getting back to normal—no more seven-hundred-dollar a gallon gas—which is nine-tenths of the battle. Official unemployment is down to twenty-seven percent, which means it's probably forty percent, but still, it's improving. All of this is part of the normal fluctuations in a market economy, although the governments made matters so much worse with their machinations. The economy needs a depression periodically to sort out all the imbalances and set up a better future. Cornell grads should be fine relatively soon, so not to worry too much."

"Uh, I transferred to another college."

"Where?" said Richard.

"Colorado College."

"Why in the name of God would you do that?"

"It's another long, boring story," said Kevin.

"Big mistake, Tessa. You know, before the baby boom, only a few percent of Americans had a college degree." Kevin put his arm down on the table and parked his head in the crook, as his father continued, "It's now somewhere between a quarter to a third, but little do people know, it's really still only a few percent. Most grads have a piece of paper denominated a degree, a piece of paper that cost upwards of a quarter of a million dollars, but with a return of virtually nil. Art history, musicology, gay studies, women's studies"—here Tessa looked down—"and on and on.

"We have ten or twenty world leading universities, but they're swamped by thousands of horrid universities and colleges with morons teaching idiots. Useless disciplines, watered down curricula, inflated grades, students who arrive woefully unprepared academically and too damn lethargic to do anything other than smoke weed and have sex." Here Richard looked at Kevin, and Kevin raised his eyes to look at him. "Lazy professors doing little teaching and less research, and halfwit administrators letting them all get away with it. The great majority of students graduate without anything approaching a marketable skill. And all at usurious prices impervious to rationality or economic circumstances. Such was the American sensibility—our craze for credentials regardless of underlying value. Utterly insane. I hope the depression works its corrective magic and wipes out all the useless colleges."

"Mine's already gone," said Tessa.

"Mine, too," put in Mort.

Richard said, "Come back to Cornell and finish a real degree, Tessa."

"Can't afford it."

"She owes two hundred grand," said Kevin.

Richard shook his head.

At Kevin's behest, Richard called his other son, who lived in Denver, to talk about his wayward brother who was wanted for murder; he left the bug in. Richard told Jeff he hadn't seen Kevin, didn't expect to, and didn't want to. "As you know, we've had nothing to do with each other for years, so I can't imagine he'd come here."

Kevin thanked his father and felt safer staying the night.

Kevin suggested burying C-4 in front of the house, but Richard wouldn't hear of it. He said he didn't believe he was in danger, and even if he was, he couldn't conceive of blowing up anyone. He did take the Smith & Wesson, reluctantly.

That evening, they sat talking at the kitchen table in candlelight—candles were a staple these days with blackouts common—on various subjects, except the economy, which Kevin declined to entertain. Kevin refused to make eye contact with Tessa.

The three travelers had showers. When the power returned, they washed their clothes. Kevin took a pair of pants and shirt from his father's wardrobe.

At bedtime, Tessa held out her hand to invite Kevin to sleep with her. He shook his head and went to the couch in the great room. *Give him time*, she told herself, as she went to bed alone.

# CHAPTER 15

At dawn the next morning, Kevin borrowed Richard's Accord to retrieve his arsenal. He returned to pick up Tessa and Mort for the drive to Cornell.

As they approached Ithaca, Kevin said to her, "Been back to the old neighborhood lately?" The two had lived in Cayuga Heights, a well-to-do neighborhood in northern Ithaca.

"Not for three years."

"You wouldn't recognize it. Every second or third house abandoned, old For Sale signs fallen down, lawns turned to chest-high weeds, hedges out of control, paint peeling, shingles stolen, windows gone, insides gutted; even the walls torn apart for the copper wiring. Has to be expected, I guess, when people hold a four hundred thousand-dollar mortgage on a house worth next to nothing. The houses with people still in them are shuttered and barred to keep the thieves and drug addicts at bay. And that's a well-off neighborhood."

"How did it go to hell so fast?"

"It creeps up without anyone noticing, I think. I used to visit mom every year. She'd say everything was pretty much the same, except the Fuhrmans on the next block lost their house after they lost their jobs. Next time it was the Stockers down the street who walked away from their mortgage. Next it was the Colwills next door, then the Cookes across the street, then the Logans kitty-corner. No one comes in to buy because no one has the money. And, before you know it, skids occupy the vacant houses, stealing from everyone around to support their drug habit, and you're in a ghetto."

They got to the lab and the two scientists got to work while Kevin observed. Tessa told Kevin, "Mort's mixing solutions in glass co-precipitation reactors. Cathode materials will settle at the bottom. We'll focus mainly on that to see what he recalls about the breakthrough cell."

After two hours, Kevin left them to their research for a few hours. He lined up at Target for some food, clothes, and two prepaid cell phones. He also tracked down ammunition for his rifle and handguns.

He returned as Tessa and Mort conversed about the stubborn research problem. Apparently things weren't progressing well.

"You're jumping all over the place. At least let's try eliminating some possibilities. What can't it be?" said Tessa.

"It can't be everything but what it is," said Mort.

Tessa rejoined, "That's deep, Mort. Deep shit."

Kevin said, "We have a production problem, and it's called Mort."

"Shut up and let me concentrate," said Mort.

"Oops. Guess I knocked his ponderous train of thought off the rusty rails again. Tess, join me for a few minutes and leave Mort to concentrate."

Out in the hall, the frustrated woman said, "I don't know if I've ever witnessed such a genius for failure. All we know is what anode and electrolyte compounds he used, but the cathode is the key, and he's clueless."

"I watched him for a couple of hours this morning, and I have a couple of observations I want to check with you." She nodded. "It's pretty obvious he's just a technician. He's methodical and he's careful, but he merely follows recipes that your father came up with. He does it by rote, without thinking about what he's doing. He labels it and gets on with the next recipe."

"So trying to get him to remember anything useful about it is hopeless?" Tessa said.

"Yup. All this trouble protecting that useless bastard, and he doesn't know a thing."

"But why did he come to me? I don't have it."

"What? He came to you?"

"At the graveyard when I buried my father, he introduced himself, said he thought my father was murdered, and told me about his dead family. Then he told me about the breakthrough."

"Jesus, I got it all backward. Why would he think he needed you?"

"For access to the computer program?"

"But that wouldn't help him if he did everything by rote." Kevin put his head back with eyes shut as if to say, *Oh, it was so obvious all along!* He said, "He thinks you can figure it out."

"Me?"

"He knows you spent years working on batteries with your father. He knows you devised the software to shortcut the testing process. Mort thinks you're the key to this. You're not using him; he's using you!" She gawped at him. He continued, "Can you figure it out?"

"God, Kev, I don't think so. I haven't been involved for coming up on three years now."

"So what? You have the brains, knowledge, and drive to finish what you and your dad started. He was just following the trail you set out. You said it yourself; your computer program narrowed down the candidates."

"There's a lot more to it than that. What you put into the computer model is the key. That was my father's knowledge."

"Let's worry about output for now. At the most basic level, your father was systematically testing what your computer model spit out, giving simple recipes to Mort. He tested them like a robot, having no idea of the underlying science. So, where did they leave off in South Dakota?"

"That's what I was hoping to find out working with him."

"Any clues at all from what Mort was doing?"

"It seemed random. At one point I was thinking it looked like something I had suggested to dad ... No. Dad said it was too radical."

"Remember what Mort said at one point when I was grilling him about his phone? He said he told his contact about Tessa's battery. He immediately corrected himself and said he meant your dad's battery, but maybe it wasn't a mistake. Maybe your father called it Tessa's battery. Is that possible?"

"Maybe ... Come to think of it, Mort also told some of the killers that I was the one who knew how to make the battery. I thought it was just to save his skin, but maybe he was telling the truth. On the other hand, it wouldn't make sense that Mort wouldn't just tell me if it was my idea."

"No? What use would he be, then? You'd have dealt him out right at the beginning. He's probably wracking his tiny brain figuring out how to get your idea without letting you know it's your idea, so he doesn't wind up with nothing."

She nodded.

"Think, then. What battery would your father call yours?"

"I need to explain a few basic concepts so my answer makes sense to you. Dad's work focused on the lithium-air cell. It uses carbon in the positive electrode, which reacts with oxygen from the air to produce an electrical current. Its theoretical energy densities are over a thousand times greater than lithium-ion, almost as good as gasoline! Theoretical. There were a lot of problems to overcome. The ultimate answer involves complicated chemistry, engineering, and probably nanotechnology. That's what we were pursuing at Cornell. My software modeled chemical interactions down to the level of quantum mechanics. I won't go into the technical details, but I had a novel idea I wanted to test.

"But I couldn't convince my father to try it. Our budget had been cut heading into the year, and supercomputer time for testing these things was expensive, developing prototypes even more so, so we had to be choosy. We had a big argument over it. It made sense to me, but he was dubious. He had blinders on in some respects; not open enough to different ways of thinking about the problem. I think it was his age or the booze or his extra-curricular activities, because when he was younger his research ideas were certainly radical. My idea was a small leap of faith off the path he'd blazed. Anyway, the

242

university shut down our program the next week, so it all became moot."

"Do you think your dad had a change of heart?"

"Well, what Mort was doing looked like what I had in mind, but he went way off base."

They walked back into the lab. Kevin went up to Mort, grabbed his shirt collar, and said, "Lie and you die! Did Tessa's father call the breakthrough Tessa's battery?"

Mort lowered his eyes and said, "Yes."

Her eyes opened wide. "I know what to do!"

*

Tessa used her software on Cornell's advanced supercomputer to design the molecule she'd theorized for validation. Printout in hand, she went back to the lab and gave it to Mort.

Kevin asked what the next step was.

She said, "He'll prepare the cathode material based on what I've given him. Then he'll wash, dry, mix, and heat it. It ends up as a black powder, which he'll put into silver pouches to make our test battery. We don't have the time, money, nor equipment to actually test our battery, but we can bring it to potential buyers."

By the time they left the lab that evening, Tessa and Mort had completed the early steps in the fabrication process. Tessa needed Mort's help for this and assured him she would give him a slice of the pie, though with all the trouble he'd caused, it would only be a sliver.

Tomorrow, Tessa would draw up the specifications on the computer to enable her to patent and sell the battery. She knew her father would have ensured the battery passed all the tests before declaring it the breakthrough he'd been seeking—and Mort confirmed the battery had passed all the tests—so she wasn't worried about further testing. That would be the responsibility of the company she sold it to.

All were in a joyous mood that evening at the dinner table. Tessa enthused to Richard what this battery would mean to the country—all the benefits of energy self-sufficiency—and to the world.

Richard said, "When you patent your battery, Cornell ought to award you a PhD. Hell, a Nobel isn't out of the question. I always knew you were exceptional, Tessa, but I've obviously underestimated you. You really are in a class by yourself."

She smiled and thanked him, but gave her father most of the credit.

But Richard, being Richard, went on. "I wonder, though, if you're being a little naïve about what this means. Long-term, you're right; this battery would be a boon to mankind, but think of the short-term implications, not just for the oil and gas industry, but for everyone who relies on it for their living. Saudis trying to stop you might only be the start. The American oil and gas industry has grown tremendously in the last decade; our proven reserves are far greater than Saudi Arabia's. The industry pays tens of billions a year to government coffers. And think of how many jobs depend on the industry; it must be in the millions. How will losing those jobs help our employment situation?"

"Dad," said Kevin in a tone that insinuated, *shut up!*

"And just restricting the picture to politics in America, think of how much money the oil and gas industry pays to elected officials for re-election and likely under the table to a lot of the sons-a-bitches. When you consider it, it's awfully naïve to expect the United States government to be on your side. They're probably aware of the Saudi initiative and are turning a blind eye. Who knows; maybe they're helping the assassins."

Kevin said, "Okay, Dad. Christ, you sure have a way of sucking the air out of a room. Cheer up, Tess. Dad's astoundingly cynical. It can't be that bad."

"No, Kev; he's right," said Tessa. "My dad probably knew it, too; that's why he kept it to himself, and why he kept me in the dark. Knowing dad, I bet he planned to keep everything secret for his own protection until he sold the patent. But Mort ruined that."

Here she gawked with hatred at Mort, who didn't notice as he ate spaghetti and garlic toast.

Tessa went on, "All I was thinking of was bringing this to fruition for my dad and, yes, for the world. But if I'd just stopped to think for one second, it's so obvious that too many people lose too much in the short run for this to survive. Even with our prototype in hand, I'm doomed. There are literally millions of people who would want me dead!"

She began crying.

"Tess, calm down. There must be a way around this."

"We have to run; all of us," Tessa said.

Richard said, "Maybe I overstated it, Tessa. The U.S. would have to worry about another country coming up with this technology and cornering the market, costing us the chance for energy self-sufficiency. If they're forward-looking enough, they should want this."

"But they aren't forward-looking, are they?" replied Tessa.

"It's easy to forget that the government isn't a single entity; it's thousands of agencies and departments and millions of people. I would imagine the great majority would be behind you, both out of self-interest and the nation's interest. Only the political types who can't see beyond the next election and the nefarious types who benefit from the energy status quo will be against you. Unfortunately, they have the power and control the purse strings, and they'll employ people like him," he said, gesturing to Kevin with his head, "to ensure they don't lose power or money."

"Yup, I'm just a mindless drone at the beck and call of the nefarious," said Kevin.

"Mindless, hardly. You're easily the smartest uneducated person I know."

"Thanks, Dad. You're the smartest pompous ass I know." Turning to Tessa, Kevin said, "Sell your battery. That removes the pressure on you."

*

On the way back to Cornell in the morning, Kevin asked what the next steps were. Tessa answered, "After I get the specifications down, I'll go to a lawyer to file a patent application. After that, we find a buyer."

"Okay. How long will all this take?" said Kevin.

"To get the patent? Used to be at least a year."

"A year!"

"More like two or three these days," Mort said from the back seat.

Kevin said to Tessa, "This is your fucking plan? Are we supposed to hide out for three goddamn years?"

"Don't get mad at me; I don't control the US Patent and Trademark Office."

"I was hoping I'd at least have your problems off my back with enough money to get away and stay away."

"My problems? It sounds like you plan on getting away without me."

Pretending to be her, he said, "Let's see. Door one: riches beyond belief, Nobel Prize, solve global warming, all the men on the planet wanting me. Door two: running for my life with a perennial loser, one step ahead of the law, two ahead of the outlaws, three ahead of starvation; very unlikely to live out the month. Hm. What ever shall I do?"

"Well, I choose you because I *love* you."

"Well, I won't let you because I love *you*."

"All those wonderful benefits you mentioned assume one of the millions of people who would lose from this battery doesn't kill me; that's wishful thinking. I want the mockup so I can find a buyer right away. We'll have to accept a lot less for the battery, probably, but I'm okay with a small percent and a down payment enough for *us* to get and stay away."

"I will *not* ruin your life. Once you're safe, I'm gone."

"Let's not have this argument now. I have a buyer in mind, and they're right here in Ithaca. Primet was one of our partners in EMC². " He looked at her quizzically. "Energy Materials Center at Cornell. Primet is near Ithaca College. I know the chairman and director; they tried to recruit me every time we met. They'll jump at the chance for the battery. I just hope it doesn't put them at risk."

They dropped Mort off at the lab to continue work on a rough prototype, and Tessa spent the morning typing the precise specifications into the computer. She saved it in several different, secure locations.

Kevin kept an eye on Tessa and on the Islamic Center website. There had been no update.

*

On the way back to check on Mort's progress, Kevin's phone rang. Only his father knew the number. He looked at Tessa with worried eyes. Pushing the button, he said, "Dad?"

"They're here," said his father.

"Who?"

"Asians. Two of them."

"Jesus, Dad, get the hell out of there!"

"Too late. I'm trapped."

"Did you call the cops?"

"I dialled 911 as soon as I saw the Geely come down the driveway. I'm on hold on my land line as we speak. Took them a good two minutes to even put me on hold. I'm talking to you on the prepaid phone you gave me so they won't know about you."

"Kevin?" asked Tessa.

"Triad at dad's place," he said as he ran to the car. Tessa ran with him.

Speaking to his father, he said, "Wait till they get in the house and catch them off guard. I'm on my way."

"Kevin, I love you," said Richard.

Crying, Kevin said, "I love you, too, Dad. I'm sorry for … everything."

"Me too."

"Let's not give up. When they're both in the house, shoot. Not till then."

"I'll try."

Kevin and Tessa got to his father's Accord. "Stay here," said Kevin. "This might be too dangerous."

"I'm coming!" she said.

They peeled out.

Richard whispered, "They're at the door." The dog started barking.

"Hide, Dad. Shoot first, don't ask questions."

Richard spoke up, "Hello, I have an emergency." Kevin was confused for a moment, but he realized the 911 call had been answered. His father said to the 911 operator, "Two men with guns are … Hello? Hello? Useless pricks!"

"Dad?" said Kevin, as his heart pounded.

"I got cut off."

The dog's barking continued. Kevin heard a shot. The barking ceased.

"Dad?"

Two more shots.

"Dad? Dad! Oh, Jesus!"

\*

"Dad?" said Kevin, running through the open front door, rifle in hand and stepping over the dead dog. He looked over and saw his father sprawled on the kitchen floor. "Dad!" he yelped, darting to him. He stood above his father, whose head was lying in a pool of blood. For a few moments all he could do was stand above him staring. There was a card left on the body that said, *A father for a son.*

Tessa said, "Kevin, I'm so sorry." She was crying.

Kevin fell to his knees, lifted his father under his arms, sat, and cradled his father's head. Tears streamed down his face. "I did this."

"No, Kev, it's not your fault."

"I ruined everything."

"No—"

"Yes! He was a great father, but I was such an incredible asshole to him. I ruined our relationship. You said it yourself, and you were right; I ruined their marriage."

"Oh, Kevin, it was a lot more complicated than—"

"I ruined her life, too. She died loving him, but he would never take her back because he thought she chose an ungrateful, good-for-nothing son over her husband. He never forgave her."

"That was his choice, not yours."

"It was my fault! And now look at him." He hung his head and repeated softly, "Look at him."

Tessa knelt next to Kevin and embraced him as he continued to cry. "You warned him, Kev."

"Why should a fifty-six-year-old man give up his home and his livelihood, and go on the run because his son is a fuckup?"

"You're the best man I know."

"God help you then."

After a few more minutes, Kevin lowered his father, kissed his forehead, and whispered, "I'm sorry, Dad. I love you." He got to his feet, took a deep breath through clenched jaw, and said, "The Triad did this."

"How do you know?"

"The Geely, the Asian men, this card. You heard Chan; he said I killed the boss's son, Sheng's son. This is payback. Well, it doesn't end here!"

"Kevin?"

"It ends with Sheng like this!" he screamed, pointing to his father's corpse.

"What can I do to help?"

"Stay as far away from me as possible."

"It'll be extremely dangerous; maybe I can help even the odds."

"Find out where Sheng lives, and get me everything on the neighborhood you can."

"What else?"

"Then I drop you at the university to get the rough prototype and sell it while I go to Syracuse. Come on. The police might show up at any time—or maybe it'll take them days."

The two quickly gathered a few supplies, including a shirt to replace the bloody one Kevin had on.

He looked sadly at his father one more time, and they ran out to the Accord.

# CHAPTER 16

Their hearts pounded as a police car came up behind them with lights and siren going. It had been hiding behind an old billboard.

"What should I do, pull over?" said Tessa.

"You know I'm wanted for murder."

"No one would know it's us driving your father's car. He's probably just stopping us because I was speeding."

"They might think we murdered him and stole the car if they connect the 911 call to his car."

"He didn't even get to report his emergency before they cut him off."

"But they must have got his number and address. Sooner or later they'll put two and two together … But probably not this soon. Pull over."

As Kevin watched intently with his hand clutching the 1911 in his pocket, the officer sat in his car. Tessa warned, "Kevin, do *not* shoot a cop."

"If he arrests me, I'm dead. The rifle that shot the bullets that finished the lieutenant governor and two other assholes is in the trunk. Open and shut case."

"God, Kevin, we can bet they take murdering cops seriously. And I'll be considered an accomplice, so I'll be wanted for capital murder! Please don't shoot him!"

"I get arrested, you're defenseless; you'll be dead in no time. It's him or us."

"Shit. Here he comes."

"Calm down, Tessa. You look guilty of killing Jesus. His hand isn't on his revolver. That's a good sign." He put his gun under the seat.

The officer walked to Tessa's window and said, "License and registration, ma'am."

Tessa and Kevin looked at the trooper. He was a balding, paunchy man. Kevin fished the ownership papers out of the glove box as Tessa gave him her license. "Do you know how fast you were going?"

"No, sir," she said as she handed him her license.

"Well, Miss Sharp, the fine for going thirty-seven miles per hour over the limit is a thousand dollars."

"A thousand! Newbucks?"

"Yes, ma'am," he said, as he started to write out the ticket.

"Uh, what about, uh, a hundred cash?" she stuttered.

"That better not be a bribe attempt, ma'am. New York State Police are not corrupt; we're professionals."

"Two hundred?" said Kevin.

"That does it. Both of you out of the car; you're under arrest."

Kevin got out of the car and stomped around to the officer. "Kevin!" shouted Tessa as she, too, exited the car.

The trooper put his hand on his gun and said, "Stay back, sir!"

But Kevin was upon him in no time. He grabbed the man's arm, twisted him around, and put his arm around his neck. He took out the trooper's gun and tossed it aside.

"You're making things much worse for yourself," said the officer in a distinctly less authoritative voice.

Through gritted teeth, Kevin said, "You fat, useless piece of garbage. My father called 911, but he was cut off. He was murdered soon afterward."

"I don't know anything about a 911 call."

"You wouldn't, no. *The police took five minutes to answer the fucking phone then they cut him off!* Here you are not even five miles from his house handing out speeding tickets because your professional police force is desperate to get cash to pay all you fat, lazy, over-the-hill cocksuckers *to hand out fucking tickets*. How long have you been here trapping speeders? Were you here when he was shot?"

"I don't know when he was shot."

"A half hour ago. Were you here?" Kevin repeated at top volume.

"You're choking me. Let go or—"

"Or what?" The alarmed man said nothing. Sweat poured off his brow.

"Kevin, calm down," said Tessa.

Ignoring her, Kevin continued, "Answer my question."

"I don't know!"

"You were here, weren't you?"

"Kevin!" said Tessa.

"You have the fucking nerve to claim to be a professional, writing tickets while desperate people phoning for help are being ignored? What is your price, anyway, Mr. Fucking Professional Police Officer, sir? Three, four hundred?"

"I've never accepted a bribe in my life."

"Good for you. Ever bothered to try and stop a *murder*?"

"Yes! That's what I should be doing, but the brass tells me I need to meet my quota for tickets because the state doesn't give us nearly what we need to do our job. Let me go, for Christ's sake." Kevin released him. "You think I like this? Handing out tickets on patrol at age fifty-fucking-four? I was supposed to retire next year, but now retirement age is sixty-goddamn-seven—thirteen more years of this. Christ, pick up my gun and shoot me now. They laid off pretty much everyone under age forty, so people with decades of policing experience have to do this shit!"

"Alright, calm down. I have no intention of hurting you, but we now have a problem, since I've collared a cop."

"Get the hell out of here, and we'll forget this, and I'll go investigate this murder. Who was it and what's the address?"

Kevin told him the address but said the name "Richard Cahill."

"I'll drive," he told Tessa.

"Thank you, Officer," said Tessa as she went around and got into the car.

With one leg in the car, Kevin turned back to the trooper and handed the officer the card that was left on his father's body. "The murderers left this on his body."

"A father for a son?"

"Two weeks ago in Syracuse, I stopped the kidnapping of a teenage girl. I worked security for the Loomis Hill Neighborhood Association in Syracuse. I ended up killing both kidnappers—Syracuse Police investigated and cleared me. One of the kidnappers was Sheng Wei, who happened to be the son of Sheng Gang, upstate ringleader of the Triad."

"Triad?" said the officer with a concerned expression. Kevin nodded. "Shit."

"Kind of makes your head turtle and your bag retract, huh?"

They paused as a car passed by.

"So they killed your father for payback," concluded the officer.

"Yup. And nothing against you, Officer, but I'm not holding my breath waiting for the state police to swoop down on them and haul him off to prison."

"Well, I'll pass this information up the line."

As Kevin turned to get back into the car, the officer picked up his gun, pointed it at Kevin, and said, "Hands up! You're under arrest for the murder of Lieutenant Governor Warner."

"Asshole," said Kevin.

"Out of the car, lady."

Tessa got out, put both hands, which held the Colt 1911, on the roof of the car, and said, "Drop your gun or I drop you!" The officer sighed and obeyed.

Kevin picked up the weapon and said, "Wow, woman, you've found your calling."

She flashed him a go-to-hell look as she continued to point the gun at the trooper.

Kevin's expression turned furious as he marched to the officer, grabbed his collar, and pointed the gun at his temple.

"Kevin! Don't hurt him," ordered Tessa.

Kevin said to the officer, "Tell me why you're worried about the killing of a scumbag who was obviously on the payroll of the Mexican mob, and not my father who never broke a law in his life."

"The police will investigate both murders. You're wanted in connection with that murder and those of two businessmen—"

"Businessmen! They were Mexican mob bosses, you moron. People who murder Americans every day, including my *mother*! But the cops didn't worry about that either." Now Kevin was livid.

"Kevin, stay calm," said Tessa.

"I was just doing my job."

"Your job was to help my father. He dialled 911, but you cut him off!"

Kevin screamed this with such ire, the officer began to panic for his life. "I have two children!"

"Children my age don't count," Kevin growled as he moved the gun around to the back of the man's head.

"Kevin!" screamed Tessa. She ran around the car to grab his arm and settle him down. She said, "I love you, but I won't stay with a cold-blooded killer. *Do not cross this line.*"

He stood for a moment looking at her, then nodded. Turning the officer to face the car, he said, "Put your hands on top of the car." The man did so, and Kevin frisked him. Finding no weapons, he confiscated the radio, handcuffed his hands behind his back, and led the man back to his cruiser. He opened the trunk and looked for something to gag his prisoner. A roll of duct tape provided the solution.

"I'm kind of claustrophobic," said the man.

Kevin extended his lower lip and replied in a childish voice, "Ah, gee, I wish I had a teddy bear and some warm milk in a Sippy cup to soothe your poor little feelers." He gagged the officer, put him into the trunk, and closed it.

The two discussed what to do with the police officer. Tessa said leaving him in the trunk was cruel and maybe even dangerous if it got too hot. Kevin suggested handcuffing him to a tree deep in the woods, but Tessa argued he might never be found. "How about your father's basement?" she said. "They'll get there sooner or later."

"It might be too soon. We need to get away."

They determined their best option was to handcuff him to a post in an old barn. Kevin knew just the one, about a half mile from his father's. Speaking loud enough for the officer to overhear, Kevin told Tessa, "We need to get out of the state right away. They might be on the lookout for my father's car. Let's get to Ohio and steal another car there, then get to the West Coast somewhere."

Kevin drove the police car back toward his father's house, with Tessa following in the Accord. But about a mile from his objective he brought the car to a quick halt. He tossed the police radio out the window, turned the car around, and motioned for Tessa to follow.

They sped away, taking several turns to shake anyone who might be following. Kevin pulled into a dirt driveway on a forsaken farm and pulled into a derelict barn. Tessa stopped outside.

"What happened?" she asked.

"Over the police radio I heard them say the Defense Intelligence Agency was at the Idle place. I couldn't respond, obviously, so I threw the radio out."

"Why the DIA?"

"Excellent question. They must've been listening in on the 911 call. They don't give a shit about a few dead mobsters, so it must have to do with your battery. Maybe looking for you to offer help. Or to kill you, if dad was right. Whichever, I can't go near them. You'll have to decide for yourself."

"I'm staying with you."

He opened the trunk, hauled the cop out, and handcuffed him to a post.

The man shook his head. Tessa removed the gag. He said, "You can't leave me here. I might never be found."

"I'll tell someone once we're safely away," Tessa said.

The man tried to argue, but the two left him there. Kevin drove the police car a couple of miles down the road to impede any search for the officer. To Ithaca they rushed in the Accord to get the test battery and try to sell it to Primet.

*

Finding no trace of Mort or the prototype cell at the lab, Tessa and Kevin proceeded to Primet. Asking to see the director, they were shown to a meeting room. Michael Walsh showed up just two minutes later.

He opened with, "Tessa! Oh, now this is starting to make sense."

"Pardon me?" she said as she shook his hand.

"A Mr. Wood came by about an hour ago with an 18650 battery cell, trying to sell it."

"That son of a bitch!" said Tessa.

"He made some incredible claims for this battery. I didn't believe him because he couldn't answer any of my questions about its characteristics."

"It's my battery; well, mine and my father's."

"That I believe."

"Where is he?" asked Kevin.

"Oh, Michael Walsh, this is Kevin Idle."

The men shook hands, and Michael answered Kevin. "He left maybe a half hour ago."

Kevin said, "He took the prototype?" Michael nodded. "I'll go find him."

Kevin left.

Michael said, "Please tell me this breakthrough is true and you want to partner with Primet."

"Mike, my father is dead; I'm pretty sure the Saudis had him killed."

Michael's face showed his shock. "Shit, Tessa, I'm sorry."

"And they've been trying to kill me and Mort."

"Christ. How does Wood fit into this?"

"Dad's lab assistant in South Dakota. He built and tested the original prototype, which the killers stole. We're only alive because of Kevin. I want nothing more than to sell Primet this battery, but I can't let you buy it without knowing the risks."

"This is a lot to take in. I need to call some people in here to discuss this. Do you have the specs?"

Tessa took out a USB flash drive and handed it to Michael.

He said, "Energy density as good as gasoline?"

"Yes."

"Tested thoroughly?"

"My father directed that, yes, and Mort assured me it passed everything, but the killers destroyed the data. You'll need to do all the testing again."

"My God, Tessa, this is what we've spent our working lives striving for. What would you want for this?"

"Whatever you think is fair."

"We'll work something out. We need to move fast on this if Wood is trying to sell it to one of our competitors."

Michael called the chairman, his senior scientists, and his lawyer into the room. As the two waited for the others, Tessa looked at the Islamic Center website and Michael looked at the battery specs. Their jaws dropped in unison.

*

Kevin had left Primet and headed north toward Cornell, keeping an eye out for Mort. As he neared Cornell, flashing lights came up behind him. His heart beating fast, he took the next turn and held his breath, looking in the mirror. The police cruiser passed by. Kevin took a deep breath and pulled a U-turn. He drove up to the intersection only to see another cop car race by, followed by an ambulance.

He decided to take the risk of driving to his intended destination, the Cornell engineering quad, which was the only place he could think of to look for Mort. Passing by the commotion, he glanced over and saw a fat man sprawled on the ground in a lake of blood.

*

Tessa had sprinted to the front entrance of Primet to look for Kevin when she saw the Islamic Center webpage flashing Ithaca, NY. She knew the chances of seeing him were slim, but she had to do something to warn Kevin. But what? He always kept his phone off unless he expected a call, just in case. She'd tried it, of course, but he hadn't answered.

As she ran out the front entrance to do nothing more than look up and down the road for him, the Accord screamed to a stop right in front of her.

"Get in!" he said.

"I haven't finished here yet."

"Mort's dead; we need to leave right now."

After a few moments taking in this latest news, horror-struck, she said, "You said my only chance was to sell the battery. Primet wants it. We need to take the chance of staying for a little while."

He reluctantly agreed. Tessa ran back to the meeting room while Kevin parked. He attracted negative attention from the security guards with his Accuracy rifle on one shoulder and an M4 on the other, but the director said it was okay that this man stand guard at the front entrance.

In the meeting, concerns were raised for the safety of the firm's employees, but they were drowned out by the prospect of tens of billions of dollars. This was the Holy Grail dropped on their doorstep, and they weren't about to shut it out.

The scientists were wowed by the potential of the molecule and were anxious to start testing.

Given the risk and the desperation of the inventor to sell the rights to the battery, the company began with a lowball offer. Tessa immediately agreed to a twenty-five percent share of the profits from the battery. They drafted a letter of agreement right away, specifying that the battery had to pass all the standard tests for the agreement to hold. It was all completed within the hour.

Tessa asked for and received three perks: an annual salary of a hundred thousand new dollars, a laptop, and the use of a company car to hold her over until the revenue started coming in; that would likely be at least three years. These were added to the agreement as a loan. If the battery wasn't what everyone thought, she'd have to return the car and the cash. She left the meeting with a signed copy of the agreement, keys for a 2019 Ford Fusion, a Dell laptop, and a ten thousand dollar advance.

She checked the website once more and was shocked to see the reward raised to fifty million new dollars for her life alone. Mort's picture was already removed.

She took a moment to send an anonymous email to the police informing them of the location of the officer in the barn.

She dashed out to Kevin with the news of the sale and the new bounty on her head.

"They found the prototype, no doubt," said Kevin. "They know you've recreated it. We have to get the word out about the sale to Primet—"

"No," said Tessa.

"What?"

"It would shift pressure to them. The battery and all the people here are much safer if they can keep this under wraps for the time being."

"Tough. Keeping the focus on you leaves you extremely vulnerable."

"I already agreed to it. It was my idea."

"Jesus, Tessa! What was the fucking point of selling, then?"

"To bring the battery to life."

"For the world?"

"You say that as if I'm an egoist. Well, maybe I am. It's my invention, and I'm damn proud of it. If this is all I ever accomplish, it's more than enough. It'll make the world a much better place for everyone, eventually. If I have to die to bring that about, so be it. And it's not my right to pass my problems on to a whole new group of people."

"No, just me."

"You don't have to stay with me if you don't want."

"Really? I can walk out that door free from you?" She nodded slowly, trying to disguise her fear.

"You'd be dead before the day is out. Christ, you'll be lucky to survive the day *with* me."

She showed him the cash and told him about the salary. "Let's get out of the country and stay underneath the radar for a few years. It's on me," she said with a smile.

"Much, much easier said than done. Even getting away from Ithaca is iffy. They'll be looking for a silver Accord."

She held out the Ford keys with another smile.

A security guard led them to Tessa's new car and took the keys to hide the Accord.

Kevin wouldn't entertain the thought of leaving the country without first letting the Triad boss know what he thought of having his father killed. He added one other task to his to-do list as well.

"Tess, I think we ought to pay a visit to the Islamic Center in D.C. to demonstrate our displeasure. What do you think?" he said as they drove east along Route 79, southeast of Ithaca.

"I love the idea in theory, but isn't it likely to get us killed?"

"We're likely to get killed regardless of what we do. Small possibility if we kill the bastard who put up the reward, we live another day. And if not, at least we kill the bastard who put up the reward."

"I can't believe I'm saying this, but let's get the son of a bitch."

"Use that fancy new computer of yours to see if we can find out who he is."

Tessa discovered little about the organization, but did find out the identity of the man who administered the computer system for the Center. She tracked down his address. She also got the information Kevin had asked for regarding the Sheng clan in Syracuse.

It was too late to drive the six hours to Washington that evening, so they stopped at a cheap motel in central Pennsylvania.

# CHAPTER 17

Early the next morning, they set off for Washington. At Harrisburg, they ran into a huge traffic jam, which was rare these days, even at rush hour. Tessa turned on the radio and learned that state workers had walked off the job and were protesting throughout the state capital. The government had decided to impose a four-day week along with a fifteen percent salary and benefits rollback on the entire civil service. Unimpressed, the union directed its members to defy the law, walk off the job, and stage various antics, such as lining trucks across all lanes of I-81 just north of the Pennsylvania capital and crawling along at two miles per hour.

Among the thousands stuck in the mess that ensued were Tessa and Kevin. Kevin was fit to be tied. "These sons of bitches have jobs; and if it's like New York, they only have them because they had enough seniority to screw everyone who didn't have enough seniority by refusing to accept cutbacks. So they kept their full salaries and benefits while half their colleagues were laid off. Now they're asked to share the tiniest part of the pain that we've been suffering for *years*, and they have the fucking nerve to protest? And to cause more suffering to the people who pay their salaries?"

He lined up for the next exit, but even that was crawling. They eventually found their way to a road paralleling the highway. Spotting the line of pickup trucks causing the slowdown, he stopped the car and opened his window. "Fuckers!" he screamed. They took no notice. They seemed to take the blaring horns as support for what they were doing, waving their left hand out the window.

"Not a frigging cop in sight, of course," said Kevin to Tessa.

"No, they're going to be cut back, too," pointed out Tessa.

Another line of pickups had caused a similar jam in the opposite direction. I-81 looked like a parking lot.

One frustrated driver tried to pass on the shoulder next to the rightmost lane, but he was cut off by the closest truck and driven into the guardrail. The four drivers hurled abuse: "Scab!" and other choice epithets.

"Oh, those fuckers!" bellowed Kevin.

"Kevin? What are you … Kevin. Come back!"

He ran out onto the highway and stood in front of the truck in the fast lane. It kept coming. He stood his ground. It kept coming. He stayed put.

Tessa drove a couple of hundred feet up the side road where trees hid the car from the highway to lessen the chance of anyone catching their license plate. People were bound to use their phones to video this. She ran back to see the truck against his legs, still moving. Kevin crawled up onto the windshield. Unable to see, the driver got out and pulled Kevin off the truck. Kevin punched the man in the cheek. The man tried to return the favor, but Kevin blocked it and hit him again. He went down.

A colleague got out of the truck next to his to come to the rescue. But he, too, hit the ground. Three men from the other two trucks got out.

"Kevin, watch out!" yelled Tessa.

He took out his gun and shot into the air, screaming, "Run away." They started to run. "Faster!" he insisted, sending a bullet into the ground just behind them. They sprinted.

Drivers on both sides of the highway witnessing this had stayed in their cars to this point. Kevin got into the first truck and drove it off the road onto the grass strip dividing the highway. When he did the same with the second, smashing it into the first one, commuters began exiting their vehicles and clapping. By the time he plowed the fourth truck into the third, second, and first, the cheering had hit a crescendo. He bowed to his admirers, ran back with Tessa to the car. They drove up to the next highway entrance for their exit from Harrisburg.

She laughed for half an hour.

*

A handsome, casually-attired blond man sat on a bar stool in the fancy hotel sipping a scotch on the rocks. He looked bored.

Gazing at the ice cubes and trying to forget his troubles, he noticed movement to his left. A dazzling blonde took the seat next to him. He quickly covered his wedding ring with his right hand and stealthily removed it.

She wore a slinky red dress that stopped just short of her knees, but a well-placed slit left a generous portion of her fabulous legs on display when crossed. But her legs had some stiff competition, for the dress also plunged from the top to beautifully display her comely breasts. As if bouncing between them and back down to her legs wasn't diverting enough, a glance up brought into view the most spectacular eyes he'd ever seen. *My God!*

She gazed into his eyes and said, "Buy me a drink?"

A girl this beautiful was seldom this forward, not with him at least. *A call girl*, he thought, but no ordinary one; too pretty, and too classy. Maybe one of those high-priced escort girls he'd read about who lived off politicians and top bureaucrats in Washington DC. Must be *very* expensive.

"What'll you have?" he asked.

"Martini."

He ordered it.

"You weren't very subtle," she said. He looked at her for an explanation. "Your ring. I don't care that you're married."

*She is a call girl*, he concluded.

"Uh, I don't know how to ask this—"

"Yes, I am."

"Uh, how much."

"Not so fast. A girl likes a bit of romance. Buy me dinner and let's get to know each other a little first."

"But if I, uh, can't afford—"

"If you have to ask, you can't."

She got up to leave.

"Wait! Please stay. I'll buy you dinner."

The two moved to a table and ordered dinner. She was smart and well-spoken. *Must have been forced into this by the depression*, he thought. *Probably makes a hundred times what I do*. She told him she was from San Francisco and went to Berkeley. He told her he was from Maryland, went to the University of Virginia, and worked as an advisor to a senator he wouldn't name. He admitted to being married with two children.

After dinner, they went to his room upstairs. Before going further, there was the matter of the price. It was worse than he thought. Five thousand newbucks for two hours; ten thousand would buy him the whole night with her.

"Second thoughts?" she said.

"Just working out a way to hide this from Stacy."

"Well, you work that out and I'll change." She held out her sizable pocketbook and said, "I have a red negligee, a black mini-dress, and a businesswoman's suit. If I'm staying all night I can use it all."

"Start with the suit."

"Be right back."

Five minutes later, she opened the door and stepped out. She wore black shoes with one-inch heels, a tight, black skirt that fell to her knees, a black jacket that hugged her curves, and a white blouse with the collar pulled out over that of the jacket. Her hair was pulled up into a bun.

"All night!" he said, sitting on the bed.

She sat next to him, crossed her legs, and smiled. "We can play office with me as the boss or you as the boss, or I can do a striptease—"

"Striptease!"

She selected a funk channel on the cable TV. While she waited for a song to finish, she played with his hair. She stepped back to the middle of the room.

"Blowin' My Mind" by Solo began. She commenced her dance by jutting her right hip out and unclipping her hair, letting it fall, and flipping it out over her shoulders. She ran her hands behind her ears, down her neck, and down to her stomach. Flashing him a gorgeous smile, she sauntered toward him. She stopped a few feet from him, swayed her hips back and forth to the beat, her hands holding onto the bottom of her jacket. She smiled again, strutted closer, and as she swung her hips, she spread her legs and bent her knees to bring her face level with his. While continuing to sway, she wrinkled her nose, dug her top teeth into her bottom lip, and cast a sultry look at him that hardened him immediately.

*Christ, she's good!*

She exaggerated her swaying as she stood upright and unbuttoned her jacket, all the while altering between an innocent smile and a salacious look that drove him wild. Opening her jacket wide, she put her hands on her sides and drew them up to her breasts and squeezed. Still moving her hips to and fro, she bent forward to show off her cleavage.

She took three steps back, still rhythmically moving her body back and forth and up and down to the beat; she turned sideways, pulled her right sleeve off, then her left as she stuck out her backside. She removed her jacket and tossed it onto his head. He brushed it away so as not to miss a second of this enticing entertainment.

She pranced toward him again, turned her back to him, and moved her hips in a circular motion as she tried to undo the button on the top of her skirt. It was stubborn and took her a few seconds. She opened her mouth and smiled as if to say, *It's stuck*! But she got it and smoothly lowered the zipper. She shimmied back to stand a foot from his face, bent over, and pulled down the skirt, revealing lacy pink, sheer panties. Continuing the hip rotation, she stepped out of her skirt, kicked it aside, and turned back toward him.

Taking two steps back, she resumed her swaying motion, back and forth, up and down to the beat, while unbuttoning her blouse. She opened it, pulled it off, and tossed it onto his head.

There it stayed for half a second.

She put her finger into her mouth and pretended to bite down on it, which for some reason was a turn on, especially when she closed her mouth on it, pulled it out, and drew it down between her breasts. Then she put both hands behind her head, pulled her hair up, and strode toward him, still swaying back and forth, up and down to the beat. She did the circular motion with her torso again, this time facing him. He didn't know where to look. Her perfect legs? Her perfect breasts? Her narrow waist curving out to her hips? Between her legs where he could see pubic hair through the panties? It was too much! He was desperate to ravish her.

She bent her knees so her face was within a few inches of his and mouthed, *I want you*. Still swaying, she put her palms flat against her hips, pulled them up under her bra, and pushed it up off her breasts. She held them for a minute to tease him, then removed her hands to reveal more of her perfection. She bent her knees and spread her legs again to bring her breasts to his mouth. He kissed both. She wagged her finger at him with a lascivious grin. Crossing her arms, she lifted her bra over her head and tossed it onto his head. He left that in place.

Stepping back again, she displayed herself swaying back and forth, up and down to the beat. She sashayed back to him, turned sideways, jutted out her rear to give him a side view. She turned her back to him, resumed the whirling motion of her hips, put her thumbs inside the waistline of her panties, and moved back so her butt was a few inches from his nose. Ceasing all motion, she turned her eyes back to his, then slowly bent over while pulling down her panties. She held that pose for a few seconds, enjoying his unalloyed exhilaration. He had to squeeze the muscles in his crotch to preclude coming. She turned and hung the panties on his right ear.

She stood upright again, sashayed away, and continued swaying naked before him. For the next two minutes she continued her dance, unabashedly displaying her magnificence, casting her bedroom eyes at him and using her hands to highlight different parts of her figure, now subtly, now brazenly.

Under the latter category, as the song faded down, she draped her right thigh over his left shoulder and used her fingers to give him a peek inside.

This started him shuddering and panting, so she quickly unbuttoned and unzipped him, pulled it out, and lowered herself on him. She had just absorbed the full extent of him when he exploded inside her.

She burst out laughing.

"That's by far the most excited I've ever been," he said, still panting. "I'm actually lightheaded."

"You like me as a blonde, I see," said Tessa.

Kevin replied breathlessly, "Uh huh." She grinned. He added, "but I prefer your natural color."

"Good answer. You're cuter with black hair, but I like a little variety now and then."

"Oh? Better not get married then."

"I was just kidding."

The two had decided to spend a day in Washington shopping and sightseeing, like a normal couple in normal times; a day where they would try to forget their enormous problems and just enjoy themselves. They dyed their hair to help disguise themselves. She suggested the sexual role play, which he jumped at. It was the best night of their lives.

*

The following morning, they drove by the Islamic Center to satisfy their curiosity. Next, they checked out the address for a Mr. Fahim Jamil. It was a secure apartment building downtown, risky to break in.

Just before noon, they parked a hundred feet down the street from the apartment building on Virginia Avenue, hoping to see an old grey Volkswagen Golf return its owner home for lunch. No such luck, so they went for lunch and passed a few hours in a nearby park.

At 4 PM, they were parked under a shade tree in front of Mr. Jamil's apartment building. Kevin noticed the garage door leading to the underground parking stayed open for about fifteen seconds after a car went through. When a car exited at 4:38, he raced into the structure and backed into a parking space that gave him a good view of the first level.

Eighty-seven minutes later, the Volkswagen passed by and went down a level. Tessa, who was now in the driver's seat, followed in her Ford. As a bearded man in a white headdress got out of the car, Kevin darted out, and without a word, twice smashed the man in the face with his fist. Down he went, stunned but still conscious. Kevin kicked him in the head to alter his state of consciousness. He quickly picked up the man and deposited him in the Ford's trunk. With duct tape, he bound and gagged Mr. Jamil.

Tessa hastened to the exit, crossed the Theodore Roosevelt Memorial Bridge, went up the George Washington Memorial Parkway, and turned in to Fort Marcy Park. There they admired Civil War cannons and wildflowers, hiked a bit of the Potomac Heritage Trail, and beat a recalcitrant computer programmer.

The man had thus far admitted creating and updating the webpage, and gave Tessa the information she needed to do her own update, but refused to say who had given him orders. Tessa was uncomfortable with the beating, but not as uncomfortable as Mr. Jamil.

Kevin pulled out the Colt 1911 with silencer. He pointed the gun at the man's head and asked again for the name of the person behind the assassination. "Last chance, Jamil." The man whimpered, but volunteered no information. Kevin shot him in the thigh. The hapless man cried out as Tessa winced and turned her head. Kevin quickly covered his mouth. Once the screaming subsided, he let go and pointed the gun at Jamil's right shoulder.

"Abdullah al-Najimi!"

"Who is he, and where can we find him?"

"He's an imam at the Dar Al-Hijrah mosque."

"And where is that?"

"Uh, Seven Corners, maybe six or seven miles south of here."

"What's he look like?"

"Uh, he's old; chubby; glasses; he has a long untrimmed, grey beard. I need something for the pain!"

"His car?"

"Black Mercedes."

"Did he put up the money?"

"I don't know! He just told me what to put on the website."

Kevin cracked his head with the gun butt.

He and Tessa jogged back to the car.

"I'm surprised you didn't kill him," Tessa said. "You're improving under my influence."

"He'll bleed to death soon; I didn't want to waste another bullet."

"Maybe you're not improving."

Tessa located the mosque with Google Maps, and the two drove there. They parked beside the Dar Al-Hijrah Islamic Center and kept a watch on a black Mercedes sedan.

A little before 9 PM, a man matching the description Jamil had provided got into the Mercedes. He took a left out of the parking lot and another left onto Leesburg Pike. Tessa did a U-turn and followed him. He turned right at the first set of lights. They followed the man through a forested neighborhood, where at least half the houses were still well-kept; only about a quarter had been abandoned. They ended up passing by a modern-looking house where the man parked in the driveway. Tessa parked down the street.

"Ugly house, but right on the lake," Kevin said. "Pretty impressive for a cleric."

The two walked right up to the house in the dark. Kevin knocked on the door. The imam answered.

Kevin said, "Do you have Jesus in your life, sir? We're from the Church of Latter-Day Saints."

The man looked at him as if to say, *Don't you see how I'm dressed, you fool?* He shook his head, waved a hand to dismiss them, and tried to shut the door, but Kevin put his hand out and stopped it. "Leave or I will call the pol—" the man got out before Kevin's big hand squeezed his throat and pushed him inside. Tessa followed and closed the door.

"Check the house for anyone else," Kevin told Tessa. She checked quickly and returned with the news there was no one else.

Kevin made sure he had the right man. "You al-Najimi?"

"Yes. I'm imam of—"

"I know what you are."

"What do you want?"

"You don't know my friend?"

"No."

"Does Tessa Sharp ring a bell?"

The man's eyes and mouth gave opposite answers. Kevin gave him the Jamil treatment, hitting him hard twice in the face. The man fell to the floor, bleeding and moaning.

"Who's behind this?"

The man shook his head and claimed, "I don't know what you're talking about!"

"Who's putting up the fifty million dollars to kill Tessa Sharp?"

"What are you talking—"

Kevin broke the man's nose. Blood poured out of it.

"You've put us through hell, al-Najimi. We know why, but we need to know who's bankrolling this, so we can personally thank the fucker."

Kevin pulled out his 1911 and held it to the man's head.

"If you shoot me, Allah will strike you down!"

Kevin smiled and shot the man in the thigh. He hollered in pain. Kevin looked around and said, "Nothing. No Allah."

The imam said, "If you let me die, you will burn forever in hellfire!"

Kevin replied, "That's what's in store for me anyway according to your hellish religion, so I guess I have nothing to lose by killing you."

"You can repent! Accept Allah and you will be saved."

"I can do that?"

"Yes. Accept Allah and you will go to heaven."

"Even though I already shot you?"

"Yes. His forgiveness is all generous."

"Then I'll ask his forgiveness after I kill you."

"No! Killing an imam is, uh, unforgivable."

"You're sending mixed messages here. Anyway, we've already proven Allah doesn't exist. This time we'll test Jesus. Lord Jesus Christ, if you exist, help this bullet go straight and true into this infidel's left eye."

"No!"

Kevin shot; the bullet went into the imam's shoulder. The imam again cried in pain. "If Jesus exists, he's a lousy shot," concluded Kevin.

"Try Muhammad," said Tessa.

"Ooo. Invoking him is dangerous with millions of brain-dead Muslims ready to attack at the least whiff of an insult—and this on behalf of a man who deflowered his nine-year-old wife. But I'll give it a shot."

"No! Don't kill me! Ahmed al-Zayd is providing the funds."

"Of course. Who the hell is that?"

"Ah!" he groaned in pain. "Take me to the hospital, and I will tell you."

"Tell me, and I'll take you to the hospital."

"I don't trust you."

"Then die."

"Please don't let me die."

"What are you worried about? Do you believe in heaven or not? Where's that good old Muslim blow-yourself-up-and-take-a-thousand-infidel-children-with-you spirit?"

"I ... I don't wish to die."

"No, imams never do. That's only for the moronic young zealots. Tell Allah for me, fuck you," he said as he put the gun to the man's temple.

"He works at the Saudi Arabian Embassy! Now take me to the hospital."

"Sorry to tell you, imam, but you were dead the minute I shot your femoral artery. No way you're making it to the hospital."

"You'll burn—"

Kevin shot the man in the temple.

Tessa shook her head, not so much at the latest killing as at her acquiescence. She had to admit, she felt good knowing this particular fiend was dead. The cruelty was appalling, but she felt good. She was less humane now, she knew, but that's what comes of being marked for death by evil men. Stay humane and you die.

On the way back to the city, Tessa used her skills on the computer to find the embassy, to update the website so that it now flashed Portland, Oregon, and to look up Ahmed al-Zayd. She said, "He's a Saudi, a cousin of Prince Sultan. He *is* a diplomat at the Washington embassy. He's rumored to be a heavy hitter in the Muslim Brotherhood in America and in the Council on American-Islamic Relations."

"Do we have a picture of him?"

She held up the screen, which he glanced at as he drove.

They approached the embassy slowly. Across the street was the Watergate complex. They decided against staying the night at the infamous hotel; too risky being so close to the hornet's nest. Leery of cameras that would inevitably surround an embassy, they looked for a spot down the street to park the next morning and keep an eye on the building for their quarry. Unfortunately, there was no good vantage point on nearby streets. Also, the 11 PM curfew—which Washington DC had been under for months because of incessant protests marches and rioting—was nigh, so they decided they had to take the chance of checking into the Watergate Hotel.

# CHAPTER 18

The next morning after breakfast, the two donned hats and sunglasses and walked around the block, trying to find a good place to camp out and watch for al-Zayd, but were again stymied. The Watergate buildings with private residences were patrolled by armed guards, standard in 2020 for upscale condominiums. One Watergate office building was across the street from the embassy entrance; it would have been ideal for sniping, and probably had ample empty offices, but again, security was tight.

Frustrated, the pair returned to their hotel room. Tessa checked the website and it no longer existed. They knew when neither man showed up for work that morning, the Saudis would take action quickly. That also meant that the manhunt would likely focus on Washington DC.

Around noon, they went down to the Potomac Lounge across from the main lobby in the hotel for a bite to eat. They had decided that the wise course of action was to leave the city for now. Neither wanted to give up on the idea of getting this man, but for now it was too dangerous.

As they called for the check, four bearded men walked in. Kevin's eyes opened wide. He said, "Don't turn around." Her eyes, too, gaped. "Our target just walked in with what look to be three bodyguards."

"Are they looking for us?" she asked.

"He's looking around, but his ugly eyes didn't linger on me. I doubt he would come looking for us, anyway. He doesn't get his hands dirty, I'm sure."

The men stood at the entrance to the lounge, just a few feet from Tessa, speaking in Arabic. When a waiter passed al-Zayd, he grabbed his elbow and said, "She never showed up. This will not go unpunished."

"Brittany?" asked the waiter. The man nodded. "I'm sorry, Mr. al-Zayd, but I haven't seen her."

"Then get me another one! I want her here within twenty minutes. I'm leaving the country tonight."

"I can get Sara."

"I want someone new."

"I'll try to get Alicia here right away, sir."

The five men walked out of the lounge.

"Let's get the hell out of here," said Kevin. "Three security guards confirms they suspect we're in town. There's probably a hundred assassins converging on the city."

Waiting for the elevator, Tessa said, "I have an idea. I'll be Alicia."

"Not a chance! It's far too risky."

"He's leaving the country. This is probably our last chance to get the son of a bitch."

"No, and that's final. He might recognize you. It would be the last thing you ever did."

"You've said over and over, we're both dead. This way we have a chance at least. I'll take the little gun, and you'll have my back."

"A much better plan would be to gun them all down right here."

"You have three bullets left; I have one. Counting security at the hotel, there are five or six armed men here. We'd be killed for sure." The elevator came, and they got on. "I'm doing this, Kevin; I don't need your permission."

"But you need to get away from me, and I won't let—"

"You're going after your father's killer, even though they'll be expecting you. Nothing I can say will dissuade you from that. This man killed *my* father, and he'll likely end up killing the man I love and me! Don't try to stop me."

*

A dazzling blonde in a slinky red dress strolled up to Ahmed al-Zayd, and said, "Mr. al-Zayd? I'm Alicia."

She held out her hand to shake his, but he merely said, "Follow me."

"I have a room upstairs," said Tessa.

"Follow me!"

"But it's paid for—"

"You're new, so I'll forgive you your impertinence. I pay the agency twenty-five thousand a month. In return I get a beautiful woman whenever and wherever I want, no questions asked. The whore who was supposed to come to me at noon didn't come; I'll make sure she's fired. So unless you want me to get you fired, too, shut up and follow me."

Tessa decided this was too risky and turned to walk away, but one of the bodyguards put a pistol against her ribs and dragged her down the lobby and out of the hotel.

The five walked in close quarters around the block and went into a different part of the Watergate complex. They took the elevator to a large penthouse suite. One guard stayed in the hall; the other two came in with al-Zayd and Tessa. Another man, who had been in the kitchen, greeted his boss.

As one man prepared drinks for his boss and Tessa, another installed her in the bedroom. He checked her purse, confiscated the Smith & Wesson, and left.

*Shit! I hope Kevin's not still waiting in the closet. God dammit, this was a bad idea. The best I can hope for is having that lowlife ravage me. He'll probably have me killed afterward!*

Her heart raced as she surveyed the room. It was huge, with a king bed on the north wall facing a set of windows covering the entire south wall. A couch was set against a wall of mirrors and a love seat was centered on the opposite wall. An ugly purple coffee table sat in front of the couch. There were no dressers. This room was not for sleeping. She went into the bathroom looking for scissors, a razor blade, anything that might suffice as a weapon. There was nothing. She returned to the room and looked out the windows, hoping to see Kevin and alert him to her location. Somehow. There was no sign of him. *Shit!*

The man came in habited in a dressing gown and carrying two glasses of champagne. He said nothing about her gun as he handed her a glass. *Maybe a lot of escorts carry them for protection*, she mused.

"You have a negligee?"

"Yes."

"Put it on in there," he said, gesticulating to the bathroom.

She took it out of her purse and walked to the bathroom as al-Zayd pushed a button to lower the blinds.

Shaking in the bathroom as she disrobed, Tessa struggled to keep her head. Tears built up, but she wiped them away and pulled on the red negligee. She sat on the toilet, hoping to draw this out before the inevitable.

"Come on!" yelled the man through the door.

"Just a minute," she said as she knelt over the toilet. She was so upset, she had to vomit. Afterward, she rinsed her mouth with the champagne.

He called again. She opened the door and stepped out.

The hideous man smiled through his bushy, black beard and motioned her to come to him.

She walked slowly to him.

"You're shaking. Nervous?" She nodded. "I like that. Turn around slowly."

Tessa obeyed.

"Closer." She took another step. "Bend over slowly."

She obeyed.

He clutched her buttocks. She winced. He squeezed hard. She yelped, and he laughed. Patting his right leg, he said, "Sit."

Now was the time she had to decide. What was worse, sex with this beast or death? He obviously didn't recognize her; she would probably live through this if she kept her cool and gave him what he wanted. But the thought of being so intimate with this repugnant man, the man who had her father murdered and who'd put up fifty million to silence her. It was surreal.

She sat on his lap.

"Trembling all over. Keep it up," he said as he pawed her legs.

His hands were rough, his beard scratchy, his body stinky. She gagged, but held it back.

Pushing the straps aside, he yanked the negligee down. Her breasts were pulled down by the fabric and popped up when free of it. He grabbed one with a hand and bit hard on the other. She shrieked. He laughed.

She tried punching him, which only made him hornier. He snatched the negligee and tore if off her body. He stood, picked her up and tossed her onto the bed.

\*

The Potomac Lounge waiter told a pretty woman, "I guess he got impatient and left. I'll call him, and—"

"The Arabs?" asked a man.

The waiter looked at him to convey, *mind your own business, asshole.*

Kevin went on, "They left with a gorgeous blonde."

At that the pretty woman left in a huff.

The waiter started off in the opposite direction, but he was halted by Kevin.

The waiter, a large man, warned, "Let go right now, or I'll—"

He stopped mid-sentence upon meeting Kevin's Colt.

"Lead me to the men's room right now!" said Kevin.

The man complied.

There, Kevin stepped back and pointed the gun at the waiter's face. "The woman that fucker took is my woman. Tell me where he took her."

"I don't know."

"The next words out of your mouth better be al-Zayd's location, or I'll take great pleasure in blowing your brains all over the wall."

"Penthouse suite, Watergate South."

"Turn around."

"Please don't kill—"

Kevin dragged the unconscious man into a stall and ran out of the hotel.

With no time for niceties, he decided on a frontal assault. He meandered into Watergate South.

"Oh, you guys are new," he said, slurring his words.

"What's your business here?" asked one who Kevin guessed to be another ex-Marine.

"Business? I live here, moron."

"Get out of the building, sir."

Kevin stumbled into the burly man, who twisted him around and hauled him to the exit. Abruptly, Kevin took out his handgun and cold-cocked the man in the middle of his forehead. As the ex-Marine plummeted to the floor, Kevin turned the gun on the other guard who was only then reaching for his gun.

"Don't!" screamed Kevin. "Drop it." The man let the gun fall. "To the elevator. Now!" ordered Kevin as he picked up the gun.

The man, who was slightly smaller than the Marine but a tad larger than Kevin, reluctantly complied. The elevator door opened, and an old lady gawked at the proceedings. She began quaking.

"Get out!" Kevin said.

She shuffled out, frightened eyes on the maniac.

"If you call the cops, I'll track you down," he warned.

She nodded and scurried away.

The elevator door closed, and Kevin said, "Penthouse." The security guard pushed the button.

Kevin said, "I can see you girding for a fight. You ex-army?"

"Navy."

"Me too. Navy Seal, actually. So you can try your luck, but you'll end up dead. I really don't want to kill a fellow laid-off sailor, but I will if I have to. Those fucking Arabs have kidnapped my woman. Get me into al-Zayd's apartment or die. Your choice."

The door opened on the top floor. Kevin followed the security guard out. He spotted the bodyguard at the door and put a bullet into the center of his chest with the silenced pistol. The security guard tried to take advantage of this by attacking Kevin, but a regular sailor had no chance against a highly trained Seal. He found himself on the floor. Kevin pointed the pistol at his head.

"No, please! I'm just trying to do my job."

"Master key."

The guard handed it over. Kevin knocked him cold as well.

He went to the door, inserted the key as silently as he could, and turned the knob.

\*

As al-Zayd took off his housecoat, Tessa bolted for the door. He caught her around the waist with one arm and hauled her back to the bed, laughing. When he pushed apart her legs with his knee, she kicked him in the balls.

He fell on her, cursing in Arabic. He put his hands around her neck, choking her.

She was fading fast, but then gunfire from the other room spurred him to jump up and go for his gun. He opened the door a crack, saw his target, stuck the gun out, and ...

"Ah!" screeched Tessa as she charged into him and knocked him through the door.

Kevin turned and put a bullet into his chest.

Tessa threw her arms around her man. Looking over his shoulder, she saw three dead men on the floor, besides al-Zayd, who was still alive, but struggling to breathe.

"Did he—"

"No. He was just about to when I kicked him in the balls."

He laughed. "Did he recognize you?"

"No."

He leaned down to al-Zayd, looked into his panicky face, and said, "Subhuman terrorist Ahmed meet genius inventor Tessa. Does the money trail end with you?"

He gurgled something that was probably, "Help me!" but he expired.

"Get dressed; we need to boot it. The assholes across the street will show up on their Arabian steeds any minute."

While she dressed and retrieved her purse, he checked the hall. By the time the two got to the elevator, it was two floors below on the way up.

"Quick, to the stairs," said Kevin.

Kevin picked up Tessa by the waist with a "Sh!" as two police officers exited the elevator. Had they turned their heads, they'd have seen the two disappear into the stairwell, but they went directly to al-Zayd's condo.

"Take off those high heels. What a clatter they make."

"I was just about to when I was unceremoniously hoisted."

The two had descended to the fifth floor when they heard someone coming up; they stepped onto the fifth floor. Kevin peeked through the window after the person went by.

"Another cop. Look at how fast the shitheads come to the rescue of a Saudi terrorist. Tell me they're not in his pocket."

They got to the main floor and looked out the glass to the front lobby and saw three more police officers and four Arab men.

"Let's try the parking garage or find an emergency exit."

"Wouldn't they expect that?"

"Probably, but we have guns."

"You're not shooting a cop. I have a better idea. Let's just walk out there; they don't know who they're looking for, and they wouldn't expect a couple."

"Those A-rabs might recognize us."

But as he said this, the four Saudis entered the elevator with a cop, leaving two police officers in the lobby. Tessa put her shoes on, and the two walked into the lobby arm in arm.

Tessa said, "Officer, what's going on?"

"You live here?" asked the officer.

"Yes. We looked out our window and saw all this commotion."

"A problem in one of the penthouses. We're investigating."

She nodded, and the two walked out the front entrance and around the block to the hotel. After they got to their room, Kevin was in the middle of telling her how impressed he was with her sangfroid when she broke down crying.

"It was horrible. I had a choice to screw him or die, and when I kneed him, I chose death. He was choking me to death when you showed up."

He lay with her on the bed and held her tight. She was trembling from the rush of adrenalin. Exhausted, she fell asleep.

Deciding it was probably safer to let things settle down outside before leaving, he relaxed and closed his eyes.

# CHAPTER 19

The Mexican mob was bold because no one challenged them, not even the police. Everyone knew who was in charge, but he seemed to be untouchable, at least until he was touched in the chest with a bullet.

The Chinese were more subtle. It eventually became known who was in charge in central New York State, but it wasn't advertised or celebrated as the Mexicans seemed to do. Word around town was a man named Sheng Gang had recently become the local ringleader. Chan had confirmed this to Kevin's satisfaction when he mentioned that he had killed the boss's son.

Triad headquarters in Syracuse was well known: AXA I, a former office complex that had gone bankrupt; the gang renovated it for offices and residences. No outsiders were permitted, except for meetings, and it was well guarded. Tessa's talent at hacking had not only yielded Mr. Sheng's address, but his schedule for the next week. He and his family occupied the entire top floor of the building. He was at home tonight.

Kevin drove around looking for potential sniping sites. He found one and only one, and the news wasn't good; the perch was atop another condominium complex. This building was about 400 meters from the Triad building. The problem was the building had fallen into the hands of squatters, who had occupied the units as the owners walked away from mortgages much higher than the value of the property. As more owners moved out, the value of the remaining units plummeted.

Some of the people in the units were the former owners, who had been foreclosed upon, but had never left. Most were occupied by people who had nowhere else to go after they'd lost their homes. Drug users, drug dealers, gang members, and other refuse soon took over. The police would go nowhere near the place. Mexican mob had taken control, extorting the residents for much of the little they had, selling drugs, and keeping a semblance of order.

But this was the best bet for killing Sheng. He was too well protected to get anywhere close to him or to his car with a little C-4. Tessa would stay in the car and pick Kevin up after he accomplished his mission.

On the way to the assassination, they saw heavy black smoke wafting around a rundown, three-story building ahead. When they got closer, they could see flames shooting out the first and second-floor windows. A small crowd, mostly elderly people, were milling around. One old woman was out on the street waving at cars, screaming for help. Three vehicles passed her by. "Won't anyone help her?" cried the lady.

Tessa looked up and exclaimed, "There's a little girl on a balcony up there!"

"And you want me to stop, I suppose," said Kevin.

Her expression answered him, so he pulled over.

"Please, help us! Earl's granddaughter is in horrible danger," said the old lady.

The young girl was screaming frantically. She was huddled next to the wall, trying to stay clear of the choking smoke.

"Did you call the fire department?" asked Kevin.

"At least a half hour ago. You see that useless piece of trash over there?" Tessa and Kevin looked over and saw a heavy-set man, probably in his late forties, pacing back and forth. "He's an off-duty fireman. Won't lift a finger to help. Says regulations strictly forbid his going into a building on fire without the proper equipment and backup."

Kevin and Tessa marched toward the building. The man grabbed Kevin's arm and said, "You can't go in there."

Kevin yanked his arm free and went to the front door.

"Not my fault if you die," said the man.

"But if you die, it'll probably be my fault," returned Kevin.

When Kevin opened the door, hot, black smoke poured out, knocking him back.

"What did I tell you? Hey, where do you think you're going?" the fire fighter asked Kevin as he leaped up to grab the bottom of the railing on the second floor balcony immediately below the girl.

"Chattanooga. Taking the scenic route." He hauled himself up.

"Oh, God, be careful, Kevin," said Tessa.

"Get the rope from the car," he said as he stood on the top of the railing on tiptoes and reached up to clutch the railing one floor up. As Tessa ran to get the rope, he once more pulled himself up and climbed over the railing. Coughing hard in the raging smoke, he bent over to pick up the girl. She screamed. "It's okay," said Kevin. "I'm here to help you."

Coughing, the little girl asked, "Are you a fireman?"

"Yup," he lied. "What's your name?"

"Ashanti."

"Are you ready to be really brave, Ashanti?"

She nodded with frightened eyes.

The smoke was getting thicker. They could hardly keep their eyes open. Tessa arrived with the rope. "I can't throw it that high," she said.

"Here, lady, let a professional do it," said the fire fighter. He balled up the rope and threw it up to the second floor balcony.

"You really have a flair for the pathetic, don't you?" Kevin yelled down. He turned to the youngster and said, "You can piggy back on me." Kevin put the child on his back. "Show me how tight you can hold on." She squeezed.

"Close your eyes … Are they closed?"

"Yes."

He climbed over the railing.

"Oh, no! We'll fall! We'll fall!"

"I promise we won't. Now close your eyes and hold on tight."

She held on even tighter, so tight it was hard for him to get air, but that was okay for now. He went down to his knees, grasped two vertical rails, and slid down to try and find the second floor balcony with his feet.

"A few inches inward!" hollered Tessa.

As panic began to set in with both Kevin and Ashanti, he finally found the railing and crouched down, preparing to jump onto the balcony. But as he did so, Ashanti lost her grip.

Startled, Kevin lost his balance and fell forward onto the balcony.

Inside, he was crying, *Oh, Jesus, I dropped her; I killed the little girl!* Tears poured out of his eyes, both from the smoke and from the crushing despair of losing his little passenger.

He couldn't see through the tears; he didn't want to look down anyway … But maybe she wasn't dead. The fall couldn't have been more than fifteen feet. She wasn't crying, though, so she must be hurt bad.

"I'm so sorry," he cried out.

"It's okay, Kev," said Tessa. Bringing the blurry scene into focus, he looked down and saw Ashanti alive and well in Tessa's arms. She'd caught the toddler!

Ebullient, he tossed the rope down, hopped over the railing, lowered himself, and jumped down. The small crowd applauded. He embraced Tessa and Ashanti for pure joy.

Sirens could now be heard closing fast. With that, Tessa handed Ashanti to the lady who'd hailed them, and Kevin and Tessa jogged to the car.

"Wait!" called the lady. "You're heroes. What are your names?"

"Mr. and Mrs. Dillard Blifil," said Tessa as she drove off. She held Kevin's hand and squeezed her gratification. He squeezed back and complimented her on a good catch.

The two had to postpone the assassination attempt for twenty-five minutes, so Kevin could rest his sore eyes. At dusk, she wished him luck, kissed his cheek, and dropped him off.

Approaching the building, Kevin saw armed guards at the front door; Mexican mob, judging by their tattoos. They would be simple to take out, but that would bring the cavalry, trapping him inside. He went around back. The one guard there was obviously coming down from a high. On an impulse, Kevin meandered toward the back door. The man stopped him, but Kevin just offered him the joint he had lit. The man smiled and took it. As Kevin walked in, the man said, "What you got in the bag, bro? Looks heavy."

"Just some cans of food. Wife's pregnant; she's eating me out of house and fucking home."

"Let's see."

*Shit!* thought Kevin. If he killed the man, chances were good he'd be tracked down before he could achieve his mission. He unzipped the side pocket, took out three DCC and one CCS, and gave them to the man. The man opened his mouth, likely to order Kevin to open the other zipper, behind which was his disassembled rifle, but Kevin handed him the last of his marijuana. The man smiled, took it, and walked back to his post.

Kevin trudged up the stairs, figuring the elevators were long dead. He encountered two people either passed out or dead on landings and another pissing down the stairs. Kevin had to halt at the bottom of the stairs to wait until the man finished, and when he passed the drunk, he drove his head into the wall and knocked him out. He saw litter everywhere, including a number of dirty needles and a few piles of shit, possibly canine or possibly human.

By the time he got to the thirteenth level—labeled 14 because of people's foolish superstitions—he had to lean against a wall to rest. He smelled hashish, but thought nothing of it given where he was. As he came around the final landing, he saw an armed man sitting on the top step in front of the door to the roof smoking hash. Upon seeing Kevin, he stood and told him to "Get the fuck out of here."

Kevin cursed inwardly. *They can't be guarding the roof; he's just shirking and getting high*, mused Kevin. He turned around and came out into the top floor hallway. No one was around, so he quickly assembled his rifle as he considered what to do. Waiting for the man to leave was risky because he'd sooner or later be spotted loitering, but killing the guard would be risky as well because they likely had regular check-ins. He went into the stairwell and listened. At 9:31, he heard the man's phone ring. The man answered and a moment later said, "*Jódete, estoy ocupado*," which Kevin, who knew the basics in Spanish, thought meant, "Fuck you, I'm busy."

*That's probably the 9:30 check-in*, Kevin thought. Then he heard someone out in the hall. Forced to act, he ran up the stairs to the landing halfway to the roof level, popped out and shot the guard. The man slumped back against the door. The door to the top floor opened and two men walked down the stairs.

Kevin scaled the stairs, opened the door, stepped over the body, and dragged it onto the roof, grabbed the dead man's phone, and closed the door. He looked around to make sure all was clear, went to the north side of the roof, dropped his duffle bag, and positioned himself to take the shot. Through his scope, he scanned the south side of the top floor of the Triad complex; blinds throughout except for one room. He cursed and, having no other option, focused on that one window.

As ten o'clock drew near, he started to worry that the next check-in was due any time. He'd seen no one through the target window. At 9:57, a light went on in the room. Kevin's heart beat faster in anticipation. A young woman walked in; Sheng's daughter or maybe lover, he figured. She walked toward the window. "Don't close the blinds!" Kevin yelled aloud. She didn't; she looked out the window.

At 10:02 the phone rang. "Shit!" said Kevin. He decided to chance it. He lowered his rifle and answered, "*Jódete, estoy ocupado.*"

The voice said, "*Juan? ¿Quién es este?*"

Kevin cursed again, tossed the phone aside and lifted his rifle again. The woman was still there. With gang members soon to interrupt him, he decided to take action. He concentrated and squeezed the trigger.

The woman went down. He didn't know where she was hit and couldn't tell looking, since she'd fallen to the floor underneath the window. He'd wanted to wound the woman, mainly because her cries might bring the boss running in, but also because he could practically hear Tessa say, "Do not cross this line." She was his only link to sanity.

The seconds ticked away, each bringing the Mexicans closer. His heart beat fast, but he forced himself to calm down because he needed to be accurate if his target showed up. Then, just when he was about to give up, Sheng appeared. Kevin shot. Sheng went down. Two men came in and dragged Sheng away from the window.

Not knowing whether he had injured or killed his target, Kevin quickly disassembled the rifle and put it into his duffle bag. He took out the Colt, got up, and ran for the door. As he neared it, the door flew open. Caught by surprise, Kevin took a couple of seconds to react. One of the men got a shot away, but he, too, had been surprised, and the shot went wide. Kevin killed them both before they could shoot again. He ran over and looked down the stairs. Seeing no one, he ran down. Between the fourth and fifth floors, he heard someone coming up, so he ran back up and ducked into the fifth floor hall.

A raggedy woman, who looked like she was in dire need of her next dose of heroin, saw him holding his gun and hurried into an apartment. He flattened himself against the wall. The door opened slowly and a man's head protruded. Seeing Kevin, his eyes opened wide and he pulled back his head. Kevin got down and rolled to the opposite side of the hallway.

The man jumped out, shooting at the spot Kevin had just vacated. Kevin shot and killed him. As Kevin got to his feet, another man jumped out and shot. The bullet hit Kevin's chest and threw him back against the wall. Fighting to breathe because the bullet had knocked the air out of him through the Kevlar vest, Kevin returned fire. Not wearing a bullet proof vest, the man succumbed with a hole in his heart.

Kevin struggled to the staircase and started down. The lights in the stairwell blinked. The electricity went out, and the staircase went dark. Pulling down the NVG, he hastened down two more floors, but saw flashlights and heard several more men approaching from below. He went out onto the third floor and tried apartment doors. He got to the other staircase, but heard men there, too. Trying doors on the other side of the corridor, he lost patience and kicked one open. In that ramshackle condo were two children, perhaps seven and five years old. Two candles were lit, one on the kitchen counter, the other on a coffee table in the family room. Clearly, the children had been through many blackouts and knew the routine. There was no sign of any parents. The girl cried out. He quickly closed the door, grabbed the child, and covered her mouth.

He lifted his goggles and whispered, "I'm not going to hurt you, I promise." She kept crying and squirming. "I have food," he said. Her brown eyes opened wider. "I'll let you go if you promise not to cry." She nodded. He let go.

"We're hungry," said the girl. The young brother looked on with interest.

Kevin opened his duffle bag and took out two cans of food: DMBS and CCS. He opened the former and gave it to the little girl. She got two spoons and she and her brother ate the cold beef stew voraciously.

"Where are your parents?" he asked.

"We never had a father," answered the girl with mouth full. "Our mother works in the building."

That surprised Kevin enough that he asked, "Doing what?"

"Tricks," said the girl in a matter of fact way.

He raised his eyes. *They probably think it's magic tricks*, he thought. Hearing voices out in the hall, then heavy knocking on a nearby door, he slid the barred window over and went out onto the balcony. Taking a rope from his duffle bag, he tied it to the bottom of the railing and let it down.

"Can we have the soup?" asked the girl, jutting her head out to the balcony.

"Sure."

"What are you doing?" she asked as he put the bag over his shoulder and climbed over the railing.

"Climbing down on the rope."

"Can I try, too?" asked the little boy.

"No!" said Kevin. "It's very dangerous. Bye."

The children said goodbye and went in for soup as he descended. *I can't remember the last time I had to escape from a balcony twice in the same day*, he said to himself. The rope was only twenty feet long, which meant he'd have to jump the last fifteen feet or so. The lack of depth perception provided by his goggles would make timing the landing dicey.

When he got to the literal end of his rope, he looked up and saw a flashlight pointing down at him. He let go as the man shot. The bullet whizzed by his head. He landed and twisted his ankle. With more bullets hitting the ground all around him, he limped to the base of the building, where the men above couldn't get a clear shot. Looking at his duffle bag that held his cherished rifle, he took in a deep breath, sprang out toward the bag, picked up his bag as a flashlight beam found him, and ran back to cover, only one throbbing shoulder, where a bullet hit the Kevlar strap, the worse for wear.

With a sore chest, shoulder, and ankle, he made his way along the wall to the corner of the building and crossed a short driveway, threw the bag over the fence, and hopped it as men came around the corner. Cursing, he picked up his bag, turned, and dashed as best he could with twisted ankle across the street.

All at once he grunted and fell to the ground. One of the many bullets sent his way had struck his left calf. The bullets kept coming. One hit his vest, once more knocking the air out of him.

Out of the darkness came a car. The door flew open. "Get in!" said Tessa. He lifted himself into the passenger seat. While he was still struggling to get inside, Tessa floored the gas pedal because bullets were hitting her car. Kevin managed to close the door as she turned the corner and sped away from danger. "Are you hit?"

"In the leg. Fuck!"

"We need to get you to a hospital right away."

"Are they still required to report gunshot wounds?"

"As far as I know. Cops going to drop everything to check it out?"

"Let's go, but we can't stay long." He opened the first aid kit and wound a bandage tightly around the wound to slow the bleeding. The pain almost made him faint.

*

A rickety wheelchair sat on the sidewalk. Tessa helped Kevin into it.

Wheeling him into Emergency, she shouted, "Someone help me! He's been shot." No one came. "Help!" Besides patients waiting in the waiting room there was only a fat, white security guard who didn't even bother to look her way, and a fat, black lady behind the glass partition at the registration desk. She wasn't looking too concerned either.

Tessa shouted to her, but she said phlegmatically, "Wait your turn in line."

"But he's been shot!"

The woman looked at Kevin and repeated to Tessa, "Wait your turn."

An elderly black man at the front of the line was arguing with the woman as well. "I think she's had a stroke. You have to help her."

"Unless you have the money, we can't help her," said the lady.

"Who the hell has tens of thousands of newbucks?" he screamed.

The lady waved a security guard over.

The old man said, "No, I'm not going to cause no trouble." She held up her hand and the guard went back to his post. The old man went on, "What about Medicare?"

"She's eighty-three. Coverage for major hospital care runs out at eighty."

"But you can't just let her die!"

"Take her to the free clinic."

"The lineups take at least half a day! And what's a clinic going to do about a stroke? You have to help her!"

The guard came over, took the man by the arm, and pulled him toward the exit. "We paid taxes in this country for fifty years!" he said. "Now we need the help everyone else got and you kick us out? Please help her! She'll die. Let me go! Are you human at all …" The front door closed behind them.

Tessa watched as he opened the passenger door and caught his wife as she fell out. He hugged her, crying, and pushed her back in. He went around to the driver's side and drove away.

With tears in her eyes, Tessa said to Kevin, "Maybe the other hospital will help."

He shook his head and replied, "*This* is the public hospital; the private one is worse."

By the time Tessa got to the receptionist, Kevin was white and looking awful. The lady required a credit card, but neither she nor Kevin had any credit left on their cards, and using them would alert everyone to their location. Tessa offered five hundred new dollars, which is what she kept on her, the rest sitting under the spare tire in the trunk.

"Five hundred newbucks won't even get him through the door. He'll need surgery and a hospital stay, so unless you got at least ten thousand, you can just leave."

"Aren't you required to help the poor?"

"Call the cops. Next!"

The solution she'd got used to over the last two weeks—pulling a gun—wouldn't work this time. Crying, she wheeled Kevin out the exit.

"Hey!" yelled the security guard. "Don't leave the hospital with that chair."

"Fuck you," she said as she helped Kevin back into the car. She sent the chair flying toward the guard.

She went around to get into the car, but was stopped by a man who'd been standing behind her in line. He had a gun. "Give me the cash."

She looked over at the security guard, who merely smiled. She glanced into the car, but Kevin was sitting back with closed eyes. She toyed with grabbing the gun in her purse, but the security guard was looking, and, well, it was too complicated. As she handed over the five hundred, her finger was on the trigger in case the robber made an aggressive move, but he jogged away.

"Asshole!" she hollered to the guard, who walked back into the hospital laughing.

When she assumed the driver's seat, she said, "Did you see what happened?"

Kevin said, "No. What?"

"Never mind."

"This is the end of the line for—"

"No! I'm not letting the man I love, the father of my unborn child, die."

His eyes opened wide.

"Are you sure?"

"Sure I'm pregnant? Yes. Sure it's yours? Yes. I did it on purpose. You kept saying we couldn't stay together, so I wanted a way to force you to stay, or if not, to always have a part of you with me. Let's go see Dr. Hope."

Tessa sped to Loomis Hill. Stopped at the gate, she told the security guard she needed to see Dr. Hope. It was 11:13 PM.

The guard made a phone call, then waved her through.

At the Hope residence, the doctor ran out, saying, "Heather?"

"No," said Tessa. "She's safe with my aunt. Kevin's hurt. He needs your help right away."

Dr. Hope looked in the car. "Bullet wound?"

Tessa nodded.

"Was Heather in any way involved?"

"No."

"Where is she?"

"We'll take you to her, but help Kevin first."

The two women helped him inside and put him on an old couch. The doctor got her medical kit, and after injecting a local anesthetic, examined the wound.

"I can get the bullet out and stitch the wound shut, but he's going to need saline and blood, and I don't have any."

"Just do whatever you can."

Kevin lost consciousness.

"Is he alright?" asked Tessa.

"He needs blood," Janet said as she went to work on Kevin's wound. "Tell me where my daughter is."

"As I said, I'll take you there," said Tessa. "Why are you so anxious? She's safe."

"I have a job offer in Houston. I hadn't heard from you all this time. I've been going crazy wondering where she is. You never even thought to call me."

"It was too risky. But I assure you, she's perfectly safe."

After doing what she could for Kevin, Janet went to clean up while Tessa stroked his hair.

A few minutes later in her room, Janet whispered, "Yes, they're here right now. He was shot and came looking for medical help. Please hur—"

Dr. Hope stopped talking and dropped the phone as she felt the cold metal of a gun barrel against her back.

A livid Tessa said, "Do exactly as I say, or I swear I'll kill you."

Tessa instructed her to help move Kevin to the back seat of her Ford. She kept her gun in hand in case the doctor tried anything.

Tessa told her to get into the Ford, but Janet argued she needed her car. That was a problem because she didn't trust the physician and because her car might be bugged, but Tessa knew Janet needed her car if she was to get to Houston.

How she was to sell her house and move her belongings to Houston without the Triad finding out, Tessa couldn't imagine. While checking the BMW for tracking devices, she asked. Janet answered that the house was worth less than the mortgage; she was walking away from it all except for what she could fit into her BMW. She'd already packed what she needed; she only needed to know where her daughter was.

Tessa found a bug underneath the front left fender. She continued checking, but found no others.

While preparing to leave, Tessa asked, "Why did you call the police after everything we did for Heather?"

"You're both on the FBI's most-wanted list."

"What?"

"It was on the news a couple of days ago. He's wanted for God knows how many murders. And you're his accomplice. I've spent the last two days crying because you have my daughter."

"And you just believed it."

"Do you deny he killed the lieutenant governor, those Mexicans, the Saudi diplomat, and on and on?"

"And the ten Chinese men who tried to steal Heather and make her into a prostitute in China? Yes, he killed all those people. And every one of them was to save us or to get the murderers who killed his parents, because the police, *who you called*, would do nothing! And because he saved your daughter, the Triad killed his father. And you try to turn him in?"

"I'm sorry," said Janet, clearly worried about how furious Tessa was, especially with the gun pointing at her.

"You *will* get him blood and saline, and you won't try to betray us again, or you'll never see Heather again."

Janet solemnly promised to cause no further trouble.

The guards waved both cars through the gate. They passed a police car on the way.

At the hospital, Tessa went in with Dr. Hope and picked up the supplies they needed without incident. Back at Tessa's car, Janet got blood and saline flowing.

Tessa led Janet to Keuka Lake, keeping an eye on the mirror. She stopped at one point to check on Kevin and put on the night vision goggles to try and spot anyone who might have been following. She saw no one. *God help us if the Triad are following,* she told herself.

Arriving at Bell's place after 2 AM, they were faithfully greeted by Tom, the ex-Marine. When he saw Tessa, he relaxed and returned home. Evelyn and Heather were startled by the knock at the door but smiled upon seeing their visitors.

Mother and daughter cried and hugged. Heather's hair was short and red. Evelyn said she felt this was a prudent change to make for now. Heather was still gorgeous, but less likely to attract the notice of sex traffickers.

Kevin roused for his walk in, helped by Tessa and Heather, but went back to sleep upon hitting the couch. Janet observed her daughter interact with Kevin and likely suspected the worst, that her daughter had fallen in love with one of the nation's ten most wanted, considering the lingering kiss to the lips Heather gave the sleeping man. She was clearly ill-impressed. As was Tessa.

Tessa was fatigued, but the ladies were now wide awake and curious about their situation, especially considering their popularity with the FBI, so Tessa had to provide an update. Bell nodded throughout with warm smiles at all the death. At the news of Tessa's battery breakthrough, Evelyn hugged her niece, saying how proud she was.

They retired for the night.

*

The next morning, Kevin was much improved. The ladies brought him breakfast. He shook his head at the news of making the FBI list, opining that it was good evidence for his father's cynical assessment of the government's position on the new battery.

Evelyn turned on the radio news.

The lead story: "More gunplay in downtown Syracuse last night as an unidentified man shot and killed five men at the notorious Oak Park condominium complex. Police have no suspects at this time.

"In a separate incident, two people were shot in their home last night. Mr. Sheng Gang, a recent immigrant from China, is dead from a bullet wound to the head. His daughter, Bao, was taken to the hospital with a shoulder wound; she's in stable condition. Police have issued the names of two suspects, Kevin Idle and Tessa Sharp, who are on the FBI's ten most-wanted list. Both are considered armed and dangerous."

That caused some anxious looks.

A pounding on the door got all hearts within the cottage beating hard. Evelyn answered with Tessa nearby holding a gun. It was Tom and his shotgun. He wanted to speak to Kevin and was admitted.

He marched up to Kevin, took his hand, and shook it. "I hate all those chinks and spics and towel-heads coming into my country and killing and stealing and kidnapping and drug dealing and gun running and everything else illegal under the sun. And the cops and feds let them get away with it. I think you're a hero, son. I want you to know that. I won't be turning you in, and I've got your back."

A surprised Kevin nodded.

Tom left.

Kevin said to Tessa, "We're not safe here, but our faces must be everywhere by now, so we can't budge." He turned to address the others. "Tessa and I will lie low here until the pressure subsides, but you all have to leave right away. It's not safe for any of you to be near us."

"No!" said Heather.

Her mother said, "Yes, honey, we have to get away from—"

"I'm pregnant!"

All eight eyes looking at her bulged, six of which subsequently narrowed as they focused on Kevin. Bell's eyes were shut for a nap. Janet strode to Kevin and administered a vigorous slap, saying, "You son of a bitch!"

Tessa ran out of the room with her hand to her mouth.

Evelyn shook her head and went to comfort her niece.

Heather protested, "I seduced him. I love him."

"I'll have you charged with statutory rape!" hollered Janet at Kevin, who was still in shock lying on the couch.

"No, you won't!" cried Heather. "I was worth so much because I was a virgin. It just made so much sense to give him my virginity."

"You'll get an abortion."

"No, I will not! It's my baby, and I'll never give it up. And being pregnant, then a mother should make me safe forever. Isn't that what you want?"

"Of course, but you're much too young."

"I'm staying with him."

"No!" said Kevin and Janet in concert.

Kevin went on, "Staying with me undermines the logic of everything you just said. Staying with me virtually guarantees you and the baby an early death."

Janet threatened to turn in Kevin, but that brought a stern warning from her daughter that she would run off and never return.

Kevin endured Heather's crying and Janet's hateful glower until they left for Houston later that morning. He then weathered Evelyn's disdainful scowl until she and Bell left after lunch.

The old ladies took Tessa's car because it was the only available means of transportation. Also, Tessa was worried the car would lead the Saudis to Primet. At all costs, she wanted her battery to survive. It was more important than Kevin, herself, and their unborn child.

Evelyn was to check to see if her Maxima was still where they'd left it and, if so, take it and leave the Ford behind. Otherwise, they would leave the Ford at the bus station in Syracuse, where they would take a bus to Kingston. Aunt Evelyn cried, wondering if it was the last time she would see her young niece.

With everyone else cleared out, Kevin was left to deal with a moody girlfriend. He apologized and told her, "I love you, Tess, not her."

But Tessa gave him the silent treatment for the rest of the day.

# CHAPTER 20

Six days later, while sitting on the couch surfing the net, Tessa gasped. Kevin looked at her. She was wan, her mouth agape. Tears brimmed in her eyes.

"What's wrong?" asked Kevin. Shock rendered her incapable of responding for the moment. "Tess?"

"They … they sold the company."

"Primet?"

She nodded.

"Is that a big problem? The new owners have to abide by the contract you signed, right?"

"They sold it to a Saudi prince."

His jaw dropped, too. After a moment accommodating to the news, he said, "And they'll shelve it."

"They've probably already destroyed any evidence of its existence." Her tears overflowed.

"So the fuckers won after all. Greedy battery company assholes."

"I'm guessing they didn't have much choice. I'd bet anything they were threatened. Die or let us pay you billions. They did what they had to."

Kevin grew red with rage. He eventually growled, "We can't let them get away with this. It's not only us. Our country *needs* this. We can't let those fucking sheiks keep us in their power." His eyes opened wide. "I've got it!"

"What?"

"We use the Internet to publicize your formulation ... Oh, shit."

"What is it?"

"This makes you even more dangerous in their eyes. They have to cut you off before you tell the world what you accomplished and what the goddamn Saudis are doing to quash it. Could be a hundred million on your head now. Any new news on us?"

She checked on the Internet and reported, "The FBI is appealing to me to turn myself in for my own safety. Oh, and with their other face, they're offering one million dollars for information leading to my arrest."

"What, am I worthless?"

"You're not mentioned, though you're still in the top ten."

"As soon as good old Tom hears about this, that hero bullshit will be forgotten. A million newbuck payday for one phone call."

"Should we leave?"

"As soon as it gets dark. That should improve our chances of escaping to one in a million ... Tess, you should really consider turning yourself in."

"I'm not leaving you, and I don't trust them."

"I don't either, but it's probably your best chance. They may well want to preserve the battery. Staying with me will guarantee your death."

"I'm never leaving you. Either drop it or turn yourself in with me."

"Okay, I'll turn myself in."

"What? No! I didn't really mean it. They'll give you the electric chair."

"If it saves the battery, you, and our baby, it's a price worth paying."

"Kevin—"

"Stop, Tessa. This is the only way out, and you know it. Plus, I can earn a million newbucks to take with me to hell."

Kevin picked up the phone and called the number the FBI displayed in its appeal to Tessa. He handed it to Tessa.

\*

At 7:32 PM that evening, a shotgun blast startled the pair. Numerous gunshots followed.

"Tom," said Kevin. He ran to the window and parted the curtains. He saw several cars driving into Stone Point, which he reported to Tessa.

"I hope he isn't attacking the FBI," said Tessa.

"A much better bet is he's shooting at our posse."

"The FBI tipped them off?"

"Who knows? Maybe someone in the FBI wants the millions. Or maybe the posse found us on their own—likely tapped into the phone number the FBI posted."

"It could still be the FBI."

"To kill us? Yes."

"Or to rescue us."

"Or to kill one and rescue the other. Remember the drill?"

She nodded and went to her post. She sent emails to several people and grabbed something off the wall.

Two minutes later, he said, "Shit, this isn't good."

"What?"

"Get down!"

He dashed to her and covered her body with his as an explosion of gunfire blew through the front and back windows of the house.

A fusillade tore apart the little house as Tessa screamed and Kevin cursed with bullets zipping above them. Screaming so that he could be heard over the racket, he told Tessa, "Push it!" She pushed the button and ear-splitting blasts rocked the house.

The gunfire had ceased. They shimmied their way toward the back door. Kevin got up to his knees and peered out the back yard. "Come on, quick. Like we planned."

Tessa sprinted and Kevin limped to the motorboat through the smoke, debris, and body parts. Tessa unmoored it and jumped in to get it started while Kevin knelt on one knee with his rifle. He began shooting. Two men fell dead; two others returned fire.

"Get on!" hollered Tessa.

After taking three more shots to send the men back, he hobbled over to dive on board. Tessa gunned the engine, and the little boat zoomed out into the lake. She headed for the far shore, only a few hundred yards to the east, but as they got close they saw flashes along that shore. "Jesus Christ!" wailed

Kevin. One bullet hit his vest just below his belly button, which sent him down in pain.

"Kevin!" She reached over to him.

"I'm okay. Turn south. Get down flat, but keep it going."

They got to the branch in the lake, where it widened to about two miles. Kevin stuck his head up and said, "Holy fuck!"

Tessa lifted her head and saw what was holy: four motorboats coming their way. Kevin took the driver's seat and turned north, zipping up the eastern branch of the lake at full speed. Two of the pursuers were gaining, however.

"Kevin!" said Tessa, pointing ahead to two more motorboats coming at them from the north. Kevin turned east, but more shots from the shore turned him around.

"Christ, there must be hundreds of them! Maybe it's the goddamn National Guard or something."

He looked up to the west and said, "An Apache and a Black Hawk. Fucking Army!"

Bringing the boat to a halt, he lay down next to Tessa.

"Maybe the FBI or the Army is trying to rescue us?" said Tessa.

"Maybe. Can't think of why else they'd send a Black Hawk. We'll know when we see who the Apache is aiming for; if it's us we'll know it for a split second."

"I hope they at least save my battery."

"You did everything you could."

With boats closing in on them, dozens or hundreds gunning for them from the shore and Army helicopters zooming in, the two could only hug each other in case this was goodbye.

The Apache launched four hellfire missiles.
Both said, "I love you," at the same time and kissed.
The missiles exploded.

END

# ABOUT THE AUTHOR

Novelist ROBERT POWER was born in Canada, but raised and educated in the United States. He stayed in university so long, Berkeley eventually gave him a PhD to get rid of him. Working as a consultant from home, he drove his wife crazy until he took up writing fiction in his too-ample spare time. Neither he nor his wife know what they were thinking when they decided to have four children, but they're happy they do—most days. They live in southern Ontario. Visit his website: rdpower.ca.

# ALSO BY R.D. POWER

*For Power or Love*

*For Power or Love 2*

*Forbidden*

*Taylor Made Owens*

*Thank Sophia for Sam*